A REASONABLE AMOUNT OF VIOLENCE

By Bradley Alan Stern

1

A REASONABLE AMOUNT OF VIOLENCE, Copyright 2025 by Bradley Alan Stern. All rights reserved. US
Copyright: Application: 1-114928164641 Pending
Library of Congress number: 2025910743
ISBN: 979-8-9989983-0-0

First Edition

Published in Kalamazoo, Michigan, USA

For bibliographic questions please contact the author at:
bradleyalanstern@gmail.com   Telephone: USA: (1) 916-802-4925

Table of Contents

A REASONABLE AMOUNT OF VIOLENCE

By Bradley Alan Stern

Joel Cairo: *You always have a smooth explanation ready.*

Sam Spade: *What do you want me to do, learn to stutter?*

Dashiell Hammett

Last Night

The hallway, black as a moonless sky, the walls and ceiling blending together into one limitless space. It was so dark your brain couldn't register if your eyes were closed or open. The lump lay there on the carpet even darker than the dark. There was no sound. There was no movement.

Sounds of steps, stilettos on wood, clop, clop, getting closer. Creaking as the door opens, a pop as the lights flip on. The hallway is bathed in fluorescence. Gargling noises.

"Oh my God!" Squeal. High heels, short skirt, bubble breasts, saucer eyes, staring for a couple of seconds. Heels spinning, tripping, running back up the stairs, steps echoing.

Door explodes. The marble lobby echoes with screams.

"Help! Fucking help!" Deep, heaving breaths. She screams again, hollers. People look. Burst of tears. "Call an ambulance, oh my fucking God! I think there's a dead guy in the basement!" She catches her breath. Her heel snaps, she slips and then goes down, white panties, legs splayed in an unbecoming fashion. Heave-ho; chunks splashed across marble.

Wait. did you hear that?

Chapter 1

Quick story. A couple of years back, my roommate Sean Akana, this doughy, pasty-faced sort of satellite hover-man known as Mikey the Goon (Don't call me that! My name's Mike!) and I (the great Bruce Keown!) shuffled aimlessly around the lit charcoal Weber grill in the front yard of Kurt Black's two-story on the Hill, getting ready for the daily barbecue session of teriyaki chicken, rice, and beers, lots of beers. We were at the pre-dinner dope-smoking stage of the meal, waiting and watching the coals burn. The fire was hot.

A surf hoot-style holler turned our heads. The yell was followed by the distinctive door slam of a super-sweet '72 VW Bus: tinted windows, dual-carb pie-pan engine, original mirrors, 12V, quad exhaust, the works. Kurt strutted around the corner of the house with a stupid grin, Lanikai outrigger paddling T-shirt...and a seriously busted nose. His nose was bent about 30 degrees off center, the tip swollen to the size of a marble. Not the little peewees either, we're talking shooter sized. I took two guesses; behind door A was a fight, behind door

B was rugby practice. The winner, to my surprise, was behind door B. Kurt grabbed for the doobie and took a big hit, face turning the classic beet color from holding his breath. I scrutinized him without notice. There was blood all over his shirt, caked on his chin. Some had dropped onto his running shoes.

Me: "What's up with the shnozz?"

Kurt: "Rugby practice." Inhale. He passes the joint.

Me: "Where's your jersey?" Inhale. I pass the joint to Mikey the Goon. Sean takes it away.

Kurt: "I had to throw it away, too much blood." Suck, inhale.

Me: "Waste of a shirt, can't your 'wife' wash it?"

Kurt: "Shut the fuck up, Bruce, before I make *your* nose bleed. Then we can be twins." He grins, just a joke. I smile back. He's a funny guy, Kurt.

Mikey took out a sketch pad and pencil from his backpack and started in on Kurt's bloached face. He forgot one of the golden rules—ask first. Kurt veered away from the grill and grabbed the moving pencil. The pencil resisted for a moment and then got decapitated. Mikey, watching Kurt carefully,

9

placed his sketch pad back into his pack, zipped it up. He pulled a vial of cocaine from his front pocket, spoon attached to the cap.

Goon: "Want a spoonsky? Your nose will feel better." All appeasement.

Kurt: "No." He stared, eyes like lead, no emotion. His right fist tightened, then let go.

Mikey slowly relocated himself to the other side of the grill, Converse-clad feet kicking through the dust and clumps of dried grass. He kept his eyes down. We looked away.

Kurt's girlfriend, I think her name was Tracy, walked outside with another round of Guinness, ass swaying the way she knew we all liked. And before there are any ideas, we only looked; I never bet against Black. That is, I always side with Kurt— always. For my own safety. Anyhoo, she saw Kurt. He grinned. Her face registered surprise. She stared, frowned, opened her mouth. He acted nonchalant, like it was no big deal. She closed her mouth, gave up the beers.

His meal that night was prime rib with a side of prime rib, garnished with prime rib. And one brussels sprout, which he threw at Mikey. The steak must have weighed a pound and a half, cooked. The boys ate chicken…and the rest of the soggy brussels sprouts. Kurt drank a Guinness with the meat. We watched surreptitiously, nibbling on our chicken thighs. He drank another two for good measure, one breath. We gawped.

We did bumps of Mikey the Goon's coke after dinner. I rolled a joint and Kurt got the first hit. Kurt, sitting on the stump next to the front door, burst out, "I don't think I'll go to the hospital tonight. I feel like another Guinness, some Monty Python, and then a good, headboard-banging fuck."

He looked pointedly at I think her name was Tracy. Our eyes followed his. She smirked. He'd go to the hospital in the morning.

We sat there listening attentively to his bluster because to do otherwise would cause offense. There were rules, after all. Never offend or argue with Kurt Black. His face was splotchy and red. It looked as bad as a tied-to-a-chair, brass knuckles punch out. Under that kind of torture, I would have confessed to anything, even to fucking my ultra-obese human sexuality teacher. I know, a super-fat woman with a sprout of facial hair growing out of a mole on her chin. Teaching sex. Ironic. Kurt's reaction? Nothing. Kurt was a throwback, medieval.

Kurt got up and reached for a piece of coal from the Weber...with his fingers. He used it to light another joint, then threw it away. Jaws dropped. He turned.

"Hey Goon, you're fucking annoying, you know that? Get the fuck off my property before I get pissed. You bogarted the last joint."

Mikey: "What are you talking about?"

Remember what I said about gambling on Black? Kurt took his time walking over to where Mikey sat on some firewood piled up in the dirt. Mikey literally watched as Kurt twisted around like a dervish and connected so hard with the back of his hand Mikey's backpack flew into the next-door neighbor's yard. A tooth dropped.

"Get the fuck up and fucking beat feet." We were struck dumb. Mikey scrambled to his feet, all dust clouds, and got ready to fly, only needing a Kurt-sized boot in the keister to send him on his way. And he got one. We kept the vial of coke. And that's the last time any of us saw of Mikey the Goon.

Chapter 2

September 10, 1982

Kurt Black looked out of the passenger-side window of the burgundy 1981 BMW 528i. The Rocky Mountain pines soared overhead, and Black dropped his head onto his window edge, lazily tilted his rugged face skyward, straight brown hair shifting with the breeze, wondering idly at their ages. He blinked and shifted his head slightly, angling his position to better see his friend and associate, a tall, lanky, black-haired Hispanic dude coming out of the 7-Eleven. His name was Alexander Johnson. Johnson stepped up and leaned over the car, cleaning the front window with a window squeegee and paper towel. Black smiled. Gas flowed, katik, katik. For the umpteenth time Black wondered if his partner knew that Alexander Johnson was also the name of an iconic bluesman from the 1920s who sold his soul to the devil and died in a barroom fight. Or that Alexander Johnson was the most common name in the United States. Or that he suspected that Johnson wasn't his partner's real name. Or that Black pretty much carried on a constant silent conversation with himself every time he smoked Hawaiian weed. He'd think I was nuts, Black said to himself. Better keep it quiet. Wait. The most common name in the USA is Robert Johnson. Alexander Johnson is just my partner's name. He giggled silently, took another hit. Weed was a distraction to be sure, though not enough of one to interrupt their business. He pulled the sample doobie to his lips and puckered.

Black again looked up at the cotton clouds and smiled dreamily. Idle thoughts intruded on nothing. It's good to be the general to the king, he thought. And Alex was the king. There was trust, something rare and valuable, you could even say priceless. No falling out among us two thieves, he thought.

Black leaned out the window and asked, "So what are we going to do about the Wally Cleaver situation?"

Johnson looked up from his work with the squeegee, checked the gas pump handle, and responded, "First of all, I don't much care for Mr. Cleaver, or whatever his name is. Wally Cleaver.

That's just stupid. I think a learning opportunity is in order here. If you can retrieve our assets, a trip to and long stay in the hospital for Mr. Cleaver would seem lesson enough. If things have gone further..."

Black: "When you say 'further,' what do you mean by that?"

Johnson hesitated, then replied. "Oh, I think something a little more permanent, don't you?"

Black: "Huh. Seems drastic." Pucker, inhale.

Johnson: "Only if neither the product nor the money can be retrieved. We need retribution if we have been wronged. Every fan of movie westerns knows that..." Johnson paused, and a half smile penetrated his visage. He said, "And we do live in Colorado, where all the good little cowboys sleep."

Johnson unhooked the gas handle and replaced the cap. While he went in to pay the attendant, Black let his mind play on their predicament. Black agreed that some sort of punishment had to be dished out. He was, however, uncomfortable with the ramifications of a permanent solution. In Black's experience, that kind of permanence often came with its own potential problems. He sighed, took another hit.

Compassion and kindness seem lost on me, he considered. No matter how much I want to be the good guy, it always turns out different. He pulled on the joint, stifled another cough, stared at a pine cone. Pucker, inhale, ponder. Johnson came out of the service station office and got into the car. He started the engine. The BMW purred. Johnson put the car into neutral.

"Here's the way it needs to be." Johnson stilled, then continued, dark eyes sharp. "This guy Wally Cleaver goes to Juanita's for tequila and Coronas every night, right?"

Black nodded. "Mmmm."

Johnson: "So, tonight you go over there and find him. Don't scare him. Tell him you want to bring him up to the house, that there's a party. Tell him there's a stunningly attractive girl from Huntington Beach who knows his family and wants to meet him. Buy him a beer. Be nice but not too nice, we don't want to spook him. Get him talking and find out where our cocaine is. Find out where our money is. If he has either, go to his place and retrieve our assets, and be nice. Then bring him to the house. Then we won't be nice; I'll do the honors with a baseball bat, as a lesson. Then we will drop him off at Boulder Memorial. A broken clavicle would suffice, maybe a couple of cracked ribs. If not…"

Black scowled slightly. Alex Johnson looked at him and asked, "Okay, Kurt, what seems to be the issue?"

Black said, "I get that we gotta do something. I just think killing him is bad karma. You get more with honey and all that." Pause. "Anyways, that's what I think." Black watched the wind through the trees. Inhale.

"Are you being squeamish?" Johnson said. "Dealing with this situation properly is instrumental to our business model and marketing strategy. We have a captured customer list. We keep this customer list through having the best product, an efficient distribution program, and an understanding that failure to do business ethically has ramifications."

Black: "Hmmm. Yeah."

Johnson continued, "If he has neither the blow nor the coinage, stop someplace and use the Ruger .22. Leave him in one of the alleys near the mall. Someone will think he's a transient sleeping it off. Toss the gun out in the reservoir."

Black thought of his personal journey. Oh well, there was always the next life. He was already regretting what had to be done. He looked at Alex, read the resolution in his face.

"Fine. I'll take care of it." Face now still, he got comfortable, fastened his seat belt, and watched the wind go by as Johnson, smiling, pulled the BMW into traffic, Michelin Pilot Comps rolling west toward the mountains.

Boulder Daily Express

September 11, 1982

BODY OF MAN DISCOVERED

The body of an unidentified man was discovered early this morning in the alley behind Old Chicago restaurant in downtown Boulder. According to police, the body was found by a homeless person identified as Gregory G. Rasmussen, 64. Mr. Rasmussen contacted a passing police vehicle at Pearl Street and Broadway and led police to the body. Fire and Paramedics were then called, and the victim was pronounced dead at the scene.

"I just saw this kid lying there, kind of curled up. He's young, you know? I figured he was another college student sleeping it off or something. Man, there was a lot of blood. I never saw a head with a dent like that."

Police confirm that it appeared the man had sustained a blow to the head as well as an apparent gunshot wound to the chest. The Boulder Police Department seeks any information that could lead to the identity of the victim.

This is the third downtown Boulder killing in the past year. As of this time the BPD seems stymied and there is concern among local businesses that it could be drug related.

Chapter 3

November 17, 1983

Let's take it forward a year...

The phone rings.

"Hello?"

"Mr. Black? Good. You're awake. I have a thought." Johnson's voice chilled. Black couldn't remember a time in his friendship when the guy wasn't ice-cold cucumber.

Black said, "You always have a thought. It's like you want to break your brain for the refund or something."

Johnson chuckled. "You are the witty one, a regular Dan Aykroyd." Pause. "I am thinking that we need to diversify in terms of our Boulder distribution channels. I know we have one solid downline connection, but I think we should be interviewing for another, to cover the college and young bar-hopping demographic. I would like to increase our economies of scale. What are your thoughts on the subject?"

Black, holding the phone, silent for a couple of beats. "Yeah, I think that's a good idea."

"Do you have any potential individuals in mind, Mr. Black?" Johnson asked with some curiosity.

Black: "Actually, yeah, I do. There's this guy I went to high school with might be good, and a guy from Southern California. Especially that guy. We need them both though, the connected one is kind of a flake. The other one keeps him in check." Black heard silence. Hesitation.

Black said, "Plus, they both know I could beat them into retardation if they fuck up in any way."

Johnson sniffed. "That's more than I've heard you say in a long time, Mr. Black, though somewhat callous. Why don't you ring up these two fellows and invite them for dinner tonight. I would like to meet them. If they pass muster, we'll go up to the house for further discussions and party favors."

Black: "Shall we say 6:00? Michel's? Private room? Just for clarity."

"Yes, to all three questions. Tell them that I'll get there at 6:00. You make sure that they are there, at the bar, around quarter till. It'll give them a chance to loosen up, take off their best-impression masks, and be themselves." The phone went silent, then, "Kurt?"

"Yes?"

"I want you to stay outside until I come, then wait fifteen minutes." Alex thought about it for a couple of seconds. "I need you to do some skullduggery; after the fifteen minutes, you can sneak into the restaurant through the side door, then later sneak back out again. You'll eat with us but don't get seen by the front desk or the bar."

"What about the waiter?"

"I'll deal with him. Maybe join us for dinner, then head back out and stand by my car. Later, if they ask where you went, just say the bathroom. I'll come out with them. If I decide that we are a go, I'll give you the nod. Then we all go up to the house together. If I shake my head, give a wave. Stay by the Beemer and we'll go back to the house without them, nothing lost."

Black, surprised. He kept it from his voice. "Why?"

"A, I want to get my first impression of them without your influence or forewarning. B, what I need is for you to watch my back. That means stay out of sight. Don't go into the restaurant until I've already had time to get to our private room and sit down." Alex Johnson stopped speaking. Black heard his own breath. He took the phone away from his ear, looked at it stupidly, and then put it back.

Black: "Alexander? Are you still there?"

"Yes." Again, silence. "Let them know that this is an important opportunity. When you get there, tell them to go in and hit the bar, you'll be right behind them. I'll meet you around back, near the big tree. You move my car to where you can see the front door but again, stay out of sight. At around 6:15, come in. As I said, have dinner with us to allay suspicion, then sneak back out and wait for us, but again, stay hidden until we come out. As I said, if it works out, we can all go up to the house together, one happy family. Michel knows the BMW, so I'll pick it up tomorrow. Your job in the restaurant and the car is to watch for anything unusual. Anyone following. That's it."

Black: "What are you worried about?"

Alexander Johnson said, "Nothing. Everything. We have responsibilities too, people that I answer to as well, as you know. I want to play offense on this one."

Black: "Okay, sounds like the plan. But like I said already, you don't have to worry about these guys."

"It's not 'these guys' I'm necessarily worried about," Alexander Johnson commented. "Just watch my back and we'll discuss in-depth analysis of our options later tonight."

Black nodded to himself but before he could verbally acknowledge agreement with the plan, the line went dead.

Chapter 4

Eyes cracked, stuck like gum. Nostrils caked with what felt like sand. Need...water. I finally sat up, head reeling. The room flipped. My stomach flipped. I heard the sound of a cartoon winding up outside my bedroom door, this time a Foghorn Leghorn. While I didn't want to get out of bed, fear of pissing my sheets became the motivating factor in going vertical. I stood up and two things immediately grabbed my attention. One, the bare wood floor, untreated and filthy, was polar cold on the soles of my feet. It felt like ice cubes were being held to the balls, heels, and toes, and the sensation got only more urgent. I was going to need socks, slippers, something...and pronto.

The other attention-getter was the ache caressing my head like a poisonous succubus moved from behind my eyes to the center of my forebrain. With it another wave of nausea took out my knees. I wobbled. I put my left hand out to the wall as I reached for the door with my right. I looked down at the doorknob and noticed that the coat of gold-colored plating was wearing off, exposing the dull pewter-colored knob itself. The sun caught the knob just wrong. The glint in my eyes made me feel like I was chewing foil. Not that I make it a practice of chewing foil.

I reached for the handle and turned the knob. The familiar pinch as I gave the door a good yank was followed by the creak of the middle hinge, three quick bursts. The door rolled open. The hinge creak grated my nerves; my eyes squeezed, and teeth clamped so tightly together I could have crushed lava rock. I let my jaw go slack. God, I'm so tired. I walked down the hall and the cold that chilled my feet now traveled up into my calves. The walls of the hallway were painted the same cracked eggshell white as the bedroom, though the monotony was broken up with a couple of surf posters I had cut out of a special Hawaii edition of *Surfing Magazine*. Surf stars on huge waves four stories high, looks of concentration on every last one. My memory heard the distant rumble and felt the bone-crunching impact of waves surfed and wipeouts taken. Scary stuff.

I dragged my fingers across the posters again one at a time and continued toward the bathroom. I stopped at the alcove to the living room. I looked. Sure enough, Sean sat slouching on the sofa, stretched out, legs crossed at the ankles, watching cartoons on the little 26" Toshiba with ColorTron or some such bullshit name. He looked up at me and brayed.

I should digress for a moment.

One, calling what we had a "sofa" is kind of misleading. What we called a sofa was really an old wooden church pew, stained dark brown. It even had the fold-down kneeling bench attached to the underside. We had kidnapped it from an old church in Pueblo a few years before, covered it with some Mexican blankets for disguise and so we would be semi-comfortable, and those gray, red, green, clay, and blue colors really lit up the room. Or so others had said in the past. I didn't believe it; I just thought the whole thing looked cheesy Mexican, like the stuff fat banditos would wear. I liked the fold-down bench though, a real conversation starter. Stealing that pew and smuggling it a couple of hundred miles in an open pickup truck had been a real coup.

Two, Sean's blond hair thinned on top, food for humor. How many times had I given him grief over his hair when he struck out on a date? I mean, he wore a ball cap 24/7 to hide his bald spot. Or maybe it would be better to call it a bald half-his-head, har, har. Like we wouldn't see. To compensate, he grew the sides shoulder length, so lame. Truthfully, it was only partially his laughable haircut; he just didn't have any confidence with women. Probably because of the bald thing. He was great at being friends, but when the sex bug hit him, he started talking like a fourteen-year-old with the ripping-hot ninth-grade teacher, the one his friends said they saw in *Playboy* magazine. He just ended up friends with these chicks, like they needed another friend. What they needed was a good stiff one.

What? What did I say?

Sean said, "Weeeelll. If it isn't Bruce Keown, rising from the underworld. You'll be pleased to hear that Kurt called and he's coming over. 'Shenanigans,' that was his word." His eyes sparked and a half smirk cut into his lips. The sun shone off his skull. I squinted for drama.

I said, "What does he want? I paid him for the blow yesterday."

He grinned.

"Eh, don't laugh," I said.

He laughed.

"Fuck off." I paused, got all serious while my bladder expanded as if getting ready to pull a Hindenburg. "What was Kurt's vocal demeanor? Pissed?"

Sean opened his mouth—

I formed a plan, right there and then. Out the bathroom window ass first, jump off the second-story roof to the back parking area, and run away if Kurt wanted his pound of flesh. A sprinkle of hope on the lawn of hangover woe. Then again, Kurt was a sociopath. He could easily have been laying a trap for me, Red Riding Hood–style. The better for me to meet his fists with. I puzzled it over and listened closely to Sean's take on the situation.

"I don't think you need to worry." He smiled again. "And what? 'Vocal demeanor'? Don't ever use those words in this house again or I'll be forced to beat you."

Yeah, right.

"So, if he's not coming for a pound of flesh, why give us the pleasure of a personal wake-up call?"

Sean let me sweat for a couple of seconds. I felt my bladder bulge and tensed my butt. "He said he wants to apologize. He said he realized you didn't start the fight you and he got into with the frat idiots at Pearl's. One of the frat rats went to the hospital. Check your lip, man."

I touched it and winced. So that's why it hurt. "Did we win?"

"Well, you didn't go to jail, so there's that."

"How did I get the lip?"

Sean smiled again. "Oh, you got that from getting punched by Richard."

Richard "Dick" Dickmann, asshole of the universe. And he was supposed to be on our side. Cocksucker.

Another digression, worth the pause in the story.

I hate Dickhead Dickmann with enough fire to burn down the Sears Tower. Smug, superior, lying, entitled, narcissistic, self-serving motherfucker. He's everything I hate about people. I may have a bit of an inflated sense of self-importance and a willingness to stretch the boundaries of appropriate behavior but compared to Richard (dick) I'm a piker. He's a fucking used butt plug.

So, apparently there was more to last night than drugs, there was drinking and fighting too, obviously. Nice. My folks would have been proud. What was I saying? Why should I give a shit what my parents thought? I do the drugs I do to drown out what my parents thought.

Strangely, I didn't even remember Pearl's. If I was there, I doubt I did any fighting. I probably tried to stop it. See, that's the kind of guy I am. The voice of reason, Mr. Honest, Mr. Responsible, Mr. Loyal, the rational guy who could talk to the cops and keep us out of jail. Yeah, that's it; I must have sweet-talked us out of jail again, smooth talker that I am. I tried to remember. My hangover would indicate a blackout night, so fucked up. Then I remembered the eight-ball still in my jeans. Jesus, I must have had it on me when the cops showed up. Bruce Keown, Man of Risk. Or Man of Incredible Stupidity. I felt my lip with my tongue. I would have to do something about fucking prick Dickmann.

I closed my eyes to better concentrate on my potential penis leakage.

Sean continued, unaware of my thoughts. Now his face looked serious. "He also wants to talk to us about something else." He waited a beat. "He sounded mysterious."

I did a head-fake double-take. Ouch. My eyes left their sockets, then returned. I opened them. Wait. Oh, *oh really*. Maybe another jumping-dust deal, hee, hee, hee. Could today be the day? Hooray, hooray! Kurt had been whetting our tastebuds for months with images of a real deal. A Kilo of cocaine. *A Kilo*. Maybe I'd finally meet his connection, a mysterious mountain dude with a legendary stash. He was said to have over a hundred kilos hidden on his property. At least that's what I overheard this fraternity troll tell some fat chick one night at Jamie's over a bowl of Irish stew. Nobody knew where the mountain dude's property was. Or even if he was real. Yeah, I know, it sounded like bullshit buried treasure stories, but as I eavesdropped, I wanted to believe Skip, or Chip, or whatever his name was. Just think about it. If we went to Mr. Mystery's house, would X mark the spot, like the frat-kook whispered? I was going to be rich overnight, rich. Oh. Yeah. And I guess since Sean was my roommate and partner in all things druggie, he was going to have to make some money too.

Sean must have been peeking through my eye's window and seen the avarice. The smile left his eyes, and he froze, face like granite. He turned back to the TV. The new cartoon featured Daffy Duck, the greediest of the WB Looney Tunes characters. Sean turned back, gave me a straight look, and pointed. "Daffy Duck, that's you." Busted. I felt so ashamed. Not really.

I still hadn't gotten to the bathroom. With total focus and strength of will, I put my eyes on the doorway down the hall and purposefully strode the last fifteen feet to my target. Once inside I examined the commode. Fucking Sean. Once again, he hadn't bothered to put the seat up when he took his last piss. Great.

I turned to the sink and reached for the cube-shaped box of tissue. Three should do the trick; I had to protect my hands from germs, after all. I then turned around, leaned over and studied my task. I folded the tissues into a square. I proceeded to wipe the slightly yellowed rim of the seat, going counterclockwise three times, then two more for good measure. I looked at the tissue, Dijon mustard color combined with a little horseradish tint for just the right effect. I gagged involuntarily. That's two gags so far. Why did I look? Sean heard me and cracked up again. I tossed the crumpled scraps into the slightly rusted trash can with the Denver Broncos logo on the side, slammed the toilet seat lid up, and pulled my penis from inside my tighty-whities. I stepped up a little closer so as not to pull a Sean and...ahhh. There's very little in this world more pleasurable than taking a good piss from an overflowing bladder. Even drugs pale by comparison. And bad sorority chick sex.

Another digression. I know, but it's relevant, I promise.

My psychiatrist says I have "emotional issues," that I'm "a complicated case," like they used to label troubled teens "juvenile delinquents." She keeps throwing out brain-bound titles to label me, like there's a new one every week. It's like the hit song list from that old TV series *American Bandstand*. Or was it *Casey Kasem's American Top 40*? It doesn't matter, I get mixed up. It's all part of the package. Sometimes I don't even remember what disorders she means. Nor do I care; she's obviously a quack.

Being a person with disorders gives me a perspective that nobody else can possibly have. I have anxiety issues, which lead to a case of the jitters. Some have teased me about this problem, saying that if I just stopped using coke, my problem would just go away. What the fuck do "some" know? I'm the one with the shrink. Okay, so, I am somewhat self-involved, so I take things very personally. Yeah, fuck off. I'm inherently suspicious, which occasionally becomes a self-fulfilling prophecy. I believe I was put on this earth for great things, and I also believe that you have to grab the brass ring when you think it appears. I believe in the use of drugs, lots of different kinds. Call it skull candy. Valium, quaaludes, and weed were my favorites, and of course cocaine, though these drugs aren't attained by prescription from my doctor. I get other drugs from the shrink, they're good too. The latter offset the former and Bob's your uncle, normalcy.

So, okay. Moving on.

I flushed and looked at my eyes in the mirror, letting the frying pan of brain cells cool enough to formulate memory of the day's planned agenda so I could come up with some bullshit to cover the drug-dealing activity.

The first thing I remembered was that I had a hiking date in Eldorado Canyon with my girlfriend, Jill. Jill Chenoweth is the consummate hot little Pasadena debutante blonde, great looking in a WASP way; very upstanding, prim. She studies and goes to class on time. When we are out at the bars, she goes to the bathroom with friends, like she can't pull down her underwear by herself. Okay, that was a little cruel, I take it back. I know she can pull her underwear down by herself, I've seen her do it.

I've met her parents; very upstanding, her mother's quite prim too. You'd never know of Jill's secret identity: coke monster, hose beast, and all-around twirler. Twist and shout, baby.

Dig this: the ass of a woman is the key to knowing her fuckworthiness. No Fat Chicks, that's my policy. I'd even written a song about it, performed it with a couple of other guys mostly at drunken fraternity parties. It's very popular with the ladies, as you might imagine.

The forearm-length-and-no-wider measuring stick policy for ass width is no guarantee of a good lay, just a worthy lay. And Jill rocks. I didn't know sorority girls were so hot in bed, my only experience with them before Jill was what I saw walking to and from the university—a bunch of stuck-up, twittering, gossiping Barbie dolls. They travel in packs like the Spice Girls with blonde or brunette Scary Spice haircuts. They dress in knee-length Ralph Lauren pleated skirts and little pink or powder-blue oxford shirts with the collars and noses turned up, like Robert Palmer video chicks on hormones. They have that generically annoying voice pattern, turning up their last word, like everything is a question. If it weren't for the BMWs and Porsches that they drive (gifts from Daddy for their sweet sixteen) you'd think they were hillbilly half sibs.

Wow, where did all that venting come from? Hey, I wonder if that skinny bitch Barbie's good in the rack?

Here's a funny story, at least to me. I met Jill Chenoweth on campus. Our class together was in a huge auditorium in the science building. The room probably sat two hundred and fifty people, and the class we were taking was basic moron physics, you know, basically jocks and stoners. It should have been a piece of cake but for the professor, Dr. I'm Smart and You're Little Kid Stupid, PhD. He was the kind of guy who purposely made tests so hard that nobody passed. One time he put together a test where the passing grade was a 13; you got an A if you scored a 23. Out of 100. I know what you're thinking, Bruce's making it up, but I'm not. I figured that the only reason someone would do this to young, impressionable college students was because he was a pseudo-academic with an inferiority complex. Hell, it doesn't take a psychology degree; a half-trained cat could figure that out. Or a guy like me who sees a shrink twice a week.

To say Professor "I'm Smart...Not," PhD, and I abhorred each other is to do an injustice to the word "abhor." I suspect it was my slouching attitude and lack of a shirt. Hey, there wasn't a sign that said no shirt, no shoes, no lecture; don't judge me. Yeah, I gave him the occasional sneer and smirked at him a lot, trying to throw him off his game. Sitting in the front row, I taunted him, stretching my legs out into his lecture space, wiggling my toes. He called on me nearly every day, "And so, Mr. Keown, we come to you and your amazing knowledge of physics. Please grace us with your intellect. If you know the speed and trajectory of an item of known mass, is it possible to calculate the distance and time it will take said projectile to travel in a circle?" The answer is, "Only if you know the angular trajectory and speed." I mean, the answer is yes to all the above, solved with a combination of geometry and algebra but why answer him when a question is infinitely more annoying? I think it really irritated him when I got his queries right, doing the calculations in my head, no notes. Childish, I know. Sue me.

Yes, I digressed, twice now. Back to Jill. Jill sat two rows behind me in class and I noticed her right away—a stunner. Every once in a while, I would look over my shoulder and see her look away. Oh well, other fish. Then one day during the fifth week of the semester, she followed me out of class.

"Bruce? Is that your name?"

"Um-hmm."

"I need a study partner. Do you want to be study partners?" You have got to be kidding, I thought. Tanned legs. Freckles between her breasts; oh, so hot. Her blue eyes flashed. She smiled a little smirk like, "I know what boys want..."

I thought about if for about less than two seconds. "Um, sure, I guess. When and where do you want to meet?" Playing it cool.

She surprised me with her candor. "How about tonight? My house. How's 8:30?"

"Sure, okay." Playing it a little less cool. She had started a little kindling in my crotch.

"I have to tell the house mom that you're coming. What's your last name?"

"It's Keown." Wait. What? House mom?

"House mom? Are we going to need a chaperone?"

She seemed a little surprised at my question but answered, "She's just supervision. To look over our 'man friends.' Stupid." Pregnant pause. "But you're going to come over, right? I really need help." A little old granny with a nosy nose wasn't going to sway me from my objective.

"Umm-hmm. I'll be there with brain flipped on." And body *turned* on. I smiled just to show no hard feelings. Well, there would be hard feelings, but more like the physical kind; I smiled and showed teeth. The better to eat her with. "Where is your house, exactly?" Just like that. We studied for real for one day. Then our work turned more hands-on. A year later and I'm still eating her.

Chapter 5

Jill and I would not be hiking today, of that, I was sure. Oh well. I continued to examine the damage from last night's bingeing. Just a discoloration smudge under my eyes, a little redness on the rims of my nostrils, and the split and fattened lip but otherwise, okay. All the rock-climbing and outdoor endurance training helped in situations like the one I was now facing. Tanned and ready. Looking good, feeling like shit.

Don't even say it, I know what you're asking yourselves right about now. What kind of an athlete does cocaine and mistreats his body like that. The answer is…my kind. I don't see anything wrong with it. I'm off-season and able to delude myself into thinking I'm a better outdoor athlete than I really am. A serious athlete consuming copious amounts of drugs? No problem, and the fact that I could do it only proves my point.

I turned on the water, being careful to balance the temperature just the way I liked it, leaned over, and proceeded to wash my hands. I picked up the grainy bar of green soap sitting next to the cold tap and spun it through my fingers. Thirty seconds of hard scrubbing, then rinse. I turned on the shower. The sound of the water pouring out of the spigot was abrasive to my ears. It sounded like a waterfall from thirty feet down, looking up, thunderous and constant. I wanted to go back to bed and surround my head with the pillows again, cocoon-like.

Still, I stepped in and slid the shower door closed with a click, sealing me in like a locking closet, only me and the now-hot shower water running down my back, making the muscles that were tight, loose. I poured some of the Herbal Essence shampoo onto my scalp and massaged away. I like Herbal Essence shampoo; it reminds me of when I was a teenager tripping around with my across the street neighbor Stevenson Oliver Lowery. Stevenson, his brother Frederik, and I used to go under another neighbor's house and smoke joints of Colombian Gold. This was before we had the money to buy the better Hawaiian weed like Maui Wowie or Kaua'i Electric. The Colombian sold for about twenty dollars a quarter ounce, enough pot to roll at least fifteen joints. Also, Stevenson's mom, Maddy, was a liberal-minded pothead and often turned us on to Vietnamese hash she would bring in from Thailand. We would sprinkle a little hash with the ganja, twist a fatty, and forget that we were smoking what I later learned was basically bunk weed. The thing was, Maddy—thirty-seven, thin, blonde, tanned—was great to peep from a fifteen-year-old point of view, and she used Herbal Essence. And I hated my own mom. Do I need to paint the picture any clearer?

What? What did I say?

So, there I was, decompressing. Through the bathroom door to the other end of the living room and at the front door, I heard the heavy feet and somewhat scratchy, medium-pitched voice of Kurt Black. I turned off the shower and got out.

Chapter 6

Kurt Black wasn't a huge man by normal standards. He didn't stand six-foot-seven, nor did he weigh three-hundred pounds. He was maybe six-one/two and weighed about 195, maybe two-hundred. That's about eighty-nine kilos for you on the metric system, just over 14.07 stone for the Poms. He just thought like he was bigger. Granite. I had learned from experience that this observation was both actual and figurative. Kurt had arms like full firehoses, legs like concrete supports, and he was stronger, tougher, and crazier than anyone that I knew. His mannerisms reflected his mood; the grinning center of attention one moment, the very next, *the very next*, his serious face, a fearsome scowl that always preceded a no-holds-barred donnybrook. Excellent with his hands and feet, Kurt was a regular whirling dervish in a fight. Scary, vicious, and impressive all the same. We always joked that he was born in the wrong millennium.

You don't believe me? When we were sophomores, we took our fake IDs, walked to the Boulder Mall, and strode into a place called Juanita's. You shot pool there, and they had pretty good tacos. After the fourth shot of tequila, Kurt got it into his head that a fight, just for practice, would be a great idea. To Kurt, fighting for practice was always a good idea. You know, just for drills.

"A fight. Absolutely, that's what we need. A good fucking beating on some fucker. I'm doing it." His eyes blazed and his grin got huge. We tried to talk him off the ledge.

Sean mumbled, "This is a bad idea, Kurt."

I said something like, "You've got to be kidding. Bud, we are going to get thrown out and when the cops show we'll be arrested. I don't have bail money; I only have enough for tequila." Everybody snickered at the priority list. There was more protest. He laughed. I watched as he rolled up to the bar, turned to the next guy (a giant of a guy, a bit scrawny but at least a head taller), he goes "Hey," and threw his drink in the guy's face. It was a premium, an añejo, $12 a shot. What a waste. The guy just stood there, dumbfounded.

Kurt: "What are you looking at? I owe you money?"

Guy: "No." He gave Kurt a once-over and said, "Sorry?"

Kurt: "Yes you are. And you said I was an asshole. Then you knocked my drink out of my hand. Fucker."

Guy: "Ulp."

Kurt then stepped back and hit the poor fucker square in the jaw with a ridiculous right fist; the guy's head twisted at least ninety degrees and rocked him back against the bar. His head lolled, eyes lost focus. Legs wobbled; head dropped. Kurt hit him again, a right cross, perfect, knocking his head into the edge of the bar. Blood shot out of his left nostril and sprayed across the peasant top of the redhead standing next to him. She looked at her blouse. She screamed. The guy went down. Kurt just looked at him. Something passed across his face. Like maybe he was sorry or something. That's when Dickmann kicked the poor guy in the neck for good measure, making sure that his toe connected cleanly with the guy's chin just left of center. The guy's head snapped back into the foot bar under the stools, and I saw his eyes roll back to white. The guy was out, maybe dead, that's what it looked like. The episode couldn't have lasted more than ten seconds, and the guy's previous space at the bar was now a void. You could almost see his shadow as it followed him to the hardwood floor. The part that made me sick was that the poor trashed guy was wearing a Grateful Dead T-shirt. He was probably a hippie stoner and a pacifist. Kurt had spun the wheel, hit on Black, and the Grateful Dead T-shirt guy was a loser. The prize was an invitation to the hospital. Or the morgue. Great fight,

Kurt Black versus a defenseless punching bag. We took off, but not before Dickmann took the guy's money off the bar and put it in his pocket. Asshole. We got to the street unscathed but could see a couple of Boulder's finest approaching a couple of blocks away. The bar was pandemonium and screams could be heard through the windows. Kurt eyed Dick.

Kurt: "What did you do that for?"

Dickhead: "Do what for?"

Kurt: "You know what. And why did you take his money?"

Dickhead: "What money?" Kurt glared. The cops were getting closer. Dickhead gave him the classic Dick smile, all phony but bright, like a single headlight glinting off the streetlamps. Kurt shook his head and we took off, back to the cars parked in the lot at the Boulder Bank.

When we got the doors open, Kurt turned back to Dickmann. And hit him square in the face, sledgehammer style. And Dick stumbled. Kurt hit him again. Dick shriveled like the Wicked Witch of the West. And we left him there, but not before Kurt had a parting message.

"Don't ever do that again, hit a man while he's down or steal from him while he's down. That's just not cool, Richard, and you know that. If I see it again, we won't be sharing words for a while. I'll break your jaw." And with that, we took off. Minus Dickhead.

Chapter 7

I heard the front door bang open, and Kurt bellowed his most carefree greeting. "Sean, what's the happenings?" He turned toward the screen and, "Bugs Bunny again? I dig that cartoon." Another ping-pong thought from Mr. ADHD. "I am sooo hungry! Where's Bruce? Bruce!" he yelled, bigger than life. "Let's puff out!" Ahhh, I thought. Marijuana. *Sweet.*

"And what, you got weed?" Sean inquired in his quiet but not-so-subtle way. Dullard, I thought to myself as I toweled off and grabbed for my clothes.

Kurt retorted, "Of course I get weed, I'm edgumacated. I know proper spagettiquette. Since when do I say, 'let's puff out' and not have weed? Akana, goon, what? Who do I look like? Winner of the 'act like Richard Dickmann' contest? Fucking idiot." Then Kurt muttered a bunch of sounds under his breath that I couldn't understand through the closed bathroom door.

I heard Sean respond, "I always like it when you use the word 'fucking' all the time, it shows off your college, what did you call it...your edgumacation?" Sean continued, "A regular Einstein. Copernicus, even." Then I heard him say something like, "(garble, garble), Bruce's in (garble garble) room, (garble) masturb (garble, garble, garble, garble) his sister (haa, heee, heee, garble garble)."

"I heard that, motherfucker," I yelled from behind the bathroom door. "And I don't care if that makes me sound like a retard, swearing can be very expressive. For example," I yelled through the door, "the word 'asshole.' It's a great word, describes you both perfectly. If the word 'asshole' were in the dictionary, your pictures would be next to it as a definition." There, that'll teach him to screw with me. Clever repartee is my middle name.

Ohhh. My head hurt. A doobie actually sounded pretty good, I thought, so I hurriedly put on my jeans and kelly-green Patagonia sweatshirt, my favorite. I strolled out feeling about as good as it was gonna get. As I came around the doorway into the living room, there Kurt stood, grinning, smoke swirling from the lit joint, clouds pluming around his head. It obscured all sight of his face but for the grin. The gap where he got his bottom front tooth knocked out made the whole sight comical, in a hangover-influenced sort of way. I smiled, kind of shook my head like an adult wondering after a prodigal child. The smoke was so heavy it made my eyes water from twenty feet away. The beautiful, sweet smell of carefully babied marijuana bud wafted my way, and I felt like Bugs Bunny in the Ali Baba cartoon. That's the one where Bugs is in ancient Arabia and the sheik tries to have him beheaded. In one scene, Bugs gets wooed by a bunny harlot using a specially made potion. The smell of this floral potion makes Bugs float on air, body undulating like a magic carpet, drifting along to some vaguely familiar Indian sitar tune. He comes to rest on his face right in front of a giant hooded executioner brandishing an axe about four feet wide. Of course, he says, "Ah, what's up, Doc?"

Anyway, that's how it felt, minus the axe.

I walked over and took the joint from Kurt. As I brought it to my lips, I spun the doobie around in my fingers until the least-burned end was on top. That way the joint would burn there first because fire burns upward. Obviously. It would even out the burn pattern, which spoke to my OCD-driven sense of balance in the world.

I watched Sean watching me with what looked like a mixture of humored smirk and subtle disdain. Best friends—like brothers, we were really close. Along with this familiarity came the obligatory undercurrent of resentment, I guess. I'm pretty sure it was from my overall laziness and my disrespect for my own gifts. Also, my girlfriend, Jill. I think he wanted to fuck her but, well, I already told you about that.

Here's another thing you should know about me. Not that this should only be about me but...So, I have this ability for spatial thinking on the fly, you know, like seeing the results of actions before I—or others—act and calculate the ramifications of said behavior. This ability got us out of a lot of trouble. I think underneath it all Sean was pissed that my calculating protected me from the shit I did. So, yeah, Sean and I have an undercurrent of...something, but it's all on him. I got no problems, you know?

Kurt and I, on the other hand, didn't have such issues. I don't know. Maybe for some reason, Kurt actually considered me a friend, as opposed to a mark, and often brought over assorted toys, including women, for sport fucking. I guess it was my winning personality and unwillingness to take any of his intimidation shit. Just because I was scared of him didn't mean I had to show it.

Kurt said, "Where's our little freshman gerbil friend Bone? Now that fucker owes me money." No mention of our previous night's shenanigans. Kurt continued, "If he doesn't turn up in the next fifteen minutes, I hope he's prepared to lose some teeth." Kurt looked right at me, eyes burning a little. "I thought you said he was going to be here." He scowled, then arched an eyebrow, expecting an answer, eyes glaring.

Wait. What? I paused in the middle of the hit, lips trembling from trying to keep the smoke in and not cough and choke for the next thirty seconds. When did I say that? Since when did Bone owe Kurt money? How come I don't know about it, and why is it my fault he's not here? Did everyone in the city owe Kurt? I didn't have any recollection of telling Kurt that Bone would be at our house. It must have been another thing about the last night that I blacked out on. This was bad news, for me and Baby Fucking Bone. Kurt has been known to make up debts to bring his bottom line into the black, and then collect on them as if they were legitimate. His debt-collection quiver consisted of one arrow only...marked "violence" if the supposed debt went unpaid, or worse, the victim denied the debt entirely. If Bone didn't show up and have a legitimate reason, it would be on me, and a punch in the chest was the usual punishment. For Bone, things would be worse. In Kurt World, things always went the way he thought they would. Not should, would. If there was a need for flexibility, Kurt was not your guy.

I answered honestly, "I don't have a clue what you're talking about. If I told you whatever about fucking Bone last night, I must have been drunk. What little I remember of the night was that we went to a bar, which one I don't remember, had some tequila, type I don't remember, and apparently had a good time...which I don't remember. And it's barely 10:00, so just wait."

Sean glanced up again, but still said nothing. He was at the bar the evening before, of that I was pretty sure. What had he seen? What the hell happened? What the hell did I do? I glanced back at Sean. "What?"

Kurt's eyes drilled holes in my forehead and he grumbled, "Fucking smart-ass. You think you're so smart, yeah?" I quickly swiveled my head, the move driving a proverbial stake through my left ear and into my brain. I really needed to take some Advil. Kurt glared, fumed. "You fucked up, and now Little Bone won't show his face around for a month. I needed that cash, you fucker." He sighed and I watched with growing terror as his head and shoulders dropped in a sign of resignation. Fuckety fuck, here we go. Let the beatings commence.

Kurt balled his right hand into a fist so tight his knuckles turned white. He sighted and aimed for the meaty triangle above my left nipple, just below my collarbone. He twisted back just enough to generate some acceleration and got his hips and shoulder into the punch. He swung away. I watched it coming and prepared for the impact. It was like feeling the same powerless horror as when you see a train crush a car. It was going to hurt like being hit with a small cannonball. I watched his fist connect. The impact sounded like a slap and a thump at the same time, like someone swinging a wooden baseball bat at a bag of bananas. The bananas were me. I felt the shock, then an overwhelming ache that went from my wrist to my neck, into my gut, then back like a pinball going from one flipper to another. My left eye fluttered and my jaw started to ache. I wanted to throw up. I just knew that was going to happen. One of my favorite sayings is, "No good deed goes unpunished." I think I'll have it tattooed on my middle finger.

I caught my breath and gasped, "Fuck, what is your major malfunction? Did I ask for that? No. Did I fuck you over? No. Do I look like a punching bag from the gym? No. Wait, don't answer back on that one." I forced a slight smile.

Kurt just looked at me with some curiosity, like he didn't understand English. I think he was a bit surprised I didn't hit the ground. Probably questioning why he held back. Sean busted out laughing. After a couple of seconds, Kurt started to chuckle. A quick check of internal vital signs; Astronaut Bruce A-OK. I finally put a smile on my face but privately seethed. There would be payback, oh yes.

Still laughing, Sean said, "You are an idiot, Private Pyle." It was a reference to one of Sean's favorite old comedies, Gomer Pyle, USMC. I pretended I didn't know what he meant. It was not one of my favorites, you see. Idiocy, stupidity, and a gay main character. From Sean's point of view, what's not to like? Oh, I know. A punch in the chest from Kurt the gorilla man.

Sean said, "And that's what you get for being an idiot. Whenever coke disappears up your nose, you always forget what you did. It's a good thing we're friends or I'd have to beat you myself."

Right.

At this point, I decided to deny the whole thing ever happened, abandoning the previous strategy of ignorance. "Whatever it is you think I said or did, I deny everything. I didn't say it or do it, except for the shots of añejo. Those I did do, I think. I definitely didn't do anything else, including getting us all out of a jam with the cops. I know I didn't do that because I know spending the night in the pokey is my dream, I wouldn't miss something like that for the world. As a matter of fact, boys, jail and police abuse sounds so appealing, I don't know how I resisted. If that's in fact what happened, I deny it all. Besides, I don't think the cops had anything to arrest us for anyway. Given all that, I still didn't do it or anything else you're accusing me of. That's my story and I'm sticking to it." I let out an exasperated breath and spoke resignedly, "You fuckers are so ungrateful." I neglected to tell them about the eight-ball baggie of pink-tinged marching powder I knew was still in my jeans front right pocket, or the one-gram bindle I gave to the Boulder beat cop to ignore the rest of it. I remember.

Kurt said, "Fuck it. Get your shit, bro-ham, we're grinding out lunch at Ernie's. Chicken Cutlet day today. I buy. You drive. Oh," Kurt declared, "and I need your car later." He didn't even look at me, just started down the stairs. Huh. Now what's this about? My Spidey-sense tingled.

Wait, let's digress for a minute. My car is a 1982 Turbo Saab 900, bought brand new. Leather heated seats, original beige carpeting, sun and moon roof. Everything in it is in perfect condition. Bose twelve-speaker sound system, Pirellis, and a sweet custom midnight-blue paint job. I have it detailed every month. You could eat off the hood and watch your food as you forked it into your mouth. After snorting up the last car I had, I ordered the Saab while on a skiing trip to Oregon, to save on the sales taxes. The car ran perfect, but it did have a tendency toward the small occasional breakdown, just like its owner. It fit my personality like a glove.

Now, what would Kurt need with the Saab? More tingling. And how did he get to our house without a car? I should have asked him, right then. Kurt wasn't one to take the bus; he would have been so impatient he would have threatened the driver with bodily harm if the vehicle was traveling slower than eighty. I could just see the guy...

"Fucking step on it, you fucking bus driver fucker. And you fucking people in the back, shut the fuck up! Hey, you. The guy with the nitwit cowboy hat. Yeah, you. Dickhead. If you keep staring, I'll come back there and put your fucking eyes out. Then you can stare out of black sockets. Only you won't be able to see to stare. Ha, ha...ha. Hmmm." Then the glare that turned other people to stone.

So, if he did get to our place by car, whose car? And why couldn't he use *that* car for whatever nefarious plan he had for the evening? See? I know, a bit compulsive, and this extends to analysis of what all my friends think and do. I guess you could consider it bordering on paranoia, but I disagree. Of course. In Kurt's case, I figured I had good reason to be concerned. As I have said before, with friends like Kurt, you just never knew.

I decided to put my concerns aside for now and test the questions out on him at lunch instead. Sean was coming with us, part of the deal-making team. That was good. That way, when Kurt answered my carefully worded queries, I could silently communicate my belief or disbelief in the answers and get Sean's nonverbal reactions. I trusted his judgment. Of course, Sean would never let Kurt know of our silent conspiracy; Kurt would punch us both out for disloyalty. As a matter of principle. Kurt was big on principles. And honor. Like a twelfth-century knight. With a big-ass sword and a willingness to swing it.

It was just like Kurt to be so insistent about my car too. On top of all his other behavior peculiarities, he was very into being the alpha male, and his attitude screamed "DO IT!" And we would too, like the good little soldiers we were.

I went back into the bedroom, sweatshirt off, fresh polypro undershirt on, sweatshirt back on. Everyone living in Boulder knew that if you didn't like the weather, just wait fifteen minutes. One time I went to class on a sunny fifty-five-degree day and when I came out an hour later it was snowing. Sure, it's true about the weather, but what a cliché. You probably heard that said about a lot of places, people feeling clever for saying it. Those people are lame.

And I guess that made me lame too. As an ex-friend of mine, another guy I knew from Newport Beach used to say, "Oh well..." but I felt a different way. Like the Boy Scouts say, "Always be prepared." That's my motto. Fuck my Newport ex-friend.

I straightened my favorite brown woven leather belt and took three deep breaths. It felt like my head was clearing but I still had a subtle ringing in my ears. Was it tinnitus? Maybe I'd see the doctor later, or tomorrow after I got straight. Can't be seeing the professional now if I can't even fool the simple amateurs. I sat down on the edge of the bed facing the standing mirror and put on my gray wool socks, then my lace-up Nike Waffle Trainers. I had kept them in great condition for years. They were the originals too, blue with yellow swoosh, not the lame color combinations that Nike came up with later. I stood up, gave myself a good shake, and took a once-over look in the mirror behind the door. God, my eyes looked like shit smudges. I went into my open closet and grabbed my lightweight North Face jacket and took my tortoiseshell Vuarnet Cateyes from on top of the dresser. I put them on. One more glance; looking good, ready to rock whatever scheme Kurt had in mind. I shut and latched my bedroom door and went back into the living room, where I found the two of them taking hits and waiting. I wasn't sure they were actually waiting for me; they seemed to be preoccupied with the swirling in the carpet fibers of our tattered tan-and-red Persian carpet. So, like an idiot, I started to stare at the carpet. Perhaps there was some sort of critter hiding in it, and they were scanning like cats for the morsel. I considered the ludicrous situation. Like we should care about the carpet. I doubted the rug was even Persian, it had only cost us forty-five dollars new. Funny how smoking pot will make you do that, think and act like a moron. I looked outside at the oak trees next door. Sean mumbled, "Let's go already, food is calling and I'm hungry for anything edible." The two stood up without so much as an afterthought and we proceeded out the front door and down the winding staircase. As I locked the apartment door, Sean's black-and-brown wolf-dog came bounding up and jumped on me, knocking me into the door. He then took off back down the stairs like a jackrabbit. In Morley's case, this jackrabbit weighed about a 120 pounds and could take out an NFL running back if given a five-yard start. I know, you ask, "What's a wolf-dog?" It is just like the spelling, half wolf, half dog. In Morley's case, Belgian shepherd. He's a great dog but if he detects fear, he can just stare at you like you're his next meal. I finished locking the door behind us and followed Sean down the steps. I flashed on Sean, Morley, and the whole I Think Her Name Was Tracy situation. Who's Tracy, you ask?

Chapter 8

I'll tell you a story. One time I dragged myself home late from a party that had ended two days before, the taste of some girl named Suzy Whatever still on my tongue. There sat Morley, quietly next to Sean on the pew, watching some cartoon with a dog, a rooster, and some kind of bird. I swear Morley understood and smiled when the dog was the center of the action. If he could, Sean would have named him Acme, like in the Road Runner cartoons, instead of Morley, but the name came attached to the pooch. Besides, after careful consideration, Sean agreed that Acme sounded like an idiotic name for a dog.

Sean inherited Morley from a girlfriend of Kurt's who I think was named Tracy. Actually, he inherited Morley from Kurt, who inherited Morley from a woman we'll call Tracy, Tracy Thomsen. Tracy was easy on the eyes, simple in the head. And this is what happened.

What happened is that she cheated on Kurt with this other guy we knew, who we called Jimmy Fuckhead. Wait, that's not the beginning, let's try that again.

Something like two years ago, Kurt was making a living between classes dealing mostly pot but also some blow. He kept the stash in a brushed-silver, two-lock Zero

Halliburton briefcase in his closet, under the floorboards, just like in *Scarface*. Kurt's prideful pretentiousness with that stupid case always made me laugh, though not to his face; I wanted to keep mine intact. Anyway, the pot came from Hawaii, from friends of his who shipped it with packages of Kona coffee to cover the smell. What does this have to do with the story? I'll tell you. It all started with the case. See, Kurt was carrying this case when he went into The Broken Drum for breakfast and first saw Tracy. He noticed her looking at the case, she noticed him noticing her looking at the case, he looked at her ass hidden behind a pair of tight jeans, she noticed him, she turned so he could have a better look; her ass was spectacular. So, we sit down at a table overlooking the street (the better to see potential villains) and Kurt orders five eggs, toast and double-order hash browns, and a Guinness. And stares at Tracy's ass. He looks over and grins at me, arches one of his eyebrows; his tongue hit the floor, right then and there. Gaga for the chick, I think you would call it.

Kurt was not known for his sentimental side and his ability to understand chicks was remedial. We all knew it, including him. As I have said before, the guy was a Neanderthal throwback. Still, at that moment, he kind of wilted. He asked her out. She said yes while staring at his

64

crotch. They started dating and pretty soon we would see her with him everywhere. The two had become one, even on the drug deals. After a couple of months, I think for him it started to look like the real deal, though he still played his cards in close. And here's the rub, Tracy didn't seem to mind. In fact, she rolled with the punches when she heard of his messing around, whether girls, fights, whatever. After a couple more months, Kurt realized that Tracy didn't care about his bullshit. He went the other way and became exclusive. It shocked us. Tracy treated him like the husband of a traditional, dutiful wife. She cared for him when he got hurt, stuck up for him, cooked and cleaned for him, and from what he said of her, fucked like a porn star. He fell in love with Tracy Thomsen and, after a quick powwow with us, had her move in. He brought her into the business, and she made deals and took care of inventory while he was busy cleaning out suckers with bunk weed and trampled-on coke. In business, Kurt was ruthless and malicious; he once rolled a pimp on Forty-Second Street in New York City. When he told us the story, he made it sound like the pimp was going to roll him first, so he had to defend himself. Not very likely since Kurt began the story by admitting his need for cash to catch a cab back to his hotel.

So, anyways, Kurt and Tracy had this great business going. Fall came to Boulder, and Kurt decided to take some of his profit and go home to Hawaii for a few weeks. He didn't invite I think her name was Tracy, maybe because he wanted some time alone with his family but also because he wanted to spend time paddling canoe and drinking out with his childhood friends. No girlfriends allowed. And (let's just call her) Tracy, to her credit, got it. So, Kurt left, saying to us all that he would be back in about a month, and that Tracy had the business. If we needed anything, he said, we should talk to Tracy.

You know what? We need to go back about six more months and start again a second time. There was this guy named Jimmy. He was a tall, dopey guy with a pretty-boy face and an easy smile. Kind of uncoordinated, like he was the one kid in elementary school that got picked last for kickball and shoved into a locker after showers. We met him while picking up girls at a bar called Pearl's. Jimmy found out that Kurt was a dealer, and through a middleman that we had nicknamed HardOn, he bought some blow and somehow glommed onto the group. He was at our house when we barbecued and brought cases of beer to our parties and always bought drugs from either Kurt or Tracy that he generously shared. Sometimes he ran out of blow after laying out lines. He just reached into his back pocket for his nylon Velcro wallet with the hibiscus flower printed on the outside, pulled out a hundred-dollar bill, and grabbed another gram.

Now that we have all the players, back to the story. When Kurt left for Hawaii, we all just sort of left Tracy alone. I mean, she wasn't one of the boys, she was Kurt's girlfriend/wife. Sean and I had our own dirty dog deals going on; I think he was secretly afraid that if he hung out with her, lust would raise its ugly head. She was truly dazzling.

About three weeks after Kurt left, Sean called Tracy to get the inside story on Kurt's real return date. Sean needed to buy textbooks for spring semester, and I think he was looking to sponge a couple of Kurt's books in exchange for some Guinness. Tracy didn't answer the telephone. Sean called three times that day and got no answer each time. He called the next day, same thing. By then Sean was concerned; you could tell because every time he hung up the telephone, he would rub his ear between his thumb and first finger. He'd also look off into space like he was contemplating the general theory of relativity. He started calling around, HardOn, another guy we called Do a Line, a friend of Tracy's we called Alycat (a very hot little kitten but with claws), even a rugby player named Sherwood Forest. "Tracy? Nah, haven't seen her." Same thing every time.

He talked to just about everybody. No Tracy.

He also called Jimmy, no answer. The only one who didn't answer. Again, Sean started calling Jimmy, three times that second day. No answer. He and I discussed Tracy's disappearance and agreed that things looked and smelled very fishy. We finally called Kurt and told him the happenings. He called us morons and told us not to call back. We were undeterred. The next day, now day three of the Tracy Situation, we drove over to Kurt's house, crawled through the bathroom window, and checked around. Almost the first thing we saw was a notepad. On the notepad were scribblings involving United Airlines, Denver to Los Angeles confirmation numbers—yes, there were two of them. At the bottom, we saw Tracy's and Jimmy's names. And, would you believe, they had adjoining seat assignments. This was beyond credible. Then we looked for the briefcase Kurt kept the coke in. Kurt had splurged on that brushed-gunmetal-gray briefcase, the kind with a guaranteed unbreakable lock. It would have been easy to find if it had been there, which it wasn't. So now speculation started to percolate as circumstances started unfolding for us. Either before or after Kurt went to Hawaii, Tracy and

Jimmy planned to go to California to have sex and do drugs, probably selling some to cover expenses. The two of us considered that we were exaggerating about the whole thing but agreed that this was a combustible set of circumstances and could explode. The best solution was the direct one. We called Kurt again. This time he listened. Kurt caught a plane that night, we picked him up in Denver, and he quizzed us on the drive back. By the time we got to Boulder, Kurt stopped quizzing. I looked in the rearview mirror and saw his eyes. Medium brown, pinned, lids hooded. No sound but breathing and the occasional mumbled swear word. He kept his final thoughts to himself, though they weren't hard to figure out.

Instead of going home, Kurt stayed with us for the couple of days, up at the Gumby House, everything easy. Then we got a call from Alycat, letting us know that the loving couple were back in town. Kurt drove up the Hill to the home he shared with Tracy and waited while we went to Liquor Mart to pick up some beers. The two thieves showed up in a cab a couple of hours later. The three of us sat in the living room, waiting for the main event, drinking our beers and watching the Stanley Kubrick masterpiece, *A Clockwork Orange*. Perfect choice for the occasion, if I do say so myself. When he heard the cab door close, Kurt slipped into the bedroom while Sean went outside to greet Tracy. I stayed in the living room and watched the festivities unfold from the picture window. Sean was masterful; he was all smiles and hugs, even holding on to her for a second too long, causing her to step back, smile, and give him a second once-over. Slut. I knew Kurt was in the bedroom doing a slow burn. On that day, for Kurt, a slow burn without making noise involved tearing the telephone book apart with his bare hands.

Tracy reached back into the cab for her psychedelically patterned, soft-cover suitcase, her oversized leather tote bag, and Kurt's briefcase. Jimmy stayed in the back seat, trying to make himself as small as possible. Tracy shut the cab door and I saw her try to distract Sean by dropping the case and bending with her ass to him as she retrieved it. She didn't succeed. As the cab pulled away, Sean walked up and said into the open window, "See you later, Jimmy." I heard him clearly.

Tracy had already turned and walked to the front door. By the time she reached up for the handle, Kurt had come out of the bedroom and opened it. She staggered back a couple of steps, dropping her tote. "I didn't expect you for another week," she said. Shoulders sagged.

"I guess," Kurt mumbled. Then he backhanded her across the mouth. That drew blood, and Tracy whimpered. He raised his hand to hit her again, but she flinched and turned her back to him. He glowered at her and said in a low voice, "Get inside, we need to straighten this out." Pause for effect. "I know what you did, you fucking bitch."

At this point I was now outside, watching. When they went in, Sean and I stayed in the hot August sun for a few minutes watching air move. We considered. I nodded toward the door. Sean shook his head slightly. I sniffed. We waited a little while longer. I looked in through the front window to see if the coast was clear; it was, the two of them were in the bedroom. We snuck in and closed the door quietly behind us. Sean opened up a couple of Guinness, one of which he gave to me. We sat down and turned on the stereo. Some Steely Dan, *Aja*. Great album and it sounded so clear in Kurt's system. I took sips of my beer. On the fourth swallow, a loud scream from the bedroom. Sean's head snapped. His eyes bulged and he licked his lower lip. I just shrugged. Getting in Kurt's way as he settled the Tracy Situation would have been a very bad idea.

We heard nothing for a couple of minutes, just some low whispering and an occasional growling noise that could have come from a bear. I reached for a freshly rolled joint and the cheap BIC lighter sitting on the coffee table. I gave the joint to Sean and was about to thumb the lighter when we heard another sound from the bedroom. It was unmistakable. Tracy pleading, "No, Kurt, please." We froze, and within a few seconds we heard a sharp "uhnn," and then a sound I would have never expected: the sound of Tracy's head smacking against the headboard as Kurt fucked her. Well, raped her is a more accurate way to put it. I gagged. This was so wrong, I thought. Sean and I again looked at each other, this time silently communicating. I said to Sean, "Forget it. I'm not going in there. No fucking way. You go; you've been friends with him longer than me." Coward.

"Yeah, but he likes you better, and he told me to watch out for her before he left. I'm going to catch shit from him later. You've got to do it."

I said, "To tell you the truth, what's going on in there scares me. Kurt scares me, the guy's in caveman mode. Forget it. No way." Yella coward.

"You and I both know this is so fucked up. Kurt could go to prison for this if she presses charges. We gotta stop it. It's wrong, and you know it. We'll go together."

"You go." Double Yella coward.

So, shaking his head, Sean got up and went over to the door. He knocked but didn't wait for an answer before he opened the door, went in, and closed it again. The sound ended. I sat there, ashamed of myself, and listened for any word to give me a clue of what was going on. I heard Kurt exclaim, "Fuck you." More murmuring, crying.

Kurt: "This is on you, you, bitch."

Then Sean came back out. He shut the door with a quiet click, looked at me with unmasked disdain, and said, "It's over. You're a pussy."

Not really, just a survivor. And maybe a little cowardly.

Kurt came out a minute later wearing only a pair of jeans and went to the kitchen. He opened the fridge, reached in, and brought out another Guinness. He popped it open with his teeth and slowly ambled over, kind of plopped down next to me and took a long, really long pull. Half the beer was gone, just like that. Tension poured out of him, so invasive that you could have felt it in Kansas. He reeked of it. It was like he was vibrating at a totally different level. His hand was steady, but his face twitched every couple of seconds. I don't think I ever saw Kurt this upset, angry, pissed; you pick it. Tracy finally came out of the bedroom. She had gotten into her jeans and T-shirt. Her eyes were red, and there looked to be a welt on her right cheek where Kurt hit her. She carried her shoes in her left hand, her bra and socks in her right. Kurt seethed. He laser-stared at her, brown eyes glowing, I swear it; she looked down to the ground.

"Get those clothes off," Kurt said on a monotone so low he sounded like Lurch in *The Addams Family*, only not funny. Not funny at all. "I bought you those clothes, and I want them back. You can wear the sheet. I'll call you a cab. I know you don't have any money of your own since you've been stealing mine, so you don't have to pay me back. But I'm taking the dog. He's mine now."

Tracy looked at Sean and me. "Can I stay with you guys for a couple of days until I find a place?" She didn't even kick about the dog. Fucking bitch. Kurt didn't say anything, and I wondered for a second if he would relent and give her a break. What he said was, "Whatever."

Sean said, "Okay, if it's okay with Bruce."

I said, "No. You made your bed, now you live in the sheet." Look at that. I made a funny.

Both Sean and Kurt turned and gave me a simultaneously surprised look. I guess I was being callous, but the chick deserved it. I didn't have any patience for her bullshit. She broke our trust. Fuck her. I bet she was wondering what Kurt would do to Jimmy. Sean said to me, "You're a petty fucker." He looked at her. "Sorry, Tracy." What the fuck was he apologizing for? He didn't do anything.

Kurt just grunted and took another sip of his beer, then gave me another look out of the corner of his eye. He held my gaze until I looked away. Did I misread this? What if this is big show on Kurt's part and he planned on getting back together with her? What if this was another one of those toxic relationship scenarios? You know, where the couple yells at each other, husband beats wife, she screams, they split. Then two weeks later they're back together making dinosaur noises from the bedroom. Was I getting in the middle of that scene? Was that the message Kurt was giving me? Kurt has a code, for sure. So, I might as well second-guess the situation all night; let my obsessive behavior go wild. Oh man.

Tracy went back into the bedroom to change out of her clothes, now Kurt's clothes. Sean leaned over to me and quietly asked, "What's wrong with you?"

"Eh, the chick deserves it. You don't think so? If she's smart, she'll go live with Jimmy Fuckhead."

Kurt said, "I wouldn't if I was her." Fuck. Here we go again, Tracy Situation; the thing that wouldn't leave. Clearly from Kurt's point of view there was more work to be done.

Chapter 9

And there was. The next night I decided to take an evening off from partying and sales. While I still had some stash, most of my dealer buddies were good to go, it was midweek and most of the students studied while all the white-collar, midlevel-manager types slept for the next workday. I was still up trying to make sense of a passage in the Ayn Rand book *The Fountainhead*. My marijuana-addled brain wouldn't meet with Howard Roark, so I put the book down next to the wiggling hula dancer lamp on my nightstand and turned off the light. The house was silent; only an occasional loud voice came from down the street. There was a college apartment complex down there. It was the kind of place that mimics a dorm situation, two losers to a bedroom and two bedrooms to an apartment. You had to pay an inflated rent to live with someone else. In the same room. What happened if you wanted to fuck some chick? Kick the other guy out to sleep in the living room, maybe give him a pillow and his blanket? And here's what really gave me the willies. What about if the guy was a faggot? And you had to live with him. In the same room. No fucking way. I wouldn't want to be caught in a blind alley behind a fag bar in Denver either.

There was a resounding knock on the downstairs door and Sean called down, "We're asleep! You can't wake us up! You'll never wake us up! Go away!"

Kurt came around to the front of the house and called up through my window, "Hey, Bruce. Let me in. I need to talk to you." Ho jeez. Not good. I got up and went to the window that slid up into the ceiling to become a doorway, my heart rate speeding up as I considered the potential nature of Kurt's visit. An idle thought occurred to me: perhaps he was there to execute a beating over the way I treated Tracy. I know, paranoid, but...I took a deep breath, consciously calmed my hands, slid the window up, and went out onto the balcony. The balcony had a bench that you could sit on and look out over the whole street. It was a great place to go to wake up, drink a cup of coffee, and watch the sunrise. That is, if you had actually been to sleep. Not such a good place if you hadn't. I looked down at Kurt looking up at me. I decided. "Okay, hold on." I went out to the living room heading for the front door. Detouring to the light switch, I started to turn the lights on when Sean quietly uttered from his open bedroom door a couple of feet away, "Don't even think about it."

I heard him roll over.

"It's Kurt, he wants to come up. If I don't let him in and he gets pissed, you only have yourself to blame."

"You shouldn't have been such a dick to Tracy. If you open that door and Kurt's back with her, the shit's on you, not me. Now shut up and let me sleep," Sean warned.

"If he's not back with her and remembers that you were supposed to be his eyes and ears, that beating you avoided yesterday will be back to haunt you. And Kurt's an unforgiving kind of ghost." I heard a sigh and a snort, and Sean came out of the bedroom in his Jams shorts and rubber slippers. While I switched on the lights, he went into the living room and turned on the TV. I glanced at the screen as I went to open the front door and start down the stairs. How quaint, *Three's Company*. Priceless classic late-evening entertainment, 1970s cultural sophistication at its finest.

I went down the stairs and opened the front door. Kurt barged past me and took the steps two at a time, his feet making loud stomping sounds as he raced to our apartment. He was in the kitchen before I even got back up the stairs. I hit the top stair and crossed the threshold just as I heard the crack and hiss of a Harp Lager. Kurt came back into the living room. I sat on our pew; Sean sat on the windowsill and looked out at the University of Colorado tennis team house next door. Morley sat at attention, perhaps feeling the level of energy in the room.

"You guys are coming with me on a business chore I have. It's got to be tonight, so get your shit." He looked at me. "We can take your car."

I opened my mouth to ask him why we couldn't take the car he came in when he interrupted. "Don't. Just shut up, Bruce. We're going, hurry up."

I put on a pair of jeans, slippers, and a white Surf Line Hawaii logo T-shirt. Sean wore something similar. When we stepped toward the door, Kurt looked us over, top to bottom.

"That's not going to work. You guys better change. Quiet shoes and dark clothes. Hurry up."

I looked at Sean. Sean shrugged. Dark clothes, running shoes. It sounded suspiciously like we were going to scamper away from something nefarious in lickety-split time. Still, we were committed, loyalty among Hawaiians. And one Californian. No stopping without fully pissing Kurt off. And no going back. Fuuuuck. Okay, since there was no going back, we best move forward, full speed ahead. If you can't stop something, embrace it, that's my motto. We went downstairs and Sean locked the door as Kurt and I climbed into the car, Kurt in the back seat. I pulled out my coke vial and handed it over my shoulder. Kurt took out a bump for each nostril, then gave it back. I used the little silver spoon to scoop out a snootful of snow and hoovered, then screwed the cap back on the vial. I started the engine, but we had to wait for Sean to race back upstairs and close my balcony doorway. Stupid, we could have been totally ripped off while we were out doing who knows what the hell. Well, that's not quite true. Kurt knew what the hell. You are so fucking stupid, Bruce. I don't know where my brain is sometimes.

Actually, I do. I've seen it tripping the light fantastic in the bars on the Boulder Mall; sometimes it isn't even attached to my body.

The lights finally went off upstairs and Sean came down, shut and locked the front door, and walked to the car. He got into the passenger side, catching his shoelace on the running board and almost tripping as he got in. "Get in, goonie," I said. I looked through the rearview mirror. "Where are we going?"

Kurt's face, his eyes narrowing slightly.

He smoldered. He spoke in a real low voice, "Go up Broadway to Maxwell and turn left toward the mountains. There's a red-and-tan apartment building about four or five blocks up, 760 Maxwell or something like that. When we get there, I'll tell you the rest of it." We drove.

Here was the rest of it.

We pulled up to the front of the building and the two of them got out of the car. Kurt leaned in and said, "You'd better pull it around and point it the other way."

This sounded ominous. I did what Kurt said. The Saab now pointed back toward Broadway with enough room in front to make a quick getaway without having to back up first. I shut off the engine and from the interior of the car I saw Kurt and Sean standing at the curb under a tree, Kurt whispering to Sean in a forceful manner; Sean was listening just as intently. I watched for a couple of seconds, then got out of the car and started to lock the door. The two of them stopped talking. Sean turned to me and said, "Better not lock it. We may not be here long." Kurt waited for me to join them. He pulled a long-barreled revolver, like an old S&W .38, the kind the cops used to use back in the day, and mumbled, "We go. Don't say nothing, just do what I say, and it'll be cool."

We walked to the back of the complex to a narrow concrete stairwell with a metal railing. Kurt put his finger to his lips, "Don't touch the railing," and started up, taking care to be as quiet as possible. We followed, taking similar precautions. By this time, my head swam with preconceptions of this escapade. All outcomes led to horrible. I really needed a spoonsky of blow, and for a second gave some thought to stopping right there and taking a good sniff from my vial, you know, just in case I was going to freak out I wanted to be able to run like hell. Then I thought better. Kurt had a gun, and I didn't want him aiming it at me.

We crept forward as silent as leopards in the moonlight and stopped at apartment number 14. Kurt reached out with his left hand and tried the door. He had the revolver in his right, thumb on the trigger. Oh man, this was bad, this was bad. The door was locked but when Kurt stepped to the window a couple of feet away, it slid open. By silent majority, I was picked to walk point, so I climbed in over the sink and made sure there was nothing that could be disturbed when they followed. They climbed in, first Kurt, then Sean, and there we were in this apartment, standing there. I had no idea where we were, why we were there, what the fuck was going on. I was along for the ride. That's it.

The place was all dark, not a sound except our light breathing and the hum of the refrigerator. Kurt stepped past the fridge and reached out to a bowl on the counter and picked up what looked like a piece of fruit. He palmed whatever the hell it was and used the gun to point down the hallway toward the bedrooms. We started down the hallway, Kurt on point, me second, Sean last. Kurt stopped in front of the first doorway and again he turned and put his finger to his lips. The door was slightly ajar, and there was the sound of someone sleeping coming from the other side. The person had to be a cokehead. The sound we heard was kind of like a whistle. That came from cocaine sinus buildup, I knew that from experience. Maybe we were here to rip this guy off. Oh no. This was bad. Bad, bad. A burst insight, and everything came to clarity, like a spotlight illuminating a dark street corner. This was Jimmy Fuckhead's place. We were here for Kurt's retribution. Gun. Kurt pulled the piece of fruit from his side; it glowed in the moonlight. Except it wasn't a piece of fruit, it was a potato. He squashed it over the tip of the barrel. Oh no. Gun. Potato. Suppressor. Fuck. I turned to Kurt, whispered.

"Ok, who lives here?"

"Who do you think? Jimmy, the guy that fucked my girlfriend and stole my blow." He was going to kill Jimmy Fuckhead. I reached out and grabbed Kurt's shirt. He just shook me off and bared his teeth. Oh man, this is going to happen.

I turned to Sean, but he was already heading back down the hall toward the kitchen. Kurt grabbed me by the arm and held me in place. What the fuck, I hadn't done anything. Sean was the one that had fucked up. Why was I even there? Kurt looked at me and mouthed and pointed. "Push open the door."

I didn't move for a second, and then I remembered the commitment I had made in the car. If you can't go back, go forward, full speed ahead, and I was in for the whole megillah. I pushed the door open with my fist as Kurt moved behind me and aimed the gun at Jimmy's head. I guess Kurt thought better of it; shooting Jimmy in the head, I mean. Instead, he stepped past me and into the room. Reaching the bed, quick as lightning, he raised the gun again, this time aiming for Jimmy's heart. I watched him pull the trigger. The room lit up and something warm hit my arm where I had raised it to protect myself. The sound was like hitting a pear with a hammer, only louder. It wasn't as loud as I expected though. Jimmy bolted up and hollered, "Oww! What the hell?" I almost didn't think Kurt had hit him. Then Jimmy sort of wilted back into the mattress, holding his chest. He turned toward us, and I saw his eyes open a bit as he recognized Kurt. Then it was too late. Kurt walked around and stood directly over Jimmy, pointed the gun at his head. Jimmy watched.

"You shouldn't have done it, asshole. There are rules. You fucked up. Now look at you." He pulled the trigger again. This time there was a tremendous bang, like a big firecracker, an M80 without the echo. Or whatever, something like that. We used to have M80 fights in the street on Halloween when I was a kid, so yeah, it sounded like that. My ears rang, then my head spun, and I started to lose my balance. I looked up and Kurt was past me, moving quickly to the front door. I didn't even look at Jimmy, what was the point? Nothing to see anyway. A guy with a hole in the head, brains leaking onto the pillow. Fuckety fuck.

I turned and raced after Kurt. Both Sean and he were already out the front door, waiting for me. I sprinted to the window, shut it. Then I wiped down the sink, windowsill, and counter with the dishrag hanging on the oven handle. I kept it and gave it to Kurt as I went out the door. Sean pulled the front door closed and checked the lock while Kurt wiped our prints off the outside window frame. Lastly, front door handle, and we were free. It couldn't have been more than fifteen seconds since the gun had gone off. Twice. Fucking Kurt. Sean was already around the corner as I moved to the stairs and heard Kurt right behind me. I purposely slowed down so we could be together and not cause suspicion. It occurred to me that people would have a more difficult time telling us apart if we were bunched up. I mean, the three of us were about the same height, though I was thinner. We cruised through the complex and out to the street, glancing around with a casual falseness that would have indicated guilt to the dumbest Keystone Kop. We walked to the car. I looked at my Rolex Submariner. Holy shit, it hadn't been three minutes. Sean scanned the street for witnesses, but at two thirty in the morning, we were good to go. A couple of lights were on in other apartments but no heads out windows or shadows in doorways, nothing like that. I unlocked the car doors, we got in, and it was off to sleep we go, heigh-ho, heigh-ho. Like I was going to be able to sleep. If we were caught and convicted, it would be at least ten years for me. Fucking Kurt.

I pulled onto Broadway and pushed the car up to the speed limit. I didn't want to do the speedy getaway thing. Very suspicious, total cliché. I stopped at the two stop signs as well, once again, nothing to see here. We got to Pearl Street. We were almost home. Just stay on Broadway until College, left on 13th and we would be back home, doing lines of coke, drinking Guinness, and watching *The Addams*

Family. I was so focused on just finishing what we started that my brain didn't have time to process what I'd seen and what Kurt had done. I kept my eye on the ball and stopped at the red light on Canyon. There was the Bank of Boulder. *Nice*. Hey, I needed to go to the bank. What about it? What about you get it together and get home, Bruce. Now was not the time to do something foolish, like stop at the ATM machine while dressed in dark clothes splattered with blood with two other guys lurking in the car, one also blood splattered, even more than you. I didn't think we could use the old "coming home from the debutante dance" excuse if the cops crept up on us. When the light turned green, I changed my mind, got off of Broadway, and drove west up Canyon a couple of blocks. I turned left. The hood of the car pointed us up the hill and into the college residential area. It was easy to get home the back way and had the added advantage that I could pull the car around the back of the house, where nobody would see or hear us park. We crossed three or four more blocks, and I took the last few hundred yards to the alley behind the house at a low speed. Parked. Lights off. My heart was still pounding like John Bonham on the drums. Off went the engine, click went the doors as we closed them behind us, and crunch went the gravel as we went around to the front door. I opened it. We stepped through. We climbed the creaking staircase. Sean unlocked our apartment and that was the end. Except for the part about our new companion and best friend Morley jumping around and knocking into the TV and nearly breaking a bottle of Stoli. And the part about me, brainish matter and mashed, gunpowder-blackened potato in my hair, a short trip to the toilet and the loss of my ramen-and-rice dinner. How's that for a story?

Boulder Daily Express

April 25, 1981

Loud noises lead to the discovery of unidentified body.

Fireworks were reported at 2:30 a.m. last night in the vicinity of 8th and Maxwell Streets. The Boulder Police were contacted by a concerned neighbor and upon investigation, a man was discovered with apparent gunshot wounds. Paramedics responded but the man was pronounced dead at the scene. The as yet unidentified man was discovered at 740 Maxwell Street, an apartment house catering to CU students. According to Boulder PD, there are several leads to the shooting, including witnesses who saw several individuals leaving the area. Lt. Sue Wilson, head of the violent crime task force tasked with cleaning up the drug-related crime in the downtown area, was characteristically quiet on the subject of any drug association with the crime but did ask that the public come forward with any other information that could be relevant to the case. Mayor Margaret Correlli has also asked the Federal Bureau of Investigation to investigate any potential ties to larger drug trafficking, including potential ties to Mexican and/or South American cartel activity. This is the fifth murder or alleged murder in Boulder County so far this year, compared to one by this time in 1979 and four by the end of April last year.

Chapter 10

When I stepped outside for the first time that day, Ernie's Chicken Cutlet on the brain, the crisp air caught in my throat. Cough. Ugh. Cold. I tugged on my wool-lined gloves, finished zipping up my jacket, and headed for the car parked at the sidewalk. We all got in, Sean calling shotgun like the very mature and sophisticated individual he was. I cranked the motor, waiting for that telltale purr of a well-tuned Saab engine as it warms up. I could see my breath fogging up the windshield and turned on the heater.

The windshield began to clear as we pulled into traffic and started toward a section of the city called the Mapleton Hill. The road was dry and my car's after-market racing suspension made short work of the corners. I took care of the stop signs, ignoring them.

We made the last turn at Broadway and Mapleton, finding a place to park just up the street from the restaurant. As we got out, I glanced up at the renovated Queen Anne–style house across the street from us. I sniffed and smirked, elbowed Sean, quick head nod toward the two-story abode. He snorted. Kurt looked over my shoulder, quick snicker.

One day a couple of years before, we got into a thing with the occupants over an argument at one of the football games. Our team was getting soundly thrashed by our main rival at the time, Oklahoma University, ranked number 3 in the country. Oklahoma slapped our team around for sixty minutes like little bitches. I think the final score was 84 to 6. When we left the game, we were drunk. What else were we to do but cry into our beers and then drink them? We walked to a friend's house, grabbed some aluminum beach loungers, and planted ourselves in the front yard with a view of the oncoming crowd. As a particularly rich-looking and enormously obese group of Oklahoma boosters came by, we hollered, "You may have won the game, but you're really fat, we have cocaine!" The look we got back was pure revulsion, but who cared? Well, someone did. This Dudley Do-Right, square-jawed, blond-haired, musclehead, Confederate-Flag bandana-wearing motherfucker had the hubris to tell us we were a disgrace to the school. He threatened us. I mean, HE threatened US. "If I hear you verbally hurling such vile, embarrassing garbage at visiting fair-minded sporting boosters again, I'll come back and bring a few of my brothers to straighten your shit out." He turned to the blimp-shaped Okies. "Sorry about that, folks, some people have no class."

He meant, frat brothers. Uh, yeah. Right.

It turned out that the guy lived in the very house we now scrutinized. I know because he was too stupid to see us following him. The next evening, Kurt, Sean, our buddy Colin from England, and I went over to the house and lit it up, shooting bottle rockets into the open windows of the second floor. Yelling and hollering came from inside as we took aim with our fireworks-filled aluminum tubes and screamed "Yarrr, avast! Prepare to be burned, all hands!" This southern gentleman wannabe asshole stormed out the front and came sprinting over like some heigh-ho massa ready to horsewhip us. He threatened to call the cops, all bug eyes and clenched jaw. Kurt explained the foolishness of that plan with a couple of thundering rights to said jaw and a kick to the balls. The guy went down. His buddies poured out of the house, five against us four. Make that none against four about fifteen seconds later as we took care of business. What? I never said we couldn't fight, I just suggested that Kurt was a great fighter.

The house burned. Brothers scurried for cover. We were long gone by the time the fire department showed up. We never saw or heard from the now broken-jawed and gonad-crippled idiot again, though apparently the house got rebuilt.

Back to the story. We scrambled out of the car like Keystone Kops and walked into Ernie's. The doorbell jingled. Ernie looked up from the counter and greeted us with his famous, "Ernie's Chicken Cutret today, you guys want sahm? I make special prate for you!" Ernie was a transplant from Guangdong and spoke with a pronounced Chinese accent. Those people who understood him got the special treatment, those that didn't got bupkes. He was a good guy trying to make a go of it, and I had a soft spot for him. We all did. He reminded Kurt and Sean of the little Chinese vendors in Hawaii, where they had grown up, plate lunch service in the front, marijuana sales in the back. They turned me on to Ernie's, and I never looked back. Excellent food.

As we waited for our plate lunches, we took forks, knives, and napkins and got our Cokes from the vending machine on the other side of the room. We were by ourselves. We sat down.

Suddenly, Sean blurted out, "So Bruce, how's your classes going?" I knew this was going to happen at some point; Sean, a hen checking on her chick. I found it mildly to moderately insulting. I spent time lying to my parents about my grades at the end of every semester, I didn't need the stress of lying to my roommate during the semester as well. I went with the truth.

"I missed physics and geology class today but I'm getting a B in both, I think. I never worry about calculus, that one's good as gold. Why, you think you're my moms, or what?" I'll be lucky to pass the calculus final. Of course, studying might help. I'm actually getting a D in geology. Physics is a total loss. If I don't find a way to drop it, it'll be a big F for "Flail." "Oh yeah, and I've finished my linguistics class already, got an A, so, there's that." This was the part that was the truth. Linguistics class was an experience unlike any I had faced in school, ever. It was self-paced, and you were graded based on the chapter test scores and number of chapters you completed in the semester. The way the testing went was that there were three versions per chapter, and you got three tries to pass one of them with a 70 percent or better. The higher the grade in each test and the more chapters you finished, the better the end grade.

It gets better. The tests were open book and open notes. Professor Edwards corrected them and gave you back your test to study if you failed. The next day, you could try again with another version. And it gets even better than that. Here's the scam. You go in with two other people and each takes one version of the exam. It didn't matter if you studied or not since you get the tests back corrected. You then write down the answers and trade them among yourselves, thereby providing all three would-be criminals with all three versions. The next day you take the test again, and Dr. Edwards would invariably exclaim, "Nice work, you clearly studied hard overnight. Keep it up and I'll be giving you an A." Some might call this outright cheating, but I chose to think Edwards knew what was going on. Hell, it was a jock class; everyone knew the deal.

After picking up the plates of breaded chicken, mac salad, and a cucumber and peeled carrot salad with sesame seeds, we went back outside and stood next to the car, eating and drinking our Cokes. The food was good, but it was the Coke that rejuvenated me. There's nothing like a shot of pure sugar to recharge the batteries. I would be good until dark, when it was then okay to go back to the other kind of coke for nighttime frivolities. While I was eating, I watched the corner intersection downhill and about forty yards away. This was one of the busiest pedestrian intersections in the city. College fraternity and sorority houses and several large apartment complexes were located within a few blocks, leading to a steady stream of students in the crosswalk.

I have always found it entertaining to people watch. Sometimes I would look at someone in particular and try to discern things about them that would reveal little secrets. This could be which state they were from or what they studied, or perhaps, if a woman was a hottie, what color underwear she was wearing. Maybe she wasn't wearing any at all, for that matter. Some gave off that vibe, for sure. I continued to observe the intersection and my eyes strayed to the corner store directly across from our view. It was a modified surf and skater shop, and I casually wondered for the hundredth time what a surf shop was doing in a mountain town. It seemed stupid, though I knew the surfer poseurs from Cali bought clothes there, the better to look cool. I call them poseurs because they thought they were just the greatest and that California was the center of surf and beach. What bullshit. The entitlement and arrogance of it was nauseating. Those guys were pansies, pathetic wannabes. Most had never even seen a wave taller than their dressers, let alone surfed one. Even though I was from SoCal, I had surfed small mountains with these guys; it was one of the things that bonded us. Whenever I visited them for Christmas break, we regularly got together and surfed big wave breaks like Waimea, Pipeline, and Sunset Beach, all world-renowned waves. When it got big, like twenty feet or more, people died. That's when the scrubs watched from the beach, thinking of ways to brag of their phony exploits the next day. So, I knew better. Big wave of surfing wasn't for the kiddies, nor was it for gremmie pussies from Huntington Beach. As far as I was concerned, they could take their elitist attitudes, conspicuous wealth, and their noses out of each other's asses, and go back to the ankle snappers at Santa Cruz, or wherever.

Sound hypocritical? No, I get it. So what's your point? Fuck off, I've surfed big Pipeline. Sue me.

After finishing lunch, we climbed back into the car, Sean calling shotgun again and Kurt climbing into the back. He never seemed to mind the back; he'd just put his feet up and sit sideways. He once told me privately the back seat allowed him more room to hunker down and become invisible to others. Kurt liked to keep a low profile, except when he was beating some pathetic loser's face in a bar fight.

I started up the engine and heard again that satisfying purr. We pulled out into traffic and started back down the street, toward the downtown mall. As we hit

Broadway, I ran the yellow and we blew by a couple of rice box-shaped Toyota sedans before we got to Walnut Street. I turned left, and after a couple of blocks we passed the home of Richard Dickmann. You remember Dick, right? Dick the Prick, only about two hundred times more than that. I couldn't put a finger to the word that truly described him. For me, thinking about him at all made my blood pressure go up, so I did it as little as possible. The guy was just a fucking asshole. Smug. Bullying tendencies. Homophobe. I glanced over to Sean, and I could tell he wanted to stop since he and Dick were friends. I also knew Dick was always good for a joint and a beer, even a few lines of blow. I didn't mind taking advantage of this kind of hospitality and would gladly do so even though I hated the guy. What, you've heard it all before? So? I know, seems pretty skeezy but, well, as I've said, I like cocaine. Especially when it comes from someone who doesn't want to give it to me. Besides, drugs always come before petty friendship squabbles, and we had other plans, which was also fine with me too. I glanced into his front window and noticed the spherical and triangular Plexiglas prisms he had hanging there. So gay. And Dick hated fags. Hey, maybe he was a closet fag. That would be too funny. I caught him looking out at us as we drove by and had just enough time to give him the finger before he reached up with both hands and drew the brightly colored curtains closed. Nice Victorian house though. I think his daddy bought it for him. Maybe I'd have to torch it one day.

I accelerated down the street and made a left at 28th and navigated the Saab north. I decided we would go out to this liquor store I knew in North Boulder that sold Samuel Smith's Oatmeal Stout for a buck apiece. I know, crazy, right? So, after a quick discussion and decision to play some frisbee golf at the course at 47th and Valmont, we were just getting to the edge of the city proper when Kurt spoke up for the first time since we had left Ernie's.

"After golf, let's go out to Michel's for a drink later," Kurt said. "I know the bartender; she's a monster. She's got a degree in something like chemical engineering. She showed me her Phi Beta Kappa brainiac key once." Kurt smiled, showing teeth for the second time all day. He'd fucked her, it was all over his face. I brayed, maybe a little too hard because the car got real quiet.

Fuck, whatever. I gave it a think, and said, "Michel's? Drinks are kind of steep." No sound. Another think. I was pretty good at disc golf. Better than Kurt, anyways. "Only if loser buys first round," I said.

Sean sniffed. Then he muttered, "She can't be that smart, or she wouldn't have let you bang her up against the headboard." We laughed and the ride energy shifted back to cool. Sean laughed the loudest. He liked his own jokes and I admit they were usually very funny in an ironic sort of way. I flashed on the time I was in Kurt's apartment when he had this hippie chick over for a fuck session. You know, beads in her hair, tie-dyed T-shirt, holey jeans, dazzling smile. All you could hear was Kurt's vocal exhale with each thrust, the chick's moan with the pounding, the scraping of the metal bed frame as it shifted along the wood floor, and a banging sound. It would go on for about fifteen or twenty thrusts, then stop. Then it would start up again. This happened repeatedly for about ten minutes before there was the crescendo of pants, grunts, screams, and assorted climax noise. Then silence, no mumbling or whispering that I could hear. Kurt came out of the darkened room and went for a beer in his kitchenette, leaving the door open. Of course, I looked in and noticed two things right away. The first thing was that the chick Kurt had just fucked was sitting up facing the light of the living room. She was thin, tanned in a Boulder sort of way, had sun-streaked blonde hair cut in a pixie style, and just spectacular. Drop dead.

The second was that the smell, overpowering. Really rank smelling. Running shoes, filthy clothes, blood, old pizza and French fries, who knew what else. It smelled like I imagined a cave would, and Kurt the quintessential caveman. How chicks managed to keep their food down, let alone find the motivation to fuck him in there, I had no idea. I think Sean had it wrong. The chicks that fucked Kurt were smart enough. For them, it was like a gazelle to water, only Kurt lurked below the surface. Ironic.

Chapter 11

So off we went. Unlike earlier, it had become a beautiful day, unseasonably warm given the morning, so sweatshirts worked. We got to the old nine-hole executive course that had been converted to this new game. We parked, I got three discs out of the trunk, keeping the sweet multicolored one that I like for myself, and we set off. The course was kinda busy, at least a half dozen other groups were on there in varying stages of completion. Once we started with the first throw, it was just us, talking trash and joking around like old friends can. You know, guys you trusted, guys with which you had history. In the end, Sean won low score, I was second, and of course, Kurt was last, as I had figured. A short drive to the Gym-On-The-Hill to get in a quick workout, only an hour, legs only, and it was going on five o'clock. We headed back to the Gumby House, where Sean and I showered and quick-changed for the evening. Kurt decided to stay in his day clothes, which went with his overall troglodyte style. No problem, I thought, he can sit in the back seat, window cracked open. We grabbed the rest of our stuff, including treats and accessories for the evening, and took off for Michel's. The day was ending, and the temperature was heading south; it was going to get a lot colder later. Too bad for Kurt.

We kept up the drive out north listening to an album side of the Who's *Quadrophenia*, in my opinion their best album, much better than their other rock opera, *Tommy*. As we rolled, the tires hummed along the smooth highway. After about a half an hour we passed the Beech Aircraft hangars on the left side of the road. Another ten minutes and we pulled into the gravel parking lot and parked behind Michel's restaurant.

Michel's was known as the finest restaurant in the region. Ask anybody. The waiters prepared service tableside, fancy-style. They did stuff like Caesar salad, including the anchovy grinding; Steak Tartare; and Bananas or Cherries Flambé for dessert. Most of them were in their forties, even fifties; this was their career choice, and they were at the table-waiting career pinnacle. Along with the skill and experience of being able to pronounce words like "escargot" and "Château Giscours" came the ridiculous arrogance; it was like they thought they worked in Paris or something, maybe they thought they were tableside surgeons. It was hilarious watching them leaning over the candlelight, one arm behind their backs. Obsequious, fawning, but with such an aura of self-importance it bordered on condescension. Oh please. Just bring the filet mignon medium rare and the Bordeaux, pal. You. Are. A Waiter. And you have to earn a tip, it's not an entitlement. Sucking up isn't earning.

We all climbed out of the car and strolled up to the ten-foot-tall oak double doors, Sean pulled the wrought-iron handle, and we walked into the darkened foyer. Kurt held back.

"You guys go in; I'll be right there." He turned back towards the parking lot and started walking to the car.

I called out, "Don't you need the key?" I smiled.

"Ummm. Throw them to me." I did, he caught them without even looking. Fucking guy, so damned athletic.

There was a burgundy velvet curtain in a makeshift vestibule that we had to part and walk through. I guess it was to keep out the cold. We walked straight into the enclosed bar on the other side of the hostess table and took seats facing the glass-backed liquor wall. There was a woman bartender, just as Kurt had said there would be, but she wasn't that hot. I mean, she was okay but didn't live up to the "forearm rule." Well, kind of, and she was pretty in a fresh-faced, Colorado-bred sort of way. She definitely wasn't the monster that Kurt had described earlier, so I wondered about that. Whatever, the bartender grabbed an empty bucket and took off behind the bar. I looked up at the wall of bottles glittering in the soft light, bottles flashing their delectable contents. There. On the third shelf. My favorite tequila, lounging next to the Rémy XO. The Jose Cuervo la Familia Añejo. Eighty dollars a bottle in Liquorfest, probably went for twenty dollars a shot in this place. I waited for the bartender to reappear. I've always liked women bartenders, good fun to flirt with and sometimes they'd buy you a drink. I once had a bartender take me to a Bruce Springsteen concert and fuck me in the VIP box. Excellent music, sex on demand, free blow and booze, the whole megillah.

Kurt was supposed to buy, per his agreement, the first round. Now he was gone, who knew where. Sean gave me the stare for a couple of seconds, then laughed. I guess if I wanted La Familia, it would be on my dime. Sean chose a nice single malt scotch, something like Glenmorangie. When the bartender came back with a bucket of ice for the bar, we ordered, clicked glasses silently, and each took a sip.

I know it sounded like the thing to do and I make it a habit of agreeing with just about everything Kurt says, but I wasn't sure why we had to have drinks at Michel's, of all the places. The place smelled of pomp and fake entitlement. Michel's was known as a haven for drug deals though, and perhaps Kurt wanted to dump some of his stash or make a deal. If I didn't mention it before, Kurt was a pretty extravagant Boulder drug dealer. One of the best things about hanging out with him as an insider friend was that he was incredibly generous. Whatever else he was, troglodyte or not, you couldn't fault him on the way he treated us. And he was loyal. That afternoon was a perfect example. He bought lunch, he owed us drinks that he would make good on, and I got the feeling he was at Michel's to do a deal, one that would provide us with a couple of lines of great blow to freshen up the evening. Don't let anyone tell you different; hair of the dog works with coke as well.

So, there we were, drinking our drinks, and the bartender came back.

"Hi."

I looked up from the amber elixir and gawped. This wasn't the bartender that went out with the bucket for ice. This had to be the chick that Kurt had crowed about, and though I had seen Kurt with some great-looking chicks, now that I had seen her, I figured Kurt for a bullshitter. No way had he had it on with this chick. Well, maybe he had, and she just didn't dig it. Either way, Kurt was MIA so, no harm, no foul.

She was gorgeous, and I mean *Playboy* centerfold gorgeous. I have always had a thing for strawberry blondes, freckles and all, and she fit the bill to a T. I stared at her, almost to my own embarrassment. Taller than most of the women I had seen, probably five foot-nine. She had on a long pair of Levi's and a gray tank top with a Grateful Dead skull logo on the front, right between her breasts. Her nametag said, "Patrice." Then I noticed her shoulders and back. There was nothing but muscle definition and a little tattoo of a Celtic cross high on her right shoulder blade. She just about oozed strength and femininity from the glance in her eyes to the tips of her fingers. I hadn't seen her feet yet, but she seemed the kind of woman who wore toe rings. I just found that so sexy my penis reacted. Great tits, nipples slightly upturned, about the size of my hand, perfect. She had strong-looking forearms and hands as well. In order to seem like I wasn't staring at her tits and spectacular ass, I asked her, "You have the strongest-looking hands I have seen on a woman in a long time. What's the deal?"

"I'm not sure if I should take that as a compliment." She gave me a slight smile. I persisted, thinking I had perhaps found an in with her. You never know; I had no problem with Kurt's sloppy seconds, if it meant this beauty. "I do a lot of rock climbing in Eldorado Canyon," she said.

"I've climbed in Eldorado;" I said. "I climb sometimes with a spidery Brit named Geoff Hersey. Do you know him?"

"Of course I know him, but I've never climbed with him. Everyone in the city who does any climbing at all knows him. He's world famous. How did you get to know him?" she asked. Was that a slap or just an honest inquiry?

I knew of Geoff's reputation, and thought I'd milk it a bit. "He and I hit it off at the Blue Note at a Roy Buchanan show back when the place was still open. In between sets, I saw this kind of skinny guy, about 5'6", with long black scraggly hair and beard, a bottle of Guinness, sitting there all by himself, and I just walked over." I shrugged. "We started talking about British beers and one thing led to another, an invite from him to me to go climbing sometime. I took him up on it and here we are. Geoff and I climb once or twice a week."

She gave me a slightly quizzical look before reaching for the Cuervo and pouring me another shot. "One climber to another," she whispered, and flashed her eyes.

Okay, once or twice a week was more like once or twice a month, but I was getting more confident. I thought that I had a chance, and that jammin' body of hers was just beckoning. I'd keep going with the story, see if it went anywhere. The truth was that I didn't have the energy to spend all day doing 5.11+ climbing pitches with a guy who could laugh at my pathetic skills. One of the reasons we were friends was that he never made me feel inept. He was a lot of fun to climb with and never made me feel like a beginner. One time he introduced me to climbing tools he called "friends," these handheld climbing devices that looked like a syringe you pushed in to open. When you did so you activated a retracting cam at the end. These cams were pushed into cracks and notches and then you would attach your rope into a loop on the end and anchor yourself. Without the little "friends," I would have taken several tumbles down steep, sharp rock faces, probably scraping skin, breaking bones, and losing my winning smile and fetching personality. Or just died.

It was this smile and personality I was hoping to capitalize on with Patrice. Now you're thinking. What happened to Jill? I mean, you just commented on her oral skills no more than three hours ago. What's your plan here?

Here was my plan. I'd schmooze this chick Patrice into coming out with me after she got off of work. I figured that would be around 11:00, 11:15. Then I'd meet her at the Flatirons Hotel by midnight and she would be staring at the poster on the ceiling of my bedroom by 1:00. If she could

111

open her eyes, since I would be between her thighs, munching away. If I could start something with Patrice, Jill was toast, skills or not. I'm not a complete asshole; I won't date more than one woman at a time. Well, that's not quite true. In fact, that's a total lie. My thinking was that if I could get Patrice into bed, I'd use all my skills as a bamboozler to keep the two of them apart so I could have them both. I admit it seems callous.

Again, what did I say? So? What's your point?

"What the fuck are you doing?" Sean whispered to me when Patrice turned to the end of the bar where a balding waiter with a porn 'stache stood with his little bowtie and waiter's tray, waiting impatiently for her to make him his cocktails. "You know Kurt; think about what he'll do to you if you keep it up. On the other hand, don't think about him, he might take it as a sign of aggression and do the 'I've got something to show you outside, like my foot in your face' thing. You're asking for a beating of the worst kind. What part of this don't you understand? Besides, why do you think we came all the way out here, for the drinks and view? Fuck, you are an idiot."

What a command of the language. I thought about it as Sean turned as Kurt entered.

I lowered my voice and whispered back, "Unbelievable. Is there some part of 'I saw her first and we have a common interest that I can leverage for potential horizontal activity' that you don't get?"

Sean looked back at me and muttered, "Are you kidding me? I'm not dumb enough to try and make time with her, that's your funeral. Get fucked, dingus." Okay, Sean didn't have as good a command of the English language as I thought.

At that point, Patrice came back to the bar holding two cases of Guinness. I was in lust. It was a good thing Sean and I were done with the conversation. Kurt had stayed strangely silent, just kind of standing to the side and observing the whole little drama as it played itself out. I didn't think he cared anymore; he gave signals that he had moved on to other pastures, ignoring her, leaving Patrice to us, well, to me. She put the cases down in front of the refrigerator next to the main service bar area and turned back to face us. "Is there something else you want?" She didn't say "Is there anything else I can get you," she said, "Is there anything else you want." My mind wandered to the space between her hip and pubic bone, that smooth surface, slightly concave when a woman is fit and lithe, like Patrice. I find that space unbelievably enticing, just about the most sensual place on a woman's body. Before Sean could answer, I said "I'd like your number, maybe we could climb sometime."

"Climbing. Really. That's what you want to do?" She smiled again, "Okayyy. I'm at Eldorado just about every day. Come by." No telephone number. Fuck, I blew it. She may have wanted an invitation to dinner or something. Maybe if I had been more straightforward. I should have just told her, "How about my house, sex, tonight" when she got off of work, maybe she would have said "Okay," with a different tone. On the other hand, that had only worked once before, and the chick was rancid. I woke up from that one-night stand and had to sneak out of my own bedroom in case she woke up and wanted to go again.

Patrice turned her back on me and went down to the other end of the bar. There, she took hold of a highball glass and proceeded to wipe it down. I noticed that she had a whole tray of glasses to dry so I guessed I wouldn't be talking with her again for a little while. Besides, her in-your-face response to my casual invitation was enough for me to chew on, and I needed to regroup before taking another run at her. I looked back up at the bar, four shelves stacked up about ten feet. The liquor bottles shone bright against the bottom lighting recessed into the shelves, a myriad of colors depending on the type. I'm a tequila man so my eyes drifted down about mid-bar, second shelf from the bottom. Perfect location. This told me that tequila was popular in Michel's. Besides the Cuervo I had chosen, there was a selection of about twenty other tequilas from Don Julio platas to an añejo in a bottle I had never seen before. I called down to Patrice. "Hola Patrice, do you have a second? I think I want another shot."

Patrice came down the bar, toting the towel in her slender right hand. Oh my God. I couldn't take my eyes off of her. I tried to keep looking at her between the eyes. I had heard that if you look someone in the spot just above the nose, they can't tell the difference. It didn't matter; my eyes kept drifting to her breasts underneath her tank top. The work of cleaning and drying glasses must have been somewhat demanding because her nipples were erect. Oh my God. Jesus.

"What would you like to see this time?" she asked, keeping her eyes on me. Maybe this was a subtle hint to watch myself. Or maybe it was an attempt to be clearer in my invitation. Either way, I couldn't tell if she was doing the double entendre thing or if she was just fucking with me. She had to know what she looked like. A woman that beautiful had to know. She also had to know what she was doing to me emotionally; I was in lust beyond reason. I spoke quietly. "I'd like to see that bottle up there, the one in the silver-gilded container. What is it?" To hear me, she had to lean into the bar and bend slightly toward me. In doing so, she exposed most of both breasts to my greedy little eyes. Magnificent. Just. Splendid. She stayed that way for at least a half a minute, or maybe it was just a couple of seconds. I could smell her, a mix of soap, rosemary, and a hint of red wine. Was she drinking? I couldn't tell up from down, my brain was awash in her scent. She stood up and turned around, got on her toes, and with her left hand, reached up to the second shelf. When she leaned in toward the bottles, I got an eyeful of the back end of her jeans and the ass inside them. She had to be fucking with me. There is no way a chick this hot is going to do the bump and grind with me. Out of my league. Wait. She's a bartender. A chick like that? If she were a shallow whore bitch, she would have used it to more advantage if she were so inclined. Patrice didn't seem to be that kind of woman. I was sorely tempted to say to her, "I'd also like to see your heels overhead, naked. After that we can consider our options." Instead, I said nothing. Maybe strong, confident silence was the way into Patrice's jeans, shirt, bed, and body. Or perhaps it was because I truly didn't have the nerve to take my shot. She kept looking at me with piercing eyes, and for the first time I noticed they were an amazing light-green color, flecked with gold. It was like they shone without any light on them. I swear I could see the light from this woman's soul coming through those eyes. If I weren't in love before, I was then. I got up the strength and responded, "Along with the tequila, whatever it is that you're pulling down, I'd like more than an invitation to meet you and your friends next week sometime. What I'd like is to meet you this evening at the Flatirons Hotel for a drink. Just you and me. One drink, and some conversation. I'm sure you've heard this, but you have the most amazing eyes. I was thinking to myself that I could see your soul through those windows. I'd like to find out if I'm right." The slight twist on one side of her upper lip let go and suddenly I was seeing a woman who was seeing me for the first time as a potential fuck buddy, not just a customer. Her body language changed as well. It seemed like she was more reticent, almost hidden with the assets she had used to suck me in. I thought she looked at me with fresh eyes, and she took a long breath before she answered.

"Do you think you can discover my soul in the time it takes to have one drink?"

"I don't know. It depends on how long it takes to have that drink. If we don't get far enough, perhaps we can have another one. No promises though."

She cracked a half smile, eyelids crinkled. Okay. So maybe it was only a half smile, but it was real. A slight upturn of the edges of her mouth. Though in this story it sounds like the opposite, I hadn't really looked at her too closely. Now that I had asked her out, I did. What am I gonna say? I felt like a mutt compared to her champion golden retriever. She had a strong, angular jawline, a nice softness under her neck. She had an oval face with a thin, straight nose with nostrils that flared just slightly. Some would consider her nose a bit small compared to her other features, especially her ears, which were a bit larger in proportion to the rest of her face and were visible in front of her french braid. I, on the other hand, thought they fit her. I hadn't noticed the shape of her lips before either; I was so enamored with the rest of her. Her lips were thin to go along with her smallish mouth. They were a dusty pale red with a tinge of pink and salmon. Like her eyes, I had never seen the likes of them before either. They matched the rest of her stunning face perfectly. I took a big chance and asked her what her last name was. This might have seemed presumptuous, but I had to know. Just scratching an itch, I guess.

"My last name is Charbonneax. I'm from Santa Barbara."

I said, "Would that be Santa Barbara, California, or Santa Barbara, Ireland?" I admit, not the cleverest of responses, even hokey.

She smiled again, a little bigger this time, and said, "California. But my family is originally from County Donegal, how did you know? I still have family there; their name is Byrne."

Ah. I said, "You know, I've been to Ireland. You?"

"No, never. My father was born in Dublin, though. Have you been to Dublin?" Here was my chance to really open up the conversation and guide it where I wanted, but then a tap on my shoulder caught my attention. I glanced around, saw Kurt's receding back. Where the fuck had he come from? He glanced at Patrice, then turned and walked to a doorway off the right side of the bar. He pointed to a closed door, turned the handle, and pushed it open. I looked in. The door to a private dining room; it was empty but for one occupant.

Sean, who had been listening to my clever repartee for those last few minutes, said, "Well, I guess it's time we move along. Say good night, Bruce." He yanked at my jacket collar. He said, "Finish your tequila, or not; we are having dinner. Kurt said something about having to see a guy about a horse."

I turned to Patrice and said, "Good night, Bruce." She leaned over and said, "Stop back before you go, I'd like that drink." *Nice.*

And what did that mean, a guy about a horse? I've heard that term before, but what the fuck? Just say lua, or bathroom, or head, or whatever.

The lone occupant sat back and stretched his legs from his place at the square table. All I could make out were cowboy boots, a silver hoop in his left ear, black hair, and a buzz cut. *Finally.* The Man.

Patrice, who had also been watching, now looked back at me and raised her left eyebrow. "Do you know that guy?" she asked. She indicated Buzz Cut with a nod of her head.

"No, but I'm about to meet him. I'll let you know if he tries to kiss me when we get together later."

Her smile disappeared and her shoulders slumped just that slight bit forward. She looked away. I suddenly got a bad feeling. Shit. This date was going off the tracks before I could even get on the train, sit down, and get comfortable.

Man…if I fuck this up, I'm going to be so pissed. Fucking chicks, you just never know what's going to set them off.

I heard on a radio talk show one time about a guy, just a regular doofus, probably some pencil-scribbling cube driver, who got a date with this really hot Japanese chick who had just won the Miss Nevada contest for Miss USA. Not Miss America, Miss USA. That's the beauty contest where the contestants have limited talent between their ears but suggest a great deal more talent between their legs. The chicks for Miss USA were known to be much cooler, friendlier, less likely to have a metaphorical stick up the ass. At least that's what I'd heard. Anyway, the story goes that they went out on the date with a TV crew following along, documenting the whole scene. I guess nobody thought he would get anywhere with her. The hosts of the talk show agreed that she was out of his league. Apparently, they hit it off anyway, and the chick dug him. According to them, the guy had a shot with her. And no, I don't mean a kiss, I mean wild horizontal action and breakfast in bed. Everything was going gangbusters; she laughed at his jokes and occasionally licked her upper lip with the tip of her tongue. They also mentioned that her eyes crinkled. Enough said; the guy was on his way to the boneyard. From the hot meter on the screen measuring audience approval, they thought he had the key to the treasure, too. That was until he opened his mouth just one time too many. See now, this is where chicks get complicated, and you never know what's gonna set them off. You make a benign comment like "I'm really glad we met; I've been looking forward to my first taste of Chinese. I hope you like Italian sausage." She ducked into the freezer. The guy didn't know what hit him, what to do. He was baffled, pathetic and useless. No, I get it, she's not Chinese, she's Japanese from Nevada. What a racist idiot that guy was. Of course, for all he knew, she could have been a hostess at Caesar's Palace. All those assholes grabbing her tits, you'd think she would have had a thicker skin. Needless to say, opportunity flushed. Hardy-har.

This story, I told myself, didn't alleviate the problem I now faced. Much like the loser on TV, I had to come up with something quick. Just how smart and clever was I going to be? I said to Patrice, "I hope he doesn't try anything; I like the buzz cut but I really prefer blondes with freckles and strong hands. And they have to be women, men don't count." Patrice turned back, looked into my soul, and smiled again. Ladies and gentlemen, we have a winner!

Patrice glanced once more at the private room door and semi-whispered, "I'll be done at eleven at the latest. See you at midnight. balcony bar?"

"Sounds like the plan. What do you like to drink?" I asked.

"Tequila," she said.

Chapter 12

I turned to Sean, but he had already left, leaving me to cough up the cash for the drinks. I got up from the barstool and dropped a hundred-dollar bill on the bar. Giving my face a good metaphorical backhand smack, I took a couple of uneasy steps, mostly to gauge my stability, then stood all the way up and strode down the bar, through the open solid-oak door, and into the private dining room. Sitting was a guy, thin but looked fit, easy six feet two, wearing a pair of Levi's, a T-shirt advertising "Led Zeppelin at the Forum 1977," and a pair of Tony Lama snake-skin boots, the nicest I had ever seen. He had really short hair, like a guy just out of the army or something. I did a quick-glance once-over. No weapon that I could see, not even on his ankle. This, I told myself, was the guy Kurt referred to as Alex. Rumor had it (well, according to the idiot frat-douche) that he had a stash of a hundred kilos of coke hidden on his property. A fuck-ton of blow. Yeah, this is what I had come for. I was grateful that only Alex had shown up, the rumor was that he had a "minder," as in bodyguard, some giant of a man with extensive violence in his background. Sean had taken a seat at the far end of the table. I sat down in a chair facing the door. Kurt had reappeared and was now leaning against the wood-grain wall. I looked down. There were a bunch of legible and illegible scratches in the wood in front of me and I identified three of them: "Fuck off Dad," "Dave B. from Stanford was here 1980," "Broncos suck Donkey Dick." Smile. Tacky for a pricy joint such as this one. I lifted and turned my chair around until I faced Alex directly and waited for someone to say something. He started the conversation.

"Kurt?" he asked.

Kurt looked over from his perch holding up the ceiling.

"You wanna go to the Hill for me real quick and pick up this package for me? I'll let you borrow my car, just don't get pulled over." Hardy, har, har. That's the best this guy could do? He sounded like a bumpkin.

"What kind of car do you have?" I asked. Alex glared at me.

"Man, we haven't even met." Wooo. Tough guy.

Kurt pushed off the wall and took a couple of steps to a spot directly behind Sean. "This is Sean and Bruce," he mumbled, all noncommittal. Both of us looked at our host. Kurt indicated our host with a head nod I caught out of the corner of my eye. "This is Alex."

I reached across the table to shake his hand. He had a good grip, not too strong, like a regular person. As opposed to the musclehead idiots we knew from the gym. He shook Sean's hand next.

Kurt: "What's the car and where's the car and what do you want me to get and where do I go?"

Alex reached into his front pocket and pulled. The key he brought out was unattached. Strange. No house key? He threw it at Kurt, one-hand grab. "It's the BMW 528e out back. I have a box of albums at Dillweed Dorkball's house on 8th near Baseline. Here's the address." He threw a crumpled-up piece of legal pad paper, another one-hand grab. Kurt turned, pulled the door open.

"Now play nice," Kurt said. He left, door shutting behind him with a dull thud and click.
The guy Alex looked at me with veiled curiosity. Started rubbing his hand over his head, maybe feeling the buzz cut spikes. I took this to be a sign of insecurity. Well, that was a place to start. "My name is Bruce Keown," I said to break the ice. "I'm a partner of Kurt's; he and I do business together on occasion. In this case, he brought me along with every intention of you and I meeting. If you know Kurt, you know he always has a plan, so I'm not here just to sit at the table." Bold. Establishing my position right away.

"Is that what we're doing here?" Alex's right eye twitched, just once. "I thought we were having dinner but if you say this is business, I guess it's business. What kind of business do you think we're going to do?"

I stared. What the fuck?

He turned. "Sean," he said. "Do you think this business thing is a good idea?"

"I don't know. Kurt's like my brother. Bruce's like my brother. Ipso facto, they must be brothers."

Sean giggled, our new friend smiled at the butchered Latin, and said, "Fair enough. My name's Alex. Is your real name Keown, like 'peachy keen'? You've got to be kidding me." What was the deal here? I just met this guy, and he was already insulting me? Wait; slow down, Bruce, nobody's insulting you. Turn down the paranoia and let's make a deal.

I asked, "Are you gonna have dinner? The food's the best in Boulder. I'm thinking Steak Tartare and then a New York medium rare with a nice peppercorn sauce and some brown rice, maybe some sautéed veggies. I was thinking of ordering a bottle of Château Latour, 1976. Do you know it?"

"No."

Fuck, I am screwing this up! Okay, regroup. Never, ever give up. That's from Winston Churchill. I looked at Sean, dead eyes staring back. I turned back to Alex.

"I hope I haven't overstepped here. I just like a good bottle of wine with dinner. Can I order you something else?" I know, a little like throwing in the towel but the best chess players in the world sacrifice pieces to win the game.

Alex thought about it for a couple of seconds. I could see his eyes shift and move to his lap. He then said, "Yeah, I'm in for the wine. I was just fucking with you." He threw me a smirk. "I'm not that hungry, but it is getting later, and this place looks good so yeah, I'll eat too. I like the way you put that. There would be more smooth dealings if folks lightened up and got to know their associates, so to speak."

I got up and went to the door, opened it, and poked my head outside. Patrice was standing at the bar, just as before. She glanced up at me and raised her left eyebrow in an inquisitive way. She didn't have to say anything, I got the message. Her look said, "What's going on, is everything okay?" I smiled in response, both to give her the thumbs-up message and at the thought that even though we had only just met, she felt the need to check on me. On the "Bruce and Patrice, sitting in the tree, F-U-C-K-I-N-G..." situation, things were looking up. I had a fleeting thought, though. No fucking babies in the baby carriage. She was hot but that was just wrong on so many levels. "Patrice, we're going to have dinner. Could you send someone to start us up? I think we'll start with a bottle of Château Latour, 1976. I noticed it on the menu. And we'll need four glasses, or maybe five. Would that work?"

Patrice responded, "Yes, we have the wine." Whew. I thought I was gonna have to backpedal on the wine thing too. A shadow clouded her face for a second. "What do you want five glasses for? Is someone else coming?"

"The fourth glass is for a friend who stepped out. The fifth is for you. You're allowed to taste the choices you recommended to your guests, aren't you? I mean, how can you be expected to sell something if you haven't tried it for yourself?"

She looked at me straight in the eye and held my gaze for an extra beat. Here we go again, another test. She said a very deliberate manner, "We aren't supposed to drink with the customers."

Okay. What did she mean? I looked at her with what I thought was the same intensity and responded with the same deliberation, "You won't be drinking with customers. You would be testing a bottle of wine, educating yourself on its complexity. In order to facilitate this, a small taste will be provided by an important client kind enough to purchase the wine, here at the restaurant price, and make the opportunity possible. One thing that turns dinner in a fine-dining restaurant into a dining experience is the interaction between the patrons and the restaurant staff."

She kept my gaze, thought for another couple of seconds, and spoke in a lowered voice, "Let me get the bottle and glasses. I'll open the bottle myself. Then I'll get the waiter." She raised her voice slightly and angled her face away from me and into the entrance to the main dining room. "Château Latour, a very good choice, sir. I haven't tried it myself, but I'm sure it's the real thing. If you like it, let me know, I can take a bottle with some plastic cups on my next climbing trip." Château Latour went for about $350 on the menu. Nice. Clever, snappy, agreeable, funny. Maybe she was thinking of a trip with me? Three days in Joshua Tree, just the two of us, our tent and gear, some food and a single sleeping bag. Just enough room for us to fuck and sleep, sans clothes. We could start out early and drive through the day. We could pull into a motel, get a room. We wouldn't get any sleep because fucking was better. Then we could get up with the sun and get into Joshua Tree later that day. If I borrow my friend Martha's Porsche 911, we could easily make the drive in twenty-four hours or less. Plenty of room in the back seat for our stuff. When we get there, we can even get a suite in one of the hotels. Maybe not even climb at all, just stay in the room and fuck, eat from room service, drink French Bordeaux, and fuck some more.

Damn, Idiot. Dumbass. What the hell was I doing? I considered my current situation carefully. A stunning babe working behind the bar, giving out all the right signals. She was going to meet me at a first-class bar in the best hotel in Boulder. She liked my taste in liquor. She seemed to like me, and she has a bit of an adventurous spirit when it came to breaking rules. Not only that, but here was the elusive Alex, a new potential business partner in the room with me. On the other side of the table was Sean, the guy I thought of as my best friend, someone who for sure had my back. Alex and Sean and I were getting along, and business was forthcoming, I could feel it. Maybe a quarter pound of blow for this first deal, maybe more. A bottle of Latour, to be followed by a Mouton Rothschild. What part of this scenario was not to like?

Wait. Why did I have to go all into projection mode and potentially ruin everything because I wasn't paying attention to the present? This was the story of my life, it's the manic-depressive again. The doctors told me about drinking and taking the behavioral drugs. The two weren't supposed to be mixed. Obviously, this meant for everyone else, it didn't mean me. Besides, it wasn't just tequila and wine I was going to mix, there was the small issue of the Peruvian flake that would be running through my body after dinner. I liked to combo buzz but tomorrow I'd feel guilty and depressed and suicidal all over again. I could always get a gun and stop the pain. Blow my head clean off. I'd stick the gun in my mouth, angle it upward toward my cerebellum, and pull the trigger. Lights out, Bruce has left the building, thanks for coming. But what about Patrice? That would hurt, fucking some guy and then having him blow his own head off in the morning.

Wait. Stop it. Shut up and pay attention, Bruce. This was important. I spoke up as a point of finality, "We'll just be in here, waiting patiently for your return. Just the four of us. Just us four. So, we'll need four glasses. Thanks, Patrice."

"You're welcome, sir." Another smile, eyes crinkling and pupils shining. With that, the deal for the wine and her interest was sealed.

I turned back into the room. Get your shit together, Bruce. There were Sean and Alex, sitting on opposite sides of the table, comfortable that the things we were in the room to do were going to get done. I shut the door behind me, taking hold of the handle and pulling; the click felt safe and comforting.

Chapter 13

I always liked this restaurant, this room. Something about the dark, wood-paneled walls and faux Spanish Renaissance art, the Spanish motif and furniture, room to do a little drug-addled spinning and wailing. And the smell...cigars, Armagnac, and cocaine. Well, maybe not the cocaine but the other two for sure. The coke was all in my head. My eyes drank in the scene and my mind wandered to another time, in a previous iteration, when a little drunken dinner and degradation I had planned went very, very bad.

Have I got your attention? Okay, so, I decided to celebrate a little ounce deal of the pink stuff with customary lines of blow, and the guy I did the deal with that time had a name, Timmy Gordon. Jesus, even today I have to think about it for a second or two before I remember his name.

Timmy was a kind of shorter-than-average guy, about five-seven, but he weighed a flabby two hundred, like a kid who was teased and bullied in fourth grade for being a Jell-O belly. A fat fucking tub. He had a reddish-blond baby-head. Kind of like he looked like a baby with a grown-up body. His body was soft, like Play-Doh, like you could mold him into different shapes and mash him up again.

Timmy was a nocturnal cokehead, and it showed in the pastiness of his skin color. His blubber face and neck shook when he moved, like when you see really fat people, and their bodies sort of shake under their clothes when they walk? Ha, ha. Yeeesh.

Wait. I'll come back to this story, but I gotta digress. Here's how I met Timmy. When I say he was a nocturnal coke monster, I speak of his vampire-like lifestyle firsthand. I was over at his apartment one night, doing coke, smoking pot, and drinking pretty much whatever he had in the cupboard, his or his roommates, I didn't think he even cared. All of the sudden, he got up from the Scandinavian-style black leather chair he had been sitting in and babbled,

"You gotta hear something. Do you like the Dead? I love the Dead; I've gone to two hundred and thirty-eight of their concerts. Garcia is a genius. If it weren't for Jerry, there would be no American music scene at all!" His words sped up, his statements getting harder to understand as he tripped over his own coke-numbed tongue.

"You gotta hear this! Jerry was in rare form at the shows in San Francisco in 1980. The Dead played like fourteen shows there in September and October, at the

Warfield. They were from like another planet! The show on the fourteenth was so different from the one on the twenty-fifth, the last show of the tour. There was such a difference in the way Jerry played the solo on 'Dark Hollow.' He finished it up with a great upbeat section, truly masterful. On the twenty-fifth, just the opposite, it was like he was a different person. I just want you to hear both versions, tell me what you think."

Oh my God! Babbling idiot!!! I shoved a teaspoon into the ounce bag of blow sitting at the end table, laid out a line the size of Runway 5 at Kennedy Airport, and hoovered with a rolled-up hundred. I didn't even bother to chop it down first, just used the crystal from my Submariner to crush the biggest rocks. He watched; I mean, it was *his* blow. Didn't say a word. I must have put $75 worth of snow up my beak and all he did was watch. What a laugh.

So, then Timmy fell to his knees on the stained shag carpet, kneeled into a ball, nose three inches from touching the carpet, and started combing through a large drawer stuffed front to back with hand-recorded cassette tapes. He started flipping them past his fingers one at a time. The Dead. Every fucking concert. Seriously.

"Hey, how many of the shows do you have recorded?" I asked.

Timmy turned back to me from his fetal position. "I have every show from that tour. I also have most of the '77 tour, but I'm missing the three shows at the Ocean Theater in June, but I got the ones in March." This guy was a Deadhead fanatic with a capital Fuck. Oh my god, what was I gonna do for the next...who knew how long. I pulled at my hair. I could have shot myself, but then I wouldn't have gotten to snort anymore of his coke. If I didn't think he'd be watching for my every nuanced movement, I'd try to get a little sleep. Well, I figured, I might as well suck it up. See what I did there?

"Before we start this adventure," I said to the back of his head, "let's do some more blow." He didn't even turn around when he responded with a simple, "Help yourself. Leave some for me. Could you grind it up first?" Asking me like he needed my permission, so worthless and weak.

I slid back over to the end of the couch, hand grabbing for the Ziploc. This time I also reached for the well-used coke grinder on the small glass picture frame Timmy used as a chopping table. There were the remnants of lines past done on the glass, and the grinder showed many scratches where razor blades had nicked it. I twisted the grinder open, exposing the bottom-section cup piece. This also exposed the coke inside the cup; there was a lot of it, almost coming over the sides. When I say a lot, I mean enough to fill a prescription bottle. My first thought was, 'yahoo!' Who needed the Ziploc when the treasure trove was right there?

I figured I could easily sit through this Deadhead torture for some big rails of this stuff. The second thought was that I'd rather take the grinder and the Ziploc and make a clean getaway when Timmy went to the bathroom to dig the blood out of his nose. The guy was sniffling like his brain was leaking. I just knew he had blood in his sinuses, it was just a matter of time before the blood let go and he had to clean up before hitting the blow again.

The thing about coke addicts is that nothing will stop them from the next bump, not even if their own nose was about to fall off. Why do you think there are so many people with deviated septums in Boulder, and what did they all have in common? Cocaine noses. Plastic surgeons in town made a mint on the weasel-dust dipshits.

So, I thought about ripping him off, but what I did was line up four really beefy lines and instead of doing two and passing them over, I did all four and then put more out. My jaw started working overtime and my head felt like an inflated condom. Timmy was so immersed in his search for just the right tape he looked like an entomologist studying a skunk beetle pinned to a piece of wood. After a couple of minutes, I tried to get his attention. "Timmy. Timmy...Timmy. Do you want these lines or what? I've got two nice rails lined up here with your name on them." He'd passed out, leaning over his Dead tapes. I turned back and reached for the grinder. I then took most of the rest of his blow, dumped it into the baggie, and quietly left the place. I got into the Saab, started the engine, and drove home using the side streets to avoid cops. I know. I did rip him off. To my luck and credit, he had no memory of the evening and no idea where his flake had gone. Hey, don't judge me, it was a long time ago...sort of.

Back to the story. A couple of months later, Timmy and I were in Michel's, in this very room. After dinner, we asked for the "Silver Platter" from the waiter. The silver platter was literally a silver platter, like the kind used to serve high tea. In this case, it came with a razor and a hundred-dollar bill, said hundred-dollar bill twisted and ready to be used as a snorting utensil. There was a price to this service; the bill went back to the waiter along with the equivalent as a tip as well as in cocaine, around a gram. Very few places in town offered the silver platter service, and even fewer waiters were willing to serve it.

When the platter came, we were raring to go with the snow. See, along with Timmy and me, there was my friend Ronnie from Santa Cruz, star running back for CU, and four other people in the room, all girls, all party-type hose beasts; their lizard wiggling and tongue flipping were sure to lead to at least two-on-one ménage à trois action, or so we hoped. After dinner, the girls were all milling around the table drinking the rest of the wine when the waiter came in with the platter. We dumped a pile of blow on the surface the size of a coffee cup. The girls' eyes popped, becoming saucers, shining like old pinball machines, and I remember feeling the anticipation of the rest of their bodies lighting up in a similar fashion. There was lots of tongue-tip touching between them, as if in anticipation of the sexual activity to commence. I didn't complain; it turned me on to have these chicks hot for each other. I know they were just waiting for the coke; as soon as we put the first lines into them, it would be a free-for-all. Timmy laid out seven ginormous rails and we let the girls at them. The coke was snorted up like a vacuum pulls up dirt, each of the chicks leaning back and squeezing their nostrils to make sure not to lose any. By the time we did ours, two of the girls had shimmied out of their clothes, dancing and twirling naked in front of us. The others looked greedily at the mirror. Apparently, it would take a bit more flake to get these two to play ball.

There was a knock on the door. Not the door to the bar, which we had locked, but another door, this one going into the back hallway and kitchen area. The two naked chicks held their clothes in front of them as Timmy jiggled across the room and cracked the door open. "We're having a private pa—" was all that came out of his piehole as a guy about the size of a small apartment building pushed on the door and shoved it open wide enough to duck through. He pushed Timmy back into the room, propelling him over a chair and slamming him to the floor. Gruesome closed the door quietly and put his left index finger to his lips. "Shhhh." He said, "I'm here for the cocaine. I know all about your stash so don't even start a story. Give it up now, I won't ask again." You gotta be kidding. It was like a lame crime movie. It figured. I took a seat, real slow-like, and took him in. He looked like a sci-fi character, long stringy hair, Members Only jacket, and circles under his eyes. I imagined him sitting in front of his personal *Space Invaders* game or whatever, playing for hours at a time with only a McDonald's strawberry milkshake to keep him company.

Except that this guy was a lot bigger than your average geek. He was fucking huge, and ripped, not an ounce of body fat on him. The muscles and veins on his forearms stood out like ropes and he had a bad case of acne across his forehead. You know what that's from, don't you? Steroids, that's what. Not good for us. My brain went into overdrive. There was a Gold's Gym in the next town over, he probably worked out there in between shots in his ass. I figured he told people who commented on his size that it was the "vitamins"—if anyone asked. Not that I would. Ronnie dove for the floor and rolled under the tablecloth.

Then beefcake batted his eyes. Not blinked, batted. At Timmy. Now, in hindsight, I had no reason to believe he was a fag at the time except he didn't even look at the naked chicks when he came in. They might have been hose monsters, but they were very hot hose monsters. The chicks were now putting their clothes back on, one of them quietly sobbing. I didn't take my eyes off Gruesome but kept Timmy in my peripheral vision. He had gotten up off the carpet and was just standing there, looking at the fucking guy. I glanced at him—he was shaking like a tree blowing in a high wind, weaving, and leaning to and fro. I looked down at his legs to see if they would hold him up and found to my horror that he was pissing himself. One of the chicks

142

looked in his direction as well. "Oh my God, you're peeing on yourself!" Real subtle. The others all looked, and even Gruesome looked down at Timmy's pants and the stain that spread. Timmy started sniffling, and not from the blow we had just done either. He stared at Gruesome; the smell of his fear was palpable, sour like piss and cooked cabbage. If the situation hadn't been so scary, I might have found his behavior pathetic and funny in a tragic sort of way. I might have even snickered a little. Ronnie, you ask? Well. He had crawled under the table and was quietly suffocating himself trying to stay soundless.

The girls didn't think the situation was funny at all. One of them said, "Please let us go, Mister, we don't even know these guys. We just came to party. We don't know about any coke; we just came to have a good time. I need to get home. There's a curfew. We really need to go, please." There was more than a note of desperation in her voice, but also some semblance of a cooler head in that she was thinking of the others in her plea. King Kong looked at Timmy and said, "Give me your stash and you can all walk out of here." Timmy looked down, shook his leg out, and finally found his voice. "Oh fuck, sorry about that. Shit. Fuck. Okay, the coke is in my car, under the back seat. We can get it right now. I just don't want to go out there with my pants like this. Can Bruce get it?" Everyone turned and stared.

You fucking dickhead Timmy asshole. Motherfucker. Fuckety, fuck. I looked away from the pathetic blimp I had called fair-weather friend, registered the girls and the looks they gave me, and then I turned to face the fucking ape. He hadn't moved from where he stood. He stared bullets at me, and his lips were pulled back from over his teeth, like he was getting ready to lunge at me, bite me in the head and spit out my ear. He had an ugly smile. His teeth were yellow and squashed together, like a train slowly crushing on a bent track. There was some twisting and protruding from the cramped quarters of his yackety yack cavern. His mouth looked like a cartoon accordion; yeah, that was it exactly. I smiled slightly at the thought, but only for a second. He said in a slow, methodical, slightly threatening voice, "Let's go, dickwad. Pisspants, give him your keys." Timmy fished the keys to his blue Audi 100 from inside the blazer hanging across the back of his chair. He threw them at me, but I missed catching them and they tumbled to the ground next to me. I bent down and stared at Ronnie cowering behind the tablecloth. Fuck you, asshole, I thought. There will be a reconning, douchebag.

Your little CU football pals won't be able to help you dodge what I have in store for you, star running back or not.

I picked the keys up, and as I stood, I saw that the guy had moved to a position directly in front of me. I looked up and felt his presence, like a tidal wave about to wash over me. The guy was so fucking gigantic. I doubted he could have fit through a doorway without turning sideways. He grabbed me by the back of my collar and stood me up. "Now." He turned back to the room. "If any of you tries to leave, I'll be right outside. And I will be angry. You do not want me angry. Git it?" Nods all around, except for Ronnie, still in hiding. Lurch said, "And get up out of there, boy." Ronnie crawled out.

We went out the door next to the bar. The bartender was gone, lucky for him but very unlucky for me. I had hoped to give the guy a signal of some sort. You never knew; maybe Gruesome wouldn't notice my clever eyebrow twitch and head bob, and the cops would show up and kill him. Not going to happen at this time and place. There would be no such luck.

Herman Munster and I walked out the front door, under the awning, and around the back. The Audi was parked next to a five-year-old silver Cadillac Seville, one that I hadn't noticed when we got to the restaurant. I pulled out the double-sided key and pushed it into the lock, turned it until the door lock knob came up with a pop. Steroid Freak grabbed me by the right shoulder, moved me aside like a stack of tissue paper, and opened the door.

He glared at me. "Don't move." He cocked an eyebrow. He bent down and reached under the driver's side back seat. I saw his arm slide back and forth and then stop. There was a scrabbling sound like a rat scurrying around trying to escape its final rewards, and the freak pulled out the coke. A kilo bag of coke, worth about $25,000. Shit, fuck, shit. I was getting into deeper trouble by the New York second. Jolly Green Giant got up again and this time grabbed me by the back of the neck, his hand squeezing like he was wringing out a dirty towel. I remember hoping that his next step wasn't throwing me out with the garbage. I heard him put the bag in his jacket pocket. Instead of the garbage, he and I marched back into the restaurant, paused to check the coast, past the still-empty bar, and back into the private party room. When he closed the door behind us, he let go of my neck and pushed me forward into the chairs. Unlike Timmy, I didn't fall; I spun away from the closest chair and landed on one foot, slowly placing the other down as I got my balance. Nimble as a cat, that was me. Gruesome looked at me for a second, then let his eyes brush over the four chicks, who were now fully clothed and sitting quietly. I took my eyes off the freak and observed them as well, curiosity getting the better of me. I took a few seconds to imagine what might have been. Disappointing. That evening had held such promise too. Ronnie looked dejected. Still, he would have a story to tell the team if he got to leave the restaurant with his tongue. I couldn't bring myself to look at Timmy, the guy who was supposedly my friend but had put my life in jeopardy. I briefly wondered if he had done it because of all the times I had liberated blow from his place after he had fallen asleep, but I didn't think so. That would have been ironic. Timmy was basically a coward, which point was made painfully clear to me and my aching neck and the yellow stain down his back. I mean his leg.

Gruesome zeroed in on Timmy, grabbing him by the collar and pulling him to his feet. Jolly Green looked at me. "Twinkletoes, give the man back his keys." I threw them. Timmy caught, dropped, picked them up. JG commanded, "Pisspants, let's go. Your car. Me and you are going for a ride." He smiled. Then he turned away from Tim's cringing face and looked at us with all seriousness. He said, "When my new friend and I get back, you shouldn't be here. If you are, then you'll go for a ride too. That ride won't be as fun as his will be." With that, Timmy and Gruesome left the room, Timmy frog-marching, the stain where he had pissed himself plainly visible on the inside of his pants leg.

The four girls and I looked at each other, and I asked, "Do you ladies have any way to get back to town?" One of the chicks spoke up, murmuring in a high-pitched, mousy way. "I have a car. It's the red BMW 325i in back." Another spoke up. "I have the Ferrari, the canary yellow one." A red Beemer and a Ferrari, a canary yellow one. Like there were others out there in the lot. Priceless. Rich chicks behaving badly. What a story they would have when they got back to the sorority house. Something like—

"We went out to dinner with these three guys, you know, and like, we had the BEST dinner, you know, and then we got the 'silver platter,' you know? And then there was like this mountain of coke and we all did these huge rails and Bambi took off her clothes, I think she was going to blow them so I took off mine too and thought we could like do it together you know?"

So, there were two cars for six of us, and after some discussion we split up. Three of them, I think their names were Bambi, Suzy, and Wendi, took Ronnie and would go together in the BMW, and that left me catching a ride in the Ferrari with Tina, the skinny blonde with ears that stuck out in a kinda sexy way, very Irish. Her tits were smallish but she had a really tight ass and spectacular legs. She had been down to bra only no panties when the evening took that unfortunate left turn. And she was a true blonde.

What? Ok, so about now you're thinking that Brue is just a misogynistic jerk, obsessed with sex and using women for sex. Look, I'm twenty-four years old, I'm still in school on the seven-year plan, and yeah, at this point, I see women as objects to play with, like toys. I haven't me one that is worth more of my time and attention. What of it?

I cracked open the door and investigated the bar. The bartender was there this time, but he only glanced at me before going back to drying his glasses. I spoke to him in what I hoped was a calm and forceful voice. "There's fourteen hundred dollars for dinner sitting on the table. Keep the change." It was all I could think of. After all, he was the guy who'd have to clean up the cocaine and piss.

We walked through the alcove, staying as calm as possible, past the hostess stand and out the big wood front door. The cars were parked next to each other, the only ones in that part of the lot. Ronnie, Bambi, maybe Suzy and Wendy got into the BMW, Ronnie took shotgun, Bambi driving. The engine started and Sue feebly waved at us from the rear passenger window. I gave a slight nod, Tina was unmoving. Bambi backed the BMW out of the stall, and I heard her put the car into first gear and pop the clutch. The car lurched forward and grabbed the pavement. By the time I heard the car go into second, it was out of sight around the corner.

Tina and I walked the few steps to her Ferrari. Even with all that had happened, I couldn't help but admire the car. It was spotless, even down to the rims. It looked brand new even though I was sure that that particular model, the Dino, had to be at least five years old. When we got in, I asked Tina if we could go around the back and check on Timmy's car. Tina gave the front window the thousand-yard stare for a few seconds, looking at nothing. "OK." She started up the car and we slowly pulled around the building. There, right where Timmy had parked it when we first arrived, was the Audi. It looked fine, no worse for wear. I noticed that the Cadillac next to it was also still there. There was something off about the situation, though I couldn't put my finger on the anomaly. As we were pulling away, I looked back again, just for a second, and then it came to me. The windows of the Cadillac were fogged over. Tina and I drove in silence for a while, neither one looking at the other. I didn't think she made the connection.

As we pulled into town and got to the first stoplight, she surprised me by suggesting we have a drink somewhere. "I could really use a shot of tequila. How about Juanita's?" On any other night I might have been up for it but after our adventure with the "man the size of a house," I was pretty fried. I said resignedly, "To be honest, while you seem real nice, tonight was crazy, and I thought I was gonna get my head popped off like a zit. Not to mention Timmy. I guess I kind of want to go home for the night."

Then came the real surprise. She said, "Okay, how do we get to your place, and do you have an extra toothbrush?'

Chapter 14

Although I felt that I had made a good first impression, I figured Alex would want to know a little about me, so I started in with the bio. "I'm from California originally, Newport Beach. Do you know it?"

Alex shrugged. Sean smirked. Fucker. I start telling a story.

"It's a nice place to grow up, big houses, chefs and nannies, lots of trophy wives at the country club, that sort of thing. You'd never know behind the masks that those people put on that they are as fucked up as anyone. The woman living next door to me was a gold digger named Judy. I think she's about thirty-five, and her husband is about a hundred seventeen. Anyway, she must have spotted me throwing a water polo ball around the pool at the PV Country Club one day and I guess it put thoughts into her head. The next day, or soon after, I don't remember exactly, I came walking down the stairs from my bedroom and I remember looking out at the ocean from the stairway window, which faces west. I got to the bottom of the stairs, walked across the living room, opened the French door to the backyard, and came to an abrupt standstill. I drew my head back and licked my lip. I'm sure this was just a subconscious reaction to what I saw. And what I saw was her sunbathing behind her house...and she was naked. Right there, no more than fifty feet from where I was standing. It was ten thirty in the morning. I remember it like it was yesterday. Here's the thing. We don't have fences in our neighborhood, just some palm trees and a few hedges to separate the properties. We share a backyard with both neighbors, like they had in the movie *The Great Gatsby*. So, I stood there for a few seconds, then out I went to grab my stuff. And there she was, all the sweet things exposed. Legs slightly spread, pussy uncovered, perfect tits. Great legs...great legs. She knew what the deal was. So did I, but I just couldn't bring myself to make the move. I skirted past her, staying on our side of the lawn, under the trees, avoiding any glance she may have thrown my way. I have to admit I was nervous; I mean I was about twenty feet away. Like the idiot I was, I nonchalantly walked to the storage locker at the back of the yard next to the tree that delineates our property from next door, got my swim fins and hand paddles, and took off for the garage around the other side of the house. I then promptly started the car I had at the time and drove for the Wedge."

"What kind of car was it?" Alex asked.

"A 1979 Z. Anyway, have you ever heard of the Wedge? The deadliest break in the world. People have their necks broken in the shore break. Bodysurfing only. The place is tame on small days, but when it gets big, only the bravest and dumbest people go out. Most of the gremmies and pussies stay in and watch it from the beach. Then they'll tell their pals at school the next day how giant it was and how they got barreled." I sniffed and smirked. "Whatever. But I digress. I'll admit it, I was a little intimidated by her. The neighbor, I mean. She was hot and I mean hot with a capital BABE and..." I sniffed again, this time with a bit of melancholy. "I know that sounds weak. I admit it. But that's not the whole story. The rest of the story came a couple of days later when I see her out there again, no clothes, pussy, tits, all hanging out like a Playboy playmate. Even from forty feet away I could see the slight parting of her lips and the slightly strained arch of her back, the miniscule twist of her hips as she got comfortable on the oversized blue-green towel covering her lounger. She must have known I was there because she smiled to herself, pouting her lips. All I can say, even now, tonight, is fuck. That's what I said to myself right then and there too. Fuck. I continued to stare, but I was still hesitant. I just couldn't bring myself to get past the consequences of taking action.

What if I had misread the situation entirely? What if she started screaming and it turned into a huge blowup? My folks would have been appalled. The whole country club community would have shunned us. We would have had to move to another state, for Christ's sake. I was stuck, frozen, looking but afraid to reach out and touch. I was so busy staring at my neighbor I didn't hear the screen door to their patio creak open and close with a wood bang. Not three seconds later, a friend of hers showed up."

I looked over at them for the first time since starting the story and saw the looks of incredulity tinged with hunger on both their faces. "I see the smiles on your faces. I know what you're thinking, both of you, you fucking Cheshire cats."

Sean said the first words that weren't mine in ten minutes. "You are so full of shit. You've never told this story. It sounds like something out of a *Penthouse Forum* article. Fuck you, you are such a liar," he said.

Alex echoed, "I don't even know you and I think you're full of it."

Full of it? He doesn't even know me and he's calling me out. Who does he think he is? Fucking guy. Well, fuck him. Just be aware that you can't trust him, Bruce. When it comes to the deal, watch your back. And Sean's no help, he isn't even supporting you. Doesn't he realize that the impression I give now will have a payoff later in the negotiation?

Stop, I told myself. Stop. Wait, look at his body language. Alex's body language and smile told me that he was enjoying the story. He didn't seem to care if it were truth, lie, or something in between. Okay, I have to admit now that the story did seem a bit ridiculous, even completely fabricated. Still, the truth was what it was. Okay, embellished a little bit.

"You can think whatever; it doesn't change to facts of the story. I'm not embellishing shit. This happened." I started again, backing up a bit to replay the scenario for them, kind of like a VHS tape. "This female friend looked just like Judy only a little thinner. Same color hair, same shape to her legs, same shaped tits. A light bulb went on. Sisters? Really? NO WAY!" Sean and Alex were totally committed to the story. Gotcha.

"Now I figured we were in freak world, Mars, whatever. I couldn't get my head around the situation. Did they want me to come over? Were we all going to have sex? Me and twins? Holy shit! What if they had sex with each other? Fuckety, fuck, fuck. If we all had sex together, what would I do first? Who would I do first? What if they both wanted to fuck me at the same time? What would I do then? Oh my God, oh my God.

"I stood there for the time it took for Judy's sister to sit down in the other chair and put her glass on the ground next to her. I used the time to think of a plan. I was so nervous my legs were shaking uncontrollably, like when you have a fever and your whole body shakes, and you can't control it? That was me. I said to myself, 'Self, there's only one solution. Go upstairs and get high. Then when you're calm enough, go over there and be cool. Let's just see where this goes. Don't talk except to say hi. Let them do the talking. Just be up for anything.' Hey, that's funny. Up. Hahaha.

"I turned around and raced back up the stairs to my bedroom. 'First things first,' I said to myself. 'Gotta clean up. For all I know they'll want to come back here. Maybe the husband is due back from playing Putt-Putt at the club.' I had a queen-sized bed, so I figured there would be room for three, as long as we didn't move around too much. Then I thought of how impossible that was going to be. Fuck. Plan B. The folks' room. A king, baby. A surfboard made for three if there ever was one. "OK, OK, plan's coming together," I said to myself. Now for the herb courage. I took an old box from on top of my bookcase and got ready to open it up. It was one of those puzzle boxes you get at Disneyland, with a picture of the Haunted Mansion on the top. I worked the mechanism and out popped the little drawer with the dope inside, stored in a little pill container with a sealed cap. I put dope in a container like that to keep it moist. Sometimes I even put in a sliver of orange peel for flavor. I went to the closet and grabbed my running shoes. I then reached in and got out my Proto Pipe. I pulled a little bud off the stem and filled the bowl. I lit a cowboy match against the bed frame. 'That's so cool, just like Clint.' I put light to bowl and inhaled, exhaled right away and then inhaled again. I held my breath. The pot started to expand in my lungs and force its way into my throat. I started to cough, then it got worse; I couldn't stop. I ran out into the hall and down to the bathroom I shared with my sister, put my face under the sink, and ran the water cold, drinking and splashing my face together. That stopped it, but I felt a major rush come on. I stood up and steadied myself against the sink, looked myself in the mirror. 'You're high,' I told myself. 'You fucking idiot, you're too high. Now what are you going to do?' I took two deep breaths, left the bathroom, and started down the stairs. I figured that the deep breathing would flush oxygen to my brain, clearing it quicker. I also figured that every step would give me that much more confidence. The closer I got to the door, the backyard, the next-door neighbor, and her sister, the more committed I would be. Then I'd have to see it through. Man, I was scared. No, that's not the word I want. Sean, what's the word I want?"

Sean looked at me and said, "Cowering? Shitting in your jockstrap? Heaving chunks?" Both he and Alex grinned, and I felt my story flow start to weaken. I prided myself on telling a good story.

"Okay, no, here's the word. Distressed. That's the word, and I'm sticking to it."

"You're sure?" Alex said. He was getting into the swing of things; I could tell my previous paranoia was unfounded. The guy seemed cool. "You don't want to choose 'intimidated'?"

"No, Alex, and fuck off, drink your drink, it's my story, and I want to reiterate again that it's a true story." I took another deep breath and another sip of my tequila. Where was I? "So, I'm traipsing down the stairs, taking deep breaths, getting psyched up for I didn't know what. I get to the french door, stepped outside, and looked next door for the sisters, as I now had labeled them. Problem. They weren't there anymore. The chaise loungers were empty except for the towels. The glass that sister number two had brought out was nowhere in sight. Fuck. No tits, and certainly no pussy. Not for me." Sean and Alex were howling at this point. "No, don't laugh, you guys, I was bummed. I had gotten up the courage to do what needed to be done in order to live a fantasy and then missed the fantasy. I wasn't sure whether to be relieved or totally bummed out. I just stood there for, like, thirty seconds, hoping for a reversal of fortune, and then finally went back inside."

Sean said, "But that's not the end of the story, is it?" Alex's eyes crinkled with delight, a slight curve on his lips. Sean smirked. "That can't be the end, or you're the biggest loser and since you seem to like Patrice out there, and she's coming back with our wine, I think I'll tell her what a loser you are." Sean was smiling while he threatened me with this horrific development, so I figured that I better finish, and pronto.

"It's not, as you have surmised, mon frère. I saw Judy Geezer about a week later, at the club, having dinner with Mr. Geezer. She didn't even look at me. Fuck, I knew then that I had blown it." I paused and said in a downer way, "Unbelievable. I fucking blew it. Sometimes I still can't believe it. I haven't seen Judy Geezer outside again since those two days, and this goes back a couple of years. I guess she found some other diaper child to cuddle with." This last part I said with a bit of venom, and the two of them just looked at me for a moment. The story was over. I raised my eyebrows, shrugged, and glanced at the door. Where was that wine? I could have really used a glass of the Latour right about then. Come on Patrice, I said to myself, shake it.

Sean spoke up. "You never know, another chance like that could fall into your lap at any moment, and this time you'll be so brave, like a good little soldier. Except that you're no longer a teen angel. Plus, you're a slacker drug fiend." He grinned. Alex barked a laugh. Fuck. I've said it before, that Sean, he's a funny guy. And he's really helping with the first impression thing, too. It was getting annoying.

We sat there for a few minutes, speaking of trivial things. There was a guy playing music at the Flatirons Hotel later that week, a one-man-band sort of artist who specialized in reggae. We discussed meeting for drinks, working at restaurants, dealing with surly customers and asshat bosses.

This reminded me of when I waited tables at this place on Arapahoe called Silvestri's. Silvestri's was to the Flatirons Hotel what Budweiser is to Guinness. Sean had gotten me the job, one of the first I was to have in the restaurant business in Boulder. The thing about the waiting staff business in Boulder is that you kind of all knew each other. This made it easier to get a new job when you were either fired or quit. First, everyone knew you were unemployed, which meant a job had opened up. Then when someone else stepped in, that person's job became open, allowing you another gig. Pretty much everyone was in the loop.

At this point, you're probably thinking to yourself, "What does this have to do with the guy playing at the Flatirons? In fact, what does this story have to do with Alex?" I don't know yet. I have no idea why I just took that left turn in the story, but I'll get back on track soon enough.

Chapter 15

Back to Silvestri's, and the guy who ran it, Sidney Silverstein. Get it? Silverstein? Silvestri's? It was pathetic, a Jew trying to be Italian. The food wasn't even Italian, it was shitty.

Working at Silvestri's did have its advantages, you know, the ironic kind. Sid's policy was that the restaurant closed at 4:00—in the morning. What he didn't tell unsuspecting new employees was that if a customer came in at one minute to four, you had to serve them, even if they wanted a full meal. This included appetizer, salad, entrée, dessert, and coffee, unlimited refills. I got to stay past dawn many times. That's what happened when some cocaine cowboy decided to eat before continuing the binge. It's true that I also saw the sunrise every so often during my misadventures under the influence of weasel dust. That's how I knew the deal with these other late-night douchebags. The sense of nighttime finality was very different if you kept yourself up on purpose or if someone else did it for you because he was such an asshole—like Sid. If I was high on coke, that made a difference too, though there were some nights at Silvestri's where the two combined for a really bad night and even worse sleep-off the next day.

Another advantage to working at Silvestri's, and this one was even greater, was that you had to take shit from said owner, a little fucker, not shoulder high, a guy with a Napoleon complex, a guy who felt you owed him for giving you a job. His best line, the one that got him all the rave reviews, was "If you don't like it, asshole, there's the door, and you can forget a reference."

Anyway, on the night I quit Silvestri's, I was responsible for the transition shift, from 1:00 until 6:00 p.m. This was a shift that you could either love or hate, or just love to hate. No customers except for some regulars. They were bored, unemployed, and looking for a ball game on the tube. Occasionally we would get the afternoon team-building meeting, some small company treating their employees to iced tea and the salad bar. As far as tips went, I could hear the coins dropping in the piggy bank, tinkle, tinkle. On the other hand, there was no side work, no cutting, folding of napkins, wiping down the bus station, no making coffee and iced tea. And since you knew you weren't going to make any money, at least you got out of there with the evening to look forward to.

Instead of my hasty departure at exactly 6:00, as planned, Sid the Yid came up to me at a quarter till and basically said, "I need you to stay. You've got the late station. Finish up your tables here. Then do the side work." I didn't have any tables but there was a lot of side work and the early waiter usually did it. I must have pissed Sid off. And then he said, "Then punch out. Be back at 7:00." Oh, you have got to be kidding. With the side work, I would have to punch out after I had already punched back in. Not only that, but I had a long night to look forward to, perhaps continuing until dawn, if I was really lucky.

"Sid," I said, "I have plans for this evening, I've got to study for a midterm I have tomorrow at 9:00 in the morning." I figured that if he knew I had to be in classes, he wouldn't make me take the closing waiter shift.

"Tough titty," he said. "I need you here because Anthony"—who was another waiter—"has to go to Longmont and pick up some liquor. We're short."

Now, I asked myself, since I was going to be finished with my shift, why wasn't he telling me to do it? Because he was an asshole, that's why. Of course, if he had asked me, I might have given an answer like, "Sure Sid, I'll go get it for you." Then I would have driven to Longmont, picked up the order, stashed a couple of bottles of the good cognac, and brought the rest back, feigning ignorance on the incomplete invoice. Or, I might have said yes and then not done it at all. The way Sid operated was, you had to do his stuff off the clock or "there's the door..."

It was going on 6:00, and I still hadn't gotten to the side work. I stood next to the bar at the swinging door to the kitchen and gazed at the baseball game, trying to think of a way out of my predicament. That's when the hostess, I think her name was Bitch, sat three obese rednecks in the only four-person booth in my soon-to-be section. What else would you call three guys with sweat-stained overalls and faded T-shirts stretched so tight you could see through the food stains to the blubber beneath? They all wore ball cap–style hats. One of the hats read "Commie Killer" on the label. Jesus. I got off my elbow, trooped over to the hostess stand and leaned over, looking at the bookings for that evening. I gave Bitch a quick glance and said to nobody in particular, "I wonder how those guys are gonna eat in a section without a waiter?"

Bitch said, "Shut UP! That's your *section*!" She had this annoying way of turning up the lilt of her words at the end of an exclamation, like the sorority chicks do. She started giving me the little girl business, you know, the part where the little girl begs for her way in exchange for something else? "Come on, please take themmm. Please? I like your tie." Bitch went into infant mode, with her lips and tits as the potential treats. I know she was just fucking with me; besides, that wasn't what I was interested in doing. Pathetic. I gave her about two seconds to think about it. The light bulb finally came on behind her eyes when she realized that I wasn't going to budge—no table of rednecks, no table for a blowjob, no table, period. I planned on leaving, pure and simple. I looked at her again, shrugged and smirked, and walked back to the bar. According to the Sidster, I wasn't supposed to be back until 7:00, so I figured I'd stay on the clock, snooze on the side work, and hang, eat whatever I could scrounge from the cooks. I didn't see Bitch zip behind me and sneak back toward the office, as I prepared to make house, sitting on the first barstool. The next thing I know old Sid comes walking out from the office area and marches right up to me, stopping within inches of my chin. I looked down and he glared at me from under his toupee. "Bruce, that table's yours. You're also taking a section in the bar. Punch in, you start work now." He then turned to Bitch and said, "Bruce is on the clock. See that he gets work, I hate to see him standing around." Then he turned back to me. "And finish the side work."

With that, Sid spun away and shoved through the swinging door, disappearing into the dishwashing area. "What the fuck is this?!" I heard him yell. Manolo, the dishwasher, must have blown off the last couple of bus trays, I thought. Sorry, Manolo. I smiled softly at Sid's anger. I hoped he'd have a conniption.

This whole time, Bitch had worked her way back to her little lectern area at the front door of the restaurant. She picked up her little pen, her source of power, and started crossing out spots on her map as she moved people waiting at the entrance to the tables. As more people came in, she kept seating them in my sections, both in the bar and in the dining room forty feet away. After about five minutes I was sprinting between five tables in the restaurant and another three in the bar. I looked up at the hostess stand; more people were filing in, probably to take advantage of the early-bird special. Great, I said to myself. I looked at Bitch, who had by then been rechristened in my mind "fucking Bitch." She studied her floor plan studiously, glanced up at me and gave me her thinnest smile. I could tell she wasn't finished with my punishment.

I took two deep breaths and was struck with an epiphany. I turned and walked back toward my section in the restaurant. I moved lazily, casually, proceeding to each table one at a time. Whatever it was that they wanted from me, the response was the same. "I'll be right with you." It didn't take long for the people to get upset. I then went to my tables in the bar and said the same thing. "I'll be right with you, I'll be right with you, I'll..." Nobody had ordered, no waters, nothing. I had put them all in standby mode, like planes on an airport runway, while I gave them all the brush-off, one table at a time. It was beautiful, people getting royally pissed off; such good fun. I heard the hillbilly with the red "DODGE TRUCKS" hat ask one of the busboys to get the manager. I took a position at the service bar area and watched as Sid came storming out of his office. He barged into the front of the house, slowing down just enough to put on a smile fit for Richard Nixon, eyes reeling, toupee askew. What a fucking idiot. I didn't wait for him to get to the table. I looked over my handiwork with satisfaction. People were irate everywhere; many were still trying to get my attention. I nodded and smiled at them, peeled off my waiter's smock, and dropped it behind the bar.

Nancy, the bartender, looked me in the eye, nodded slightly, and calmly asked, "Do you want something?"

"I'll take a shot of that Sauza Tres Generaciones, please," I said.

She spun around, picked up a shot glass, and casually poured my drink. She turned back to me and put the drink down on the bar, inches from my reaching fingers. "It's on the house. Call it a goodbye gift, for all your hard work. I saw what you did. Priceless. See you around."

I plucked the shot glass from the bar and hoisted the amber-colored liquor to my lips. The tequila went down with a slight bite, followed by the sweet taste of a job well done. I put the glass down. "Thanks, Nance. See you." I then made a beeline for the back door.

When I got to the parking lot, it was about half-full. I didn't recognize most of the cars, just the ones owned by other employees. Another car I recognized right away. Sid's gold Cadillac was parked about fifty feet away, in the dark, under a tree. My head swam with the buzz of the tequila and the majesty of what I had just done. I decided that there was a bit more work to do before I called it a night. A final "fuck you." A truly meaningful statement. No rest for the wicked.

I went out to my car, parked under a couple of trees, next to Nancy's little green Triumph TR6. I got in and waited for a good hour, keeping my head low. The activity of doing nothing would help move suspicion away from me. Nobody would think of me as the culprit if I had been seen leaving sixty minutes earlier. I waited quietly. No sound, not even the radio. I contemplated the timeline for the endeavor. I then took a deep breath and pulled the baseball bat from behind the back seat, in the cubby hole that doubles for a storage area. That particular bat was made of wood. It had only the *Louisville Slugger* burned into the side and was made to use in Major League games. Aged a soft medium brown and measured about three feet long, with a traditional taper and knob at the end. I found it at the softball fields off of 30th street one evening. There were people drinking beer, laughing, recalling the game a short distance away from me when I took it. I kind of figured that the bat was theirs, but I absconded with it anyway. People. If you didn't know a softball from a hardball bat, you shouldn't get to keep the bat, period. Especially a bat like this one. I think it was Sun Tzu who said that if you want something, grab it. Or maybe that was the guy from *It Takes a Thief*, the show on television, I couldn't remember. Anyway, the bat was on the heavier side as far as bats go, it probably weighed a good three to four pounds, give or take. This'll do just fine, I said to myself. I got out of the car, took it by the smaller end, and hefted it up overhead to test the weight and see how hard I could swing it. I closed the car door and purposefully strode to the passenger-side door of the Caddy, the side away from the light. I looked around for cars or passersby and waited a full minute to make sure there wasn't anyone in their car. It would ruin everything to miss a couple of blue-haired women getting ready to leave the lot, people who would see me using Sid's car for batting practice.

Now, what should I destroy first? I took aim at the door handle and brought the bat down from directly overhead with all I had. There was a loud crack, and the door handle came clean off, striking the ground so hard that it put a gouge into the asphalt. I looked up, there was nobody there. Steeeerike one! I loaded up again and swung for the side door panel. A loud bang followed, this time leaving a dent almost an inch deep and a good eight inches across. The door would have to be completely replaced. A well of deep joy came up from inside me, a happiness fed by tequila and adrenaline. I could feel the muscles of my forearms tighten, my shoulders bunch up, the joints of my fingers stiffen from the impacts. Steeeerike two! Some part of me realized that the previous swing was more than loud enough to arouse suspicion from inside the restaurant, so I ducked down and took a little time to reload. I stood. Putting myself into the classic batter's stance, I drew my weapon back for the final time and swung for the fences.

This time there was the sound of wood on glass, a crack, and then a huge crash. The windshield caved in halfway to the steering wheel, and the glass itself was spidered with cracks and splits. Steeeerike three, you're out, motherfuckin' Sid Silverstein asshole motherfucker!

I stepped back and looked at my handiwork. By then I knew I didn't have much time, maybe another thirty seconds. I was going to have to run to my car and scoot, swing around the corner, and duck into an alley about fifty yards up the street to hide for a bit. I made a last-second decision to really cement my disdain for the guy. If I had thought of it and wasn't in such a rush, I would have stood up on his hood and pissed through his windshield. However, time was short. I pulled out my butterfly knife, bent low to avoid being seen, and shoved it into his tires, front and back. The knife was very sharp and went in with less effort than I thought it would. I had a fleeting thought. I wonder if it's that easy to stab someone. Not that I would ever think of it for real, but you never know when a good knife will get you out of a jam.

I heard the satisfying hiss of escaping air. I stayed low and crab-skittered back to the Saab, crawling in through the passenger door to avoid suspicion. I slithered in horizontally and shut the door with a soft click. I then moved over, splitting my legs over the gearshift knob one at a time, and started the car. It wasn't until the engine had quieted down to its normal idling speed that I popped my head up. There were people filing out of the restaurant by ones and twos, spreading out in search of their own cars. Some had heard the noises of destruction. Classic look of perplexity on their faces, they were asking themselves, "What's going on? Where did those noises come from? Is my car the victim of some high school shenanigans?"

A sneaky person, one with experience, knows to take advantage of confusion. I did just that, keeping the lights off and rolling quietly into the street, not giving the car any more gas than necessary. I turned left at a well-timed break in traffic, and slowly accelerating for a good seventy-five yards before I turned my lights on. All that the people in the Silvestri's parking lot would have seen if they had looked would have been the oncoming headlights as cars came toward them. Nobody would have noticed the two small red taillights, a ways off, going in the other direction, west toward Broadway, and a clean getaway. Fuck Sid.

Chapter 16

We had already ordered dinner when the wine steward brought in the bottle of Château Latour with five glasses.

"What happened to Patrice?" I asked.

"She has customers but said to tell you that she would be looking in on you guys later." Ah, French accent. I wondered if it was fake.

The wine steward looked at us in a slightly pleading manner and in his accent mumbled, "Might I bring over another glass? I was hoping for a taste of this as well. I've never had it." What the fuck? I looked at the others, ready to tell the guy off. However, Alex and Sean seemed okay with it so...the three of us tacitly gave our consent.

"If you're going to drink our wine, we need to get a couple of things straight. Okay?" He stopped turning his waiter's knife in the cork and gave us his attention. "First," I said, "What's your name?"

"Marcel."

"Bien, Marcel, now that you have revealed yourself to be Frenchish, where are you from, exactly?"

"I'm from Quebec. I don't like the French, they're snobby people." This gave us all a chuckle.

"They do make good wine though," Alex said. We agreed on this as well.

Marcel didn't even blink; he just went back to turning the waiter's knife and opening the wine. It smelled wonderful; the nose was exquisite. We all took a taste and grinned at each other like hyenas.

"What do you think?" Sean asked Marcel.

Marcel replied simply, "Excellent." Marcel put his glass down next to the one he had poured for Patrice and left us to our dinner, which had come while we were debating the attributes of our Latour selection. As always, I chose the filet mignon, as did Sean. Alex decided on a veal dish with asparagus. Baby Killer, I thought, tongue in cheek. We ate in silence except for the occasional quiet sigh of approval. A half an hour later, we were well into the second bottle, the Mouton, when Patrice came into the room. She took my breath away. While I had only seen her up close, leaning over the bar while her attention was on cleaning the glasses, from ten feet away I saw the way she moved, tigerlike. Smooth, coordinated, and balanced, exuding supreme confidence in herself. This was a woman I wanted to match toes with.

I couldn't help but think of the story I had just told no more than a couple of hours earlier, about my misadventure with Judy Geezer. Alex and Sean didn't believe me at all. I knew they thought I was full of shit, telling them a big fat lie.

The thing is, a great story is always embellished, if for no other reason than for artistic license. In this case, however, the story was true. This made my commitment to Patrice all the more pressing. While the situation was different in that she wasn't cradle-robbing, Patrice was the most beautiful woman I would have had the chance to fuck, ever. As far as I was concerned, failure wasn't an option. Plus, I could prove that the Judy Geezer story had legs, build on my reputation.

"How's the wine?" she asked me. She didn't even look at the other two.

"Excellent, there's a glass of each for you. Are you allowed to sit down and drink with us?"

"I can come in and out, but I can't stop." She gazed right through me. Unbelievable. It was a *Penthouse Forum* story in the making, and I was damn sure I had the goods to close the deal. Time stood still. I didn't give a shit about Sean and Alex. At that point in the evening, they were a burden I needed to jettison. This wouldn't be true later, as I came to find out.

I said, "We're probably going to stick around for the rest of the bottle, then take care of some business." I glanced at Alex but he was nonplussed. "I'll see you at midnight at the hotel. Do you work tomorrow?"

"Now, why do you ask?" Was that a hint of a smirk I saw? Her eyes like reverse full moons, the whites clear and the blues deep.

"Curious, just want to make sure you get home before witching hour."

"Isn't midnight witching hour?" she asked with a sly grin.

I responded with a sheepish face, "You got me there; I guess we'll both be under a witch's spell." Pathetic I know, but all I could come up with.

She watched me for a few seconds. Then her lips formed the words, "I have all my faculties, so you won't need a spell." A quiet whistle from Sean.

Another smile and a glance around the table. She stretched her back, arms overhead. My jaw hit the table edge. Alex gulped audibly. Ha.

"And the answer is no, I don't work tomorrow. I want to climb some boulders tomorrow." Pause. "See you at the upstairs bar. Don't be late; I'm not in the habit of waiting. For anything." She took a sip of her wine, put it down, smiled at all of us, turned on her heel, and showed us her exquisite ass as she flowed out the door, like a panther.

Sean said, "You are so in there. That chick wants to fuck you so bad it makes me want to fuck you, just to see what all the fuss is about." We all laughed, me loudest to hide my lack of comfort with the direction of the conversation. I regrouped.

"I knew she would be into me," I said with a smirk, to signal that I in fact had no idea at all. "It's the clever repartee, works every time." Yeah, right, like I had anything to do with it. The truth was that as in all things between a man and a woman, it's the woman who chooses the mate, not the other way around. Unless we're talking Dark Ages, or whore/pimp shit. Maybe I should get a room in the old part of the hotel. One of the rooms with the brass beds, I thought to myself. I could bring a climbing rope and a couple of carabiners. She would definitely know what to do with them.

Okay, don't get carried away there, hoss.

Alex belched, grinned, and, looking at us through slightly glazed eyes, said, "I've made up my mind. Let's go up to my place and take care of some stuff. Then we can come back down here and drink another bottle." Holy fuck.

I had forgotten what the purpose of the whole evening was. I was supposed to win Alex's trust and get a coke deal together. I had thought we would do the deal right there in the restaurant, or maybe the parking lot. Instead, we were going to Alex's house. Fuck. Oh well…this was good news; as I've said, Alex was a pretty big connection, and now a deal for more than the ounce I originally anticipated looked possible, even probable. Long drive, tight timetable, but happy days.

Alex said, "I've got something to show you guys. You know, I bought this piece of property up Boulder Canyon, near Boulder Falls, about ten years ago. Great land, eight and a quarter acres, including a stream pass-through. That part of the property is my favorite. I built the house around the stream. The back porch literally sits right over it. I've made other improvements to the land as well, built my own driveway. You'll see what I mean. Heads up, my girlfriend Mary might be there. She lives with me and knows everything about my business but don't ask her about it, though. If you want to know something, ask me." He paused for a couple of seconds. "I like you guys, and I don't like too many people. Most people are too curious. I'm not a fan of too curious."

This was the most Alex had said at one time all evening. While I was reserved, I was very optimistic. Maybe we would see his mythical superstash, if there even was one. Like I said before, it was just a rumor out of the mouth of some fraternity pinhead. Oh yeah, substantiated by none other than that liar Dick the Prick.

At this point, I know, you're asking yourself, "Why is Bruce so down on Richard Dickmann?" Well, here's some background. Dick's the kind of guy who would get off on burning ants with a magnifying glass. Hell, when we were kids, I saw him hang a dead cat from a tree once. He was basically a bully who seemed to enjoy watching other people squirm. He would make up all kinds of shit to get people upset, then step back and watch the flames burn, friendships down the toilet, people's lives trashed. To add insult to injury, people like him, a regular laugh-a-minute at parties. I couldn't understand it. It was like I was the only one who saw through his veneer of bullshit to the sociopathic sadist underneath. I wondered how Alex would take it if he heard that Dick was spreading rumors about some supposed stash. I decided to find out.

We got up from the table, Alex threw five hundred dollars down for dinner, I put down three hundred for the wine, and we walked. In the lobby we passed Marcel.

Alex: "There's some money on the table for you, it should cover dinner and more. If we're short, I'll be back to square up. You know I'm good for it." Alex peeled another $200 from his roll and tucked it into Marcel's shirt pocket. Marcel smiled and nodded obsequiously.

Marcel: "Thanks, Alex."

"Shouldn't we wait for Kurt?" I asked. Alex responded, "He knows where we'll be, and he's got my car."

Chapter 17

We marched outside, jumped into the Saab, and took off like the world was coming to an end yesterday. I drove fast but carefully, and I bided my time. We had just started up the canyon road and had about ten miles to go. The road twisted a lot and was full of potholes, so I knew it would take us a good half hour or more to get to Alex's house. And here was my time. I glanced into the rearview mirror.

"Hey Alex," I said. "Have you ever heard of a secret pirate treasure of cocaine, stashed somewhere in this area? A guy we know told me about a secret stash of some sort. According to him, some guys from South America live up here somewhere and have like forty, fifty, a hundred or whatever kilos stashed on their property. Like some sort of huge drug depot or something. Have you heard of anything like this?" I wanted to start some shit for Dick, I figured to give him a taste of his own medicine.

"Why would you want to know that?" was Alex's response. He looked at me through the rearview mirror, eye to eye. He wasn't smiling, and just for a second, I became concerned for the direction of this conversation, and the tone of the evening. I thought fast and decided to go with the truth. Embellished, of course.

"This guy named Dick mentioned it at a party a couple of months ago, said something about knowing where it was and suggested a little reconnaissance to pilfer it. He was recruiting, and there were a couple of guys who were drunk enough to take him up on the offer. I mean, he was talking a lot of trash but, you know..." I could feel Sean's eyes on me from the passenger seat, probably deciding whether to stay mum about the exaggeration or cover Dick's ass. Sean slowly turned back to the windshield, and an audible exhale escaped him. I saw him settle back a little bit more into the seat. Good, he had decided to shut it, probably because he knew I was telling the truth about the rumor and because he knew Dick and I hated each other and didn't want to get in the middle of our rivalry.

"Who is this person, Dick?" Alex asked pointedly. He was still looking at me through the mirror, but his tone of voice had downshifted. I got the feeling he had become more interested in Dickfuck than the rumor, which had been my plan all along. I now had the chance to turn the knife and really put Dick into a hole.

"He's this guy who lives downtown on Walnut, in a converted Victorian his dad bought for him when we came to school a few years back." I paused for effect. "Another guy from Hawaii, likes to be the center of attention, shoots off his mouth. I do know this about him," I said, "he got into trouble with some dealers in Aspen about a year ago and they sent a hit team after him. I guess he ripped them off for a pound of Bolivian or something. These two guys showed up at my door one day looking for him. I really didn't think anything of it; they were normal-looking guys, just under six feet tall, not threatening, you know? For all I knew they were from the Franchise Tax Board or something. One of them wore glasses and was kind of skinny in an accountant way. Asking me about Dick, easy-like, just conversation. I told them what I knew, which was next to nothing, except about this guy Rodney who took care of Dick's cat when Dick was out and about. So, then they went over to Rodney's. I think the impression they gave him was very much on the threatening side. Maybe they had ants in the pants. Or they must have had a little more urgency. Anyway, they beat on Rodney a little. Punched him in the face, broke his nose, that sort of thing. The sick part? One of 'em grabbed the cat by its neck and throttled it. Then he kicked the cat out of the upstairs window and into the street. And how do I know that? Rodney told me. The cat went for the dive and hit the ground with the thud of a mud pie smacking on a rock."

That part of the story was fucked up. Sure, the guys from Aspen didn't do anything to me. For that I was grateful. But to kill a cat? That's really fucked up. I continued, "Dick blew out of Boulder fast, went to LA, and hopped a sailboat for Hawaii. Kind of a good idea, there wasn't much chance of getting killed if he were on the ocean. I guess his dad bailed him out, paid the dealer not to kill him. Anyway, Dick still lives in Boulder. Stupid, not to learn a lesson. I guess that's what having a rich daddy does for you." Alex looked. I paused. "Okay, it's true, I don't like him, as if you haven't noticed. Something about him just...oh yeah, now I remember why I don't like him. He's a liar, a thief, a bigot, a coward, a queer basher, and a bully. That's why. No character. Does that answer your question?"

Alex continued to watch me through the mirror. In a calm, almost chill voice he said, "If true, it is an interesting way to conduct a professional business." Silence. Then, "I'd like to meet this Dick sometime." Alex was quiet for a minute.

Alex: "Do you guys have any plans for tomorrow? We could meet at Jamie's, I'll buy. Sean, are you familiar with this Dick person?"

Sean: "Yes."

Alex: "Please bring him along. Yes. I would very much like to meet this person." He smiled. I put my eyes back on the road. He finished, "He sounds crazy, and I like that in people. It'll be fun." He looked at me again, eyes piercing, voice slow and clear. "You can bring Patrice too, if your date tonight works out. She's eye candy for the rest of us; we can live vicariously." He gave my right shoulder a playful shove from the back seat. I glanced again. Alex had turned away.

That was a cool thing to say, about Patrice I mean. Alex had clearly decided to commit to the friendship, whether we did business or not. It was good for me, I liked Alex too. Sean smiled. He had always been one to stay quiet and watch things unfold on their own. Everything was going as planned. Wine, dinner, and now a trip up to Alex's house for what I knew would be a deal that would put me and Sean both in clover, if I didn't snort the blow. I remembered how I had felt that morning and early afternoon. It seemed like ages ago that I had woken up, gone to Ernie's for chicken cutlet, and remembered the time we torched that frat rat's house. After another minute or two, Alex spoke up again from the back seat.

"I have this good friend Rocky; I know you guys will like him. He gets along with everybody. I'll try to bring him, too. Besides, he and I are like brothers. The only reason he didn't come tonight was that it's the last night of *Animal House* revival at the Flatirons Theater, and he wanted to see it again."

I said, "Rocky? That's his real name?" Alex let out a guffaw.

"No, but he's from Philadelphia and loves Stallone. I think he likes the name. I couldn't think of anything else to call him, and besides, he kicks major ass. That's one reason why everyone likes him."

Ahh, soooo, Confucius say. Rocky is Alex's muscle. We had Kurt. I would have felt sorry for Dick, but I didn't. Just the opposite, I looked forward to seeing the view from the hospital room he would occupy. If I had built up enough good karma to cash in, he wouldn't even know I was in the room; his eyes would be swollen shut. If I was really lucky, he'd have IV lines, I could squeeze them and make him squirm for a change, maybe squirt some little baby fag tears, boo-hoo. The thought made me anxious. I felt a slight shock in my cock.

We continued to work our way up the canyon, making what seemed to be arbitrary left and right turns as Alex called them out. It was as though Alex was taking us in circles to confuse his home's location, though in the dark, he really didn't have to; I wouldn't have been able to find it again for a hundred dollars. The time went by quickly, though. At one point, while we were listening to The Who's "My Wife" from the *Who's Next* album, Alex's hand snaked itself out from the back and did a flip-flop tap dance on my shoulder. I turned to see a cocaine bullet, fully loaded, pointing at my face.

"Here, and then give it back, I'll give you one for the other side. Sean, you don't get any because you're not driving."

Sean turned around, shot Alex a look and a smile, pursed his lips, and said, "You didn't say anything about that rule when we were drinking the Château Latour, or the Mouton, for that matter. If you're not careful, I may have to hold out on you when we get back to my house, sailor." He pronounced it "thailor," like fags do. We all cackled, Alex snorting in between breaths from the laughter. Reaching over my shoulder, I took the mechanism in between thumb and forefinger and put the nozzle end up to my left nostril. I then took a big sniff in. The coke went into my sinuses like sand down your swimsuit during a wipeout on the beach. I handed back the bullet; Alex quickly reloaded it, handed it back, and I took the coke in my other nostril.

Whooo. Yeah. The slight burn and acetone flavor, a barely audible crinkling sound in my ears. An immediate clearing of my senses and eyes, like I was driving during full daylight. Pink Peruvian flake. There's nothing like it in the world. I licked my lips and swallowed the nasal drip from the back of my throat. Within seconds, my tonsils were numb. I could feel the coke set in almost immediately, sending a flow of energy into my bloodstream. I could almost feel the blow as it worked its way into my heart and lungs, speeding everything up. I felt my body start to vibrate, like a tuning fork, absorbing the drug and redirecting it outwardly. My eyes felt like they were shining, like they were stars beaming back untold knowledge from the night sky. I saw a huge tree next to a boulder halfway buried in the road and suddenly realized where we were. There was a high-altitude lake about a mile away. The trail to the parking area was up around the corner no more than a hundred yards ahead and on the right. To get to the lake, you had to walk down a long, windy path along a slab face. You parked at an overlook area about a half mile away. The overlook, all dirt and ruts, was about the size of a football field, and you basically parked anywhere you could. There were scrub bushes, potholes, giant rock-and-dirt clumps the size of garbage cans, needle-like stickers the size of small stilettos. After a rain, when these items got buried from view, they conspired to flatten tires and puncture hoses, keeping the unsuspecting victim out in the boonies until help arrived.

One of the things that made this particular lake so great to swim in was that it had a series of rock semi-slabs that ended in sheer drops to the surface. You could hike around the back of the one, climb to the top, and jump, forty feet into the crystal clear, green-tinged lake water. There was little in the way of outcropping to block your direct descent, it was a nice, safe, straight drop. I dove to the bottom once to see how deep it was in the impact area. I went straight down and cleared my nose twice, and still didn't touch the silt bottom. It was at least twenty-five feet down.

Chapter 18

Here's another quick story. A while back, while we were in college, these three guys and I used to go up there and swim, hang out, smoke dope, and look at great chicks. The lake was very popular with those sorority girls attracted to danger and the chance to check out guys like us, fit, strong daredevils. The kind of guys those chicks would fuck in secret but wouldn't bring home for Christmas to meet the family. I knew exactly the image I projected and loved catching some sweet-looking little thing checking me out. What's that you say? Narcissistic much? Yup. What's your point? Anyway, on with the story.

Some of the other guys who showed up would climb up to the jump-off spot and look down for forever. I always knew that the longer they waited and thought about it, the less likely they were to jump. Fucking losers. If you're going to do something, do it. You might think I'd feel bad for them for crapping out. I mean, I had been up there countless times and knew the fear of looking down. That's the point. If they had to back down, all the better. The chicks wouldn't be interested in pussies like them, all the more for me. Diving from the spot was easy, I even did pikes, backflips, and one-and-a-half's, swimming easy back to the beach, channeling Mark Spitz. I loved every minute of it. When we were done, I'd race anyone back up the slope to the cars. A half mile hike, almost all of it uphill, hands and feet scrambling for purchase. Usually, the loser bought beer, but in our case, the loser twisted a joint or packed a pipe with Hawaiian bud, and we drove home with pot smoke pouring out of the windows, like a Cheech and Chong movie.

There was this one time when I had a bit more than disdain for some of the other guys up at the lake. I was up there one midmorning with Sean and Dick Dickmann. Dick wouldn't have been there except Sean was driving and, as I have said, inexplicably, they were friends. Anyway, this guy came marching down the trail from above, skidding along the gravel and loose shale in his Topsiders and cutoff jeans. I knew him; his name was Pete Ericson. He lived, curiously enough, right next door to us in a small fourplex on 13th and College. Pete was a good guy for someone from the East. Guys from Boston, Philly, Nashville, Charleston, even anywhere in Texas; they were the only ones that used cutoffs for swim trunks. The rest of the Boulder college universe used surf shorts. That's actually an inside joke at the University of Colorado. There were so many people from Southern California going to school there that the unofficial nickname of the school was the University of California at Boulder. But I digress.

Pete came down to the water's edge and looked up at us sitting on the rock. There were at least a dozen chicks from the Pi Phi sorority there, T-shirts praising their sorority and the nipples underneath. I never understood this, but all of the Pi Phis had tight little bodies (measured by the forearm), dark hair, and were just flat-out beautiful. I'm talking eye-popping gorgeous, so hot they could talk a pauper out of his last dollar with a look. There was another sorority with chicks just as beautiful, the Kappas. The difference was the Kappas were all blondes. Go figure, prejudice within the beautiful-people set.

Pete looked up and asked if there was any room left to jump from or were we all going to just sit there like trolls. We all looked down at him from our perch over the water. It was a beautiful day, no wind, only a couple of clouds lazily blocking the sun, giving us occasional shade.

"Come on up," Dick said. He turned away from the ledge as Pete started the hike up. Dick smiled that shit-eating grin of his and snickered. "That guy is an idiot. He's your friend, right, Bruce?"

Just like Dick, to try to get a rise out of me. For some reason, he found it funny. I guess it could have been, to a nine-year-old. I decided to work on a comeback that would need a setup.

I retorted, "You said once that you were related to British royalty, right? Dick? Dickmann's your last name...right? At least the one your mother told you was yours? Well, I've been thinking about it. I think your resemblance to Queen Elizabeth, the sixteenth-century Queen Elizabeth, is striking." A couple of giggles drifted up from the sorority gallery. "You even have the tits and the queen's taste in clothes. At least that's what your girlfriend said last night after I fucked her in the ass. She said you liked it like that too, and you had her pitch, you caught." No more giggles, I think the girls were appalled. The world isn't all sweets and cake, little Marie Antoinettes, I said to myself.

Dick got to his feet and gave me a knee to the shoulder as he did so. I sniffed and looked up at him. "If I have to get up too, you're going over face-first, and you won't have all of your teeth." Dick was bigger than me, but only because of his man-tits and melon head. He certainly didn't scare me. I thought that his constant attempts at laughter at my expense hid his secret fear of me. He knew me. So, instead of instigating any more shit, Dick turned and dove off, doing a passable forward flip and landing with a small, medium-sounding splash. Just then, Pete appeared, looked at us, and just ran off the edge. He formed himself into a jackknife for a straight entry but had pushed out too far, no time to straighten into the dive. As he went down, arms and legs flailing wildly, he yelled, "OH shittt!"

We looked over the edge just as he landed, flat on his belly, his body splayed out like he was skydiving. Huge splash, very loud slapping sound. Dick was treading water and saw the whole thing. He was laughing from his vantage point about twenty feet away, and we waited above for Pete to come up. At that point, we figured a very sore stomach, red skin, a headache, and really bruised ego in his immediate future, all giggle/laugh/snorts. But he didn't come up. We waited about five seconds and then Sean dove off, aiming right for the spot where we had seen Pete land. Dickhead took a fast five or six strokes over and was the first one to get to the spot. He took a deep breath and turned underwater, legs and feet disappearing well after his head and torso. Sean surfaced, looked around, and then dove for the bottom as well. We saw no activity for about another five seconds and then Dick came up, holding Pete by the chest, lifeguard-style. Sean surfaced a second later and swam over to help. Some skinny guy with a red bandana and blue-and-purple tie-dyed Led Zeppelin T-shirt went in as well, and a bunch of the sorority chicks were already scrambling the other way for the cars. I hoped they were planning to call an ambulance when they got somewhere with a phone, but I doubted it. Dick and Sean got Pete to the side of the lake and pulled him up onto the greenish-black sand. I could see gouges that Pete's heels made in the sand as he was pulled farther up and away from the water's edge. He was moving slightly, shifting side to side. That's all I remember because I grabbed Sean's car keys and took off up the footpath leading to the slab face. I sprinted my way up the slab, bounding from boulder to boulder, avoiding the hose beasts, sliding shale, and sticker bushes. Within minutes I had reached the top of the trail and continued running for the cars. There were a couple of the girls from the rock trying to get into a yellow BMW 2002. I asked them as I unlocked the car door, "Is anyone going for help?"

One girl, whose name later turned out to be Amy, said, "Our friend Roxy just left, she said she was going to the North Boulder Liquor store to call an ambulance."

I said, "The guy's okay, I saw him moving a little when they got him out of the water." I saw the relief in their eyes as the knowledge that Pete hadn't died washed over them. They climbed into their car, turned over the engine, and U-turned out of the space, sending dirt, pebbles, and dust flying. Amy looked out the back window as they accelerated away and waved. I waved back. While I had had every intention of going for help myself, two things occurred to me. One was that help was already on the way. I had no doubt that Amy's friend had done what she said she'd do. This meant that going down the hill and looking for the fire department was probably redundant. And another thing: if I took the car, Sean had no way home after this all blew over. Fuck Dickmann. No, the best choice was to stay right where I was and act as a beacon for the ambulance.

It turned out that an ambulance didn't come. Because of the treacherous location and steep climb down to the lake, the fire department sent the flight-for-life helicopter for Pete instead. By the time they got to him, a good two hours had gone by. A couple of guys climbed out of the gully to their cars while I waited, including the guy with the Led Zeppelin T-shirt. We talked about the events that led to Pete getting hurt, and they told me that when they left the beach, the EMTs were already on the job and that Pete was stable, talking and laughing at the predicament. It turned out that Pete was taken to the hospital and put under observation for a couple of days.

Our neighbors from up the street were very inquisitive about Pete's accident, and I must have told the story a couple of dozen times. For those people who knew Dick, I threw in that part of the story for dessert.

You're probably wondering why I mention this particular story; I mean, it doesn't really have that much to do with the evening's festivities. The story doesn't involve Alex, cocaine, Michel's, or the Flatirons Hotel. Here's the rest of the story.

A week later I was over at Pete's apartment, drinking bottles of Heineken and listening to Pink Floyd's album *Wish You Were Here*. We'd just gotten high from some buds a friend of mine sent me from Humbolt County. The pot was homegrown *Cannabis indica*, very rare, very potent, very sweet; it smelled a little bit like skunk, hence its nickname, skunkweed. There was a knock on the door and in walked Dickhead, grinning that stupid grin. He didn't even lose a step when he saw me and threw his usual insult.

"Bruce! Aren't you supposed to be studying your remedial English? I hear that you don't have enough stars on the rewards wall to get your cupcake. Maybe you should go on home for your nappy time."

I had to come back, so I said, "I take naps, what of it? You could use one too, it might help with your facial tic. Do you know any big-boy words?"

Pete said, "Hey, Rich. Thanks for stopping by. We just finished smoking a doobie, there's a roach left. You can have it, if you want." Pete was being generous, seeing as it was my pot. I didn't want to make a bad situation any worse, so I let it go. It turned out that Pete and fuckwad Dick had become friends after Dick saved him at the lake.

"So," Dick inquired, "howzit going?"

Pete said, "I feel really good. No problem. I even worked out yesterday, did some pull-ups, leg extensions, went for an easy run."

Dick smiled. I knew that smile, he had mischief on his mind. Dick. He said, "If you're in such good shape, let's see you do thirty push-ups, right here and now. If you do it, I'll buy you a beer. Oh, I guess you have some already. In that case, you can buy me one." And Dick walked into the kitchen, past the sink with the broken faucet, and reached for the handle of the over-under refrigerator. He opened the door and got a bottle from the second shelf, knocking a block of cheese on the floor. I watched as he picked it up and took the plastic off. He then took a bite, leaving teeth marks, and finally, he put the cheese back without rewrapping it. I looked away and just shook my head in disgust. He smacked the beer open on the edge of the kitchen table, making a depression in the tabletop. So Dick, doing his dick thing.

He came back into the room and sat down in an overstuffed black leather chair with batting coming out of the seat and left arm where your hand wraps over. He took a pull on the beer and said, "Well. We're waiting." I recognized that quote from the movie *Caddyshack*; and how lame was that?

Pete said, "Done, except you're going to buy me a six-pack, my choice. We'll go to Liquor Mart as soon as I'm done. In fact, you can do the push-ups with me. There, how about them apples?"

The two of them got on the floor, positioned their hands, and started. Dick got into a steady rhythm, but Pete went after it, as quickly as he could and still do them right. I counted nineteen when Pete suddenly stopped. His eyes bugged out, his arms gave out, and he dropped to the carpet, face kissing the polyester fibers.

Dick stopped and laughed. "Pathetic, Pete."

I sat there for a second, then reached out and pushed him with my foot. "Get up, Pete, or no more pot." Pete didn't budge. I got off the couch, scooched down next to him, and looked at his face. His eyes were wide open, but they saw nothing. I knew right away that he was dead. Fuck. Fuckety fuck. Oh shit, I thought, what to do? I looked up at Dick, who had gotten up and was standing over the two of us, smile for once wiped off his face. "Fuck, he's dead," I said in as calm a manner as I could. "What should we do? Call the cops?"

Dick looked at me, scowled then smiled, grabbed his stuff and said, "That's what you can do. I'm out of here. You explain the pot." With that, Dick turned on his heel, laughing, and walked out the door, leaving it open. I sat there in complete shock, incredulous of the events and of Dick's behavior. Unbelievable.

I called 911 and spoke to the dispatcher. I figured I had a few minutes to clean up. I picked up the paraphernalia and flushed incriminating drugs down the toilet. I was careful to avoid Pete, still on the ground, dead drool hanging out of his mouth and trailing to the rug. The inside of his pants legs looked wet, and I realized that it was urine from when his bladder gave way. The guy just dropped. One minute here, another gone, who knew where. His eyes had glassed over and he looked like a mannequin. It was really freaky.

The cops showed up about ten minutes later, followed by some paramedics with a gurney. One of them recognized Pete immediately. "Isn't that the guy we pulled out of the lake with the helicopter last week?"

I didn't give the other guy a chance to answer before chiming in, "Yeah, he was the guy. I was there. All I can tell you is that he was doing push-ups and he just collapsed, just like you see. I didn't move him."

"Why was he doing push-ups?" asked the bigger of the two Boulder Police guys.

I turned my attention to the both of them and said, "Would you believe it if I told you he wanted to prove he was completely recovered from last week's mishap?" They both looked me over, sizing me up as truthful. I got the feeling they were sizing me up for a pair of handcuffs too. While I had dumped the pot and put away most of the dope stuff, a small mirror sat on the end table. There was a twenty-dollar bill rolled up next to it and white powder residue clinging to the reflective surface. They noticed my glance and gave me another look-over. Not my house, not my blow. I was the *good* guy.

"I can see what you're thinking, but I could have dug out and left him here. Instead, I stayed and did the right thing. Who would do that if they were guilty?" I decided not to tell them about Dick, there just didn't seem to be any point. I mean, we didn't do anything. I couldn't really get him into trouble, there was no evidence that he was even there; he took his beer with him. Clever. I said, "If you have any questions, I'll be happy to answer them. These guys here actually know more about this than I do." I pointed at the paramedics. "They were the ones that got him last week. What happened here had to be part of it. Maybe his heart gave out, or an artery burst, or something."

The big cop turned his wide girth toward the paramedic who had recognized Pete.

"What do you think?" the cop asked. The paramedic, who by this time had turned Pete over and started getting the sheets ready to move him, said, "Yeah, it could have happened like that. Maybe a blown aorta. The guy took a hectic fall last week at the lake, landed on his stomach splat from a good forty feet up. The doctors will know at Memorial, that's where we're taking him."

"So, where do you live, and how do you know this guy?" the second cop asked me. He was staring at me with serious concentration. Maybe he was trying to identify a lie. Please. I lie all the time and convince theater professors, for Christ's sake. This flatfoot wasn't going to get anything out of me. Besides, I was telling the truth, with omissions.

"I live next door in the upstairs apartment. Pete and I are friends. I mean were." I shrugged. What else is there to say? "I was here when it happened."

"Were you drinking?" the cop asked.

"Yes. And we were stoned, too. I'm not high anymore though; this kind of cleared my head. Pete might be, but he's not going to complain." The joke fell flat. The cop just stared at me. As an afterthought, since we had been drinking, I said, "We're both twenty-one, if that helps." His mouth twitched. Maybe he thought of himself as T. J. Hooker, or some other lame TV cop. I had decided to stop with the question answering. Officer #4131 was way too suspicious, like he was getting ready to bend me over the squad car, legs splayed. Ten fingers on the fender. That would be so Boulder. I hated cops, especially Boulder cops. I've always distrusted cops, since little-kid days in Newport Beach. Out there, the cops were worse than the criminals. In fact, they were the criminals. I've said it a thousand times. If you wanted to get a hold of great weed, find a cop. They were racist fuckers too. They all seemed related, had at least some Mexican in them, and hated white guys, especially surfers. I once had a cop follow me for three miles around my old neighborhood, his headlights off. I'm sure he was hoping he could pull me over for something. He must have been desperate since he was willing to break the law to catch me doing the same. I didn't give him the satisfaction. I wouldn't have noticed him back there if it hadn't been for the midnight-blue flake paint job on his Cutlass. It was probably nice in the sun but gave him away in the moonlight. I finally ducked into a friend's driveway, a long dirt road leading to the guy's garage, near the ocean. Private property. Sorry, you aren't invited, fucking cop motherfucker. Try to catch me? Right, nice try. Maybe you should arrest yourself, shit-for-brains.

That was my attitude at the time. T. J. Hooker's partner gave him an easy nudge to his left side, away from hidden gun hand. I'm sure he did it on purpose, T.J. was getting a bit bothered under the collar. I gave T. J. another eyeball up/down as he turned away and followed the gurney out the door. He was wearing those lame-ass Reebok aerobic shoes, in black. I guess that made it easier for him to chase down little old ladies but didn't make the shoes any less gay. His partner said, "Bruce, if you would give us your telephone number, we could call you if something else comes up. And we appreciate your giving us a call on this; it was the right thing to do." This cop's name was Dillon. Thanking me, what a novel idea.

Dillon seemed like a decent guy, so I obliged him. I asked, "Can I go?"

"Yes, we're about done. As I said, we'll call you if we have any other questions. And Bruce? If you flushed anything else besides the pot, you need to come clean." Drugs? Of course not, Occifer. I would never flush the rest of the eight-ball of coke I was going to sell to my friend Timmy, the coke that I would have to pay for, to the tune of $250. A debt owed to another friend named Kurt, who didn't suffer fools or deadbeats. What the fuck is it with you cops anyway?

"No, Officer, you got me on that, but he really died just like I said, I swear. I told the EMTs everything."

Chapter 19

I didn't say anything to either Alex or Sean of my recognition of the place, and it turned out to be a good thing. Did Sean recognize it? Didn't seem likely, he would have said. Or maybe he was on the same wavelength as I was. I turned to look at him but got nothing.

We drove along for another five minutes at most. I continued to recognize markers, up until we pulled around a right-hand bend and passed a dirt driveway flanked by cowboy-style post fencing.

Alex yelled, "Stop! Stop, stop, stop! Right here!" We had finally gotten to the mysterious Chez Alex. "Sorry about that. Turn in here and go slow, the ruts are deep. You'll bottom out." By this time, Alex had done at least four bullets in each nostril, then given us two each. I was very high; the coke was phenomenal. Alex must have been ridiculous. Sean was sitting back in the passenger seat, eyes staring out at the dark, wide as a deer's in the headlights of an oncoming truck full of hunters. He was toast.

"How far is it to your house from here?" I asked. I really needed to take advantage of Alex's hospitality. Said hospitality included his bathroom, his liquor, his phone, and his cocaine. Three of the four were obvious. I kind of wanted the phone to confirm with Patrice that we were still meeting at the hotel. I figured that this visit might last a while, and I didn't want her to think I had blown her off.

It was 7:45 when we started down the side road to his place.

Alex said, "We go down this way for about a mile, then turn into my real driveway. I share this part with my neighbor." Great. Not only did I hear the Saab complaining about the gross mistreatment being heaped on it, I could feel it. The jarring was like being on Mr. Toad's Wild Ride at Disneyland. Jerking, throwing, pushing, and bumping back and forth. My head hit the ceiling of the car at least a half dozen times. The Saab responded in typical fashion; the car performed with valor but kicked up a fuss. The headlights reflected on all kinds of nasty obstacles. I thought we'd tip over when I veered off the track accidentally and literally drove up the side of a downed tree. If it hadn't been for Sean yelling, pointing in a very urgent manner, and finally grabbing the wheel, we would've ended up ass overhead, looking at each other with chins for eyes and eyes for asses. As stoned and coked up as we were, this might have proven to be the kind of situation that caused lasting trauma to both body and mind. It's a good thing we had stopped drinking at the restaurant. That would really have been a disaster, a mind-altering trifecta.

We backed off of the tree and right into a mud hole that buried the car halfway to the axle. This pretty much cemented us in place; we didn't go anywhere. I spun the wheels back and forth a couple of times, shifting from first gear into reverse and back again. Sean said, "I don't think you're helping. If you want to get out of here, we need to get out and put something under the tires, then pull forward and out of the hole." Sean, not only a prankster but also the most coherent person in the car. Okay, so not toast after all.

"Who's going to get out and do this?" I asked the two of them. "I'm driving so you won't get me out of the driver's seat. Alex, this is your driveway, so you're kind of responsible for the predicament we're in. You wanna get out?"

"Now why would I want to do that? I'm the one providing the refreshments, so as party king of this trip and the ultimate host of any shindig when we get to my house, no, I don't want to get out. I don't think so. Forget it."

Sean said, "I knew it." He grinned. "You fucking guys planned this from the beginning, when we left Michel's. I saw you plotting the whole time, don't think I didn't. When you put in the tape of The Who, I knew this was a done deal.

You know how I like The Who, especially *Who's Next*. Some bribe, a song on the stereo. I've got whatchucall precognotion, and I knew this would happen. Fuck." We all laughed; Sean joined after a couple of seconds.

"Yeah," I said, "but if you're prescient, you tacitly agreed to be the one to get out. Besides, the music was great, right? I mean, you don't seem to be hurting for music or party favors. Helping out, taking one for the team. It's the least you can do."

Alex chimed in, "Yeah, yeah. Go, Sean. I promise when we get to my house, I'll make it up to you."

Sean said, "Unless you can provide me with a new pair of shoes, new jeans, and a hot chick, you can't make it up to me."

Alex responded with enthusiasm, "I can do that!"

So, Sean got out of the car and immediately went into the puddle up to the tops of his ankles. "FUCK!" he yelled. "You guys suck so huge. This is definitely not the way I saw this evening going."

"Quit grumbling and whining," I said. "Find a stick or something and put it under the wheel. We can't get out of here if all you do is bitch. I didn't see anyone stop you from imbibing all the way up here. Now it's time to pay for the ride."

Alex and I laughed, and Alex said, "Well put. Come on, Sean; put your mind to it. There are tons of sticks all around here. Just grab one and let's go!"

Sean swore at the two of us in unison, "Fuck you both, while I'm out here, you guys are in there. You have no idea what I'm going through, here in the mud. Now I know what it must have felt like to fight in Vietnam." There was a moment of silence, and then we all laughed. Sean said in a dejected manner of finality, "Okay, I'll get the stick. Try wait."

I reached my head out the window and looked at our predicament. The left rear tire was indeed buried just shy of the axle. "I don't think we're going anywhere. If it's okay with you, we'll just wait here patiently while you go and GET. THE. STICK!"

"I AM! FUCK OFF!" Sean calmed. "You suck, brah." Sean took two steps, freeing his feet from the mud at the bottom of the puddle, and as he moved off to our left, his head began scanning to and fro, scouting for the best stick to do the job. The next thing, we heard a squelching, squishing sound, and looked out to see Sean standing about eight feet away, missing his right black-and-white Adidas Superstars, his favorites. Apparently, the shoe got stuck in the mud so deeply that he literally walked out of it.

"Oh, you have got to be kidding me" was all he could muster. The resignation in his voice was palpable. I began to feel sorry (but not sorry) for him, but as you've noticed, I don't concern myself with that kind of thing very often. Life is too short to worry about the other guy's bullshit. My main objective was still the acquisition of as much blow as I could get out of Alex in this first deal. I had built up enough trust to get the wheels of progress turning, I wanted to close this puppy and get back to the hotel. I had a very hot date with a talking sex puppet named Patrice. I had no doubts that we would be doing the horizontal Lindy...and that she'd be good at it.

With this objective in mind, I realized that I needed to actively participate in assisting my own circumstances. "Alex, I'm going to help that sorry sack out there." I stepped gingerly out of the car, looking for a dry area to put my feet down. And found it. Sean couldn't have been more unlucky. The dry spot was only a foot and a half from the driver's side door. Good for me, unfortunate for him. As Bugs Bunny said often enough in the old Warner Brothers cartoons, "Hardy, har, har." I put my feet down and carefully stood my ground. No problem, though I could feel the soles slip slightly as I pivoted and stepped into the brush. I didn't take more than five or six steps when I heard another scrambling and shaking of the brush on the other side of the car. This rustling was followed by a dull thump, like someone dropping a large stone into a patch of dirt. A yelp emanated from the area that Sean had gone into. It was very dark outside the glow of the headlights, and I couldn't see him. I froze for just a second, about as long as it took to realize what had happened; Sean had slipped and fallen into a prickly bush. "Sean, are you okay?"

Sean answered, "Yeah, I'm okay. I think I broke my brain. The good news is that I tripped on the perfect stick to get the car out with." Sean came shuffling out of the brush into the glow of the car's headlights and showed us the stick. It was a good stick, cylindrical, about four inches in diameter, about five feet long. We'd be able to get a good purchase on the end and lift the car out as Alex drove forward. Sean looked totally pathetic, standing there with mud all over his faded jeans, University of Colorado sweatshirt, and only one shoe. His other foot was covered by a gray wool sock, the kind you use for hiking. It was stretched and wet from the puddle and the toes were covered with mud and some black substance.

"What's that on your shoe, Sean? Oh, sorry, that's not your shoe, that's your sock. What the fuck is on your sock, Sean?"

Sean said, "It's some kind of shnu, or something."

Alex put his head out of the window. "What's shnu?" Alex asked. His eyes were wild, like he was one of those guys who could move their eyes independently. It was creepy to see, especially since we were just getting started. A lotta night to go, lotta things to do. While we were outside rooting around, Alex had climbed into the driver's side seat, I guess to rock the car back and forth while both Sean and I positioned the stick under the tire. It was a good idea, even though I regretted having him drive my car. In fact, at this point I had concerns about Alex behind the wheel of a manually powered tricycle. I know I wouldn't have wanted to be in his path. "Alex, please don't try to move the car until I say. You may be able to replace Sean's clothes and even get him female companionship for the night, but you can't replace the Saab. You just can't." I was very diplomatic; I asked him nicely. What I thought was, Don't even try. You don't know me; once business is concluded between us, whether it's tonight or in ten years, if you fuck up my car, I will fuck you up. Once on my shit list, you'll regret the day we ever met.

Sean looked up at him from behind the car and said, "You can't replace my clothes either. And I definitely expect a chick to climb all over me when we get to your house. And to answer your question, I don't know what's new. What's shnu with you?" Fucking hilarious. Another crackerjack yuk from the master of horrible humor. Sean had been telling that old one for as long as I'd known him, and the only people who fell for it anymore were elementary school kids. And Alex, apparently, though Alex had an excuse—he was temporarily insane.

I started to get irritated. I bent down and picked up the piece of wood that Sean had found in the weeds and shoved it under the wheel until I felt the tire catch. I made sure that the branch was secure and that the car would track straight when Alex started. I looked up at Sean. We both looked at Alex, who by this point had half poured himself out of the window and was staring at the sky, head bent almost upside down, arms hanging slack. There was no way he was driving the car out of the mud.

"What do you see?" I asked, ready with another quip. Alex took a deep breath. I could see his chest rise and fall, even in the low light.

"I see the stars. I see the past, the future. I see the bending of time." He took another deep breath. "I see life."

The quip dried up in my mouth as if I had swallowed a teaspoon of cinnamon. Prophetic. This guy must have had something on the ball to reference Einstein in his condition.

I'd have to pay more attention to him the rest of the way. Maybe he wasn't as fucked up as I thought.

"Alex, you're the biggest one here, you get out and help Sean." Alex popped his head back into the car, opened the door, and stepped out. I noticed that he didn't stumble when he stood up and came around to the back of the car. He looked down at the situation with his hands on his hips.

"I think I can do this myself. Get out of the way." He set his feet nice and wide and grabbed the stick, moving his hands around the grip to tighten it. I got into the driver's seat, quickly turned the car's motor over, and started the engine. The car cranked for just a second and settled into a smooth idle.

I heard Alex tell Sean, "Stand out of the way, I got this." I watched Alex get down into a low stance, the better to maximize his leverage. He settled into a classic lifter's position, like he had been in a weight room for years, practiced in the fine art of the squat. I saw him straighten and felt the car rise slightly. "So, pop the clutch, already! This is heavy!"

I pushed in the clutch and slowly gave the car some gas. The movement was delicate. I gave it a little more gas and the Saab started to roll. At the same time, I felt the back end of the car move a little higher out of the mud as Alex got more leverage on the stick. A little more gas, I said to myself. There was a slight lurch, Alex stumbled forward, and the car was out. The car settled a few feet from the sucking bog, in some grass, dead leaves, and small pebbles. Alex yelled with jubilation. I saw Sean grin and quickly move for the passenger door. As the door opened, Alex climbed in first, then popped his head back out and gave me a grin and wink. He got into the back, careful to keep his feet off the floor, then settled in lengthwise, head behind me. Sean jumped in, the seat cushion bouncing a couple of times from his weight. I got back in and revved the engine. "So? Which way are we going?"

Alex said, "Go left and loop around a hundred and eighty degrees. This time, pay attention and stay out of the ruts. The best thing is to stay slightly to the right. There's a big boulder about a mile from here, and we go right around a hundred yards after you pass it."

We drove in silence for less than ten seconds and Sean blurted, "Let's get some vibrations going. Maybe you won't make any more mistakes if we have some musical accompaniment." Good idea, but it kind of made me bristle that he would put the whole previous disaster on my shoulders. Especially since Alex and I had paid for the drinks, wine, and dinner, he was getting a free ride. In fact, he was getting a free ride throughout this whole venture. He provided some comedy asides. That was it. My money, my reputation, my contacts, my scale, Deal-A-Meal, my everything, every time. What a dick, trying to make me look bad in front of Alex, who gave no response to the quip. I tried to get a look at Alex's face in the rearview mirror, but couldn't see him behind my head, in the shadows. I glanced at Sean, who was attentive to the road ahead, face a mask of emotion and thought. He had put in the tape of the Rolling Stones' double album, *Exile on Main Street*, and we listened to the third song on the first side, first disk, called "Tumbling Dice." Great song. Great...song. It was universally taken within our peer group that this album was the Stones' best ever. I kind of thought *Some Girls* was really good, too, especially their remake of the Motown hit "Just My Imagination." My right fingers began to tap, but my brain said, Fine. Karma's going to be a bitch for you, my son. I turned my attention back to the road ahead and accelerated, looking for the boulder and the turn into Alex's driveway. Song over, we were at our destination.

Chapter 20

We got to Alex's house at about a quarter after eight. The house was a slate-and-wood modern, lots of slanted roof angles, stone fireplace, redwood siding, flat-pane windows, split into eighth sections. We got out of the car and walked the thirty feet from the end of the driveway to the front door, cutting through a small thicket of trees and mountain grasses and flowers. I had studied some of this type of landscaping in college. I remember the class really well; I just don't remember the final, which I took high as a kite flying in a strong breeze. The class was called Architecture 221, "A Timeless Way of Building." That was the name of the class, and it covered the work of Christopher Alexander, a professor at the University of California at Berkeley. The basic premise of the class was that there was a way to design anything from the smallest window dormer to whole cities that incorporated specific rules and guidelines both small and large. These guidelines were defined in the other book we used called *The Pattern Language*. It was a great class, one of the best I had taken. My grade didn't reflect my knowledge since most of the grade involved the final, which was nearly impossible to fathom. The professor put a picture of an urban street corner in a busy city on the overhead and we had to define the five main guidelines used and discuss the building patterns from the design of everything in the photograph as one entity to the smallest detail that either made or didn't make the overall design work. In two hours. Just like that. I can barely understand the question, even years later. I've always thought that the test was a setup for failure, since the space we were describing was composed of many self-contained environments, all designed by different people from famous architects to the guy working down at the city planning office who chose the streetlights based on a bidding system. We all knew of the format beforehand, and I felt confident of my understanding. Two things happened, as I mentioned. One, I got very high on pot (okay, so sue me). The other was that I didn't appreciate the depth of the professor's cruelty in the assignment. The guy had a very well-developed ego. He gave me a pretty bad grade on the final modeling project as well, the fucker. Because I didn't have the money to make my project really impressive, he fucked me on the grade, and I lost my parental funding for future semesters. I ended up having to drop out. I went into his office after receiving the bad news and tried to reason with him. No go. I'm sure he regretted it; I know he didn't see it coming, the crack in the mouth I gave him, nor did he see the explosion of balsa wood as I punted my project all over his office. He was probably cleaning up the wood for months. And I did get the last laugh. He got fired the next year for selling grades in exchange for blowjobs. I think he took a job as an adjunct drafting instructor in a community college in Iowa. Fuck him, just another asshole who made my life miserable for the short time he was involved in it. And like all those others who've fucked with me, he regretted it. Do I sound like sour grapes? Yup, but as I said, karma's a bitch.

Anyway, I really liked the way Alex had designed this part of the entrance to his place. It was a nice way to separate the driveway and outside world from the privacy of the house. He had some columbine growing, but the season was just about over, the flowers just about gone. Up in the canyon where he lived, it was cold. There was snow everywhere, from just a light layer on the driveway to what looked like maybe a foot around the side of the house, down a culvert. I could see my breath and regretted not having my fleece jacket or something. I couldn't remember where I had left it, maybe the bar. I was too fucked up. Straighten out, Bruce. It's time to get your shit together. A shake went through me. I felt my toes. They were numbing. My sweatshirt just didn't cut it, even with the base layer. I wanted to get inside as quickly as possible. I was shivering by the time we walked off the gravel and onto the brick formal entrance and stood facing the double front doors. The right one had one of those peephole windows carved into it, the little doors that you open and stick your nose out of. The little peephole was about six inches square, and had a wrought-iron latch, though we didn't see that until we got inside. Alex opened up the door with his keys, using two different keys to unlock two separate dead bolts. When he opened the door and let us in, a high-pitched siren triggered, ear-splitting. Alex sprinted to the keypad on the other side of the entrance to the kitchen, visible about forty feet away and through an arched doorway. Jesus, that was loud. I guess we came to the right place, he has security up the ass. I wonder if he has his stash in the house. Maybe in a big safe hidden in the guest bedroom closet or something. Maybe I should search it out, pretend I'm going to take a piss and poke around? What the hell are you thinking, Bruce? You're here to do a coke deal, a big one by your scale. You've done all the right things until now. Alex is ready to go. Sean's kept his piehole shut about some of the inconsistencies in your stories. Smart; he wants to do the deal as much as you do. I mean, he stands to gain almost as much as you do from this relationship with Alex. If we do this first deal for a kilo, we were going to make over $12,000, and I'd probably split it with Sean fifty/fifty; Sean would make about $6,000. I'd make him set up most of the little deals, eight-balls and quarter ounces. I planned on selling the coke in these small amounts to a large distribution of contacts who would then split the much smaller amounts into retail grams, halves, and quarters for the addicted masses. I didn't mind selling the coke that way, I knew lots of guys who had the money for an eight-ball. I thought of all the frat goons and sorority coke whores who had carte blanche living expenses from Daddy.

Like this guy I knew named Viper. I had no idea why he was called Viper; he wasn't particularly dangerous. In fact, he was a pretty passive, good-natured guy who had a terrible nose for blow. Sometimes he would come over and buy a half gram from me, then lay out two huge lines, a quarter gram each. He'd give me a bill and roll up his own, and we would race to see who could snort their line first. Demented. Still, it's true that I had a bottomless nose for coke. I didn't have any problem selling it to someone and then turning around and doing the coke I just sold to him. It was like paying a personal trainer to work out with you. I would keep a couple of grams as stash and sell that off in retail amounts as well; more profit for me, plus I could keep control of my own consumption.

So, there was Viper, Do-A-Line, a guy nicknamed Ingemar who was on the ski team and had a taste for hair band rock, another guy named T-Bone. Now, his name I understood. He had a reputation for putting the bone to every chick he could. It was crazy. Of course, it didn't hurt that the guy's dad was filthy rich, Denver oil money.

There were also a couple of others in the frat world I could depend on to get it done; I knew at least one dealer in every fraternity, even the Jewish one. Who'd have thought? I also knew a bunch of potheads and rockers, and the clubbers. These people would step on the blow I sold them with baby laxative, cutting the potency, and they'd make a good one hundred dollars on an eighth ounce themselves. Let's see. Two fifty for three and a half grams, pull out a half gram for themselves and put in a half gram of cut. Sell it for fifty a half, that would net them three hundred fifty. Minus the two fifty for cost of goods sold, that's a hundred dollars profit plus a half gram to snort. And they would want more. That was the best part of the plan; they would be back again the next day. If things went really well and they did their own stash, they would be back that night. This was the best of all scenarios, and I planned on adding incentives for a quick turnover. I love cocaine addiction, so profitable.

Sean and I exchanged glances as we scoped the place out from the foyer. "Nice place, Alex. Do you own it?" I asked. I took off my shoes and placed them next to the door to the right of the entrance.

Alex said, "You don't have to take your shoes off in here."

"Thanks, but force of habit. That's just the way we do it in Hawaii." The other two gave me the stare. "I mean, the way *they* do it in Hawaii. I just like the idea." The entrance hall opened up into a vaulted ceiling. There was a loft space where there was a Barcalounger-style chair, a standing lamp shaped like a skeleton, and a big TV. There was a VHS machine under the TV, so high tech. The stairs leading up to the second floor started from that area designated as the living room, on the far-left side of the space. The whole downstairs was basically one room with areas delineated by furniture and Oriental carpets, and the kitchen. The stairs had no railings, just kind of floated, like the Brady Bunch had in that incredibly brainless television show from the 1970s. Alex started off for the kitchen and said over his shoulder, "I'm getting a beer. Do you guys want one?"

Sean said, "What kind of beer do you have?"

"What are you, a beer snob? I have Heineken. Is that good enough for your overeducated taste buds?"

"Well, now that you ask, why yes, I am a beer snob, and Heineken will be fine, thank you," Sean said.

"Bruce? Beer?" Alex inquired of me.

I answered, "No, I don't think so, thanks. I don't like mixing beer and wine, and I have plans later. But...if you've got a nice red, I'll take a glass." They both chuckled.

Alex disappeared into the kitchen and returned about fifteen seconds later holding two opened bottles of Heineken, a glass of what he said was a Cuvaison pinot, and a razor blade. He walked about halfway into the room and called over to us at the front entry.

"What are you guys still doing over there? My house is yours. Come into the living room and have a seat." I felt the change in surface from marble to carpet as we left the space set aside for Entry Hall and made the transition into Living Room. The carpet was a beautiful Oriental, mostly royal blue in color. It was soft as velvet against my socks. I didn't know what Sean was feeling; his feet were still clad in one wet and one dry sock. He had one shoe at the door and the other was back at the puddle, hiding in the mud somewhere. And to that subject, Sean asked, "Hey Alex, you said something about having a spare pair of shoes around here. Exactly what kind of shoes are they? And socks too, please."

Alex said, "Not very demanding, are we? Okay, what size are you? No, let me guess. I'll be right back." With those words, Alex walked to the other side of the room and sprinted up the stairs, taking them two at a time. When he got to the top, he made a sharp left and disappeared out of sight. "Yes! Found them! I'll be right down." He came back from around the wall and hopped down the stairs, using each step like a ski bump, jumping and twisting as he descended. When he got to the bottom, he threw a pair of gray wool socks at Sean, followed by a pair of green Converse All Stars. Sean put on the new socks.

"Ahh," he said. He then took one shoe in each hand. "You're kidding, right?"

Alex said, "I never kid when it comes to Converse Chuck Taylor All Stars. I have forty-three pair. I'm giving you those so now I only have forty-two. You owe me a pair of green Cee Tees, size ten, payable next summer. Now, who wants to do a big-ass rail? Don't be shy, this is a good night to celebrate." He hesitated. "Wait, I have a question. Would you like to talk about a business opportunity?"

Could have read my mind. His face changed, he got serious. He took a breath. "One which I am now convinced will make us all some money. There is a lot of opportunity in Boulder and my strategic plan now seems to include you both." Why did he sound different?

Alex waggled his eyebrows like Groucho Marx. Impressive. The room silenced for a couple of seconds. I wanted to see his stash, if there even was one to see. I wanted to get the deal done; I had money in the trunk, a Tupperware plastic canister I'd buried in the backyard, under some poison oak I had planted to ward off curious passersby and sneak thieves. If I needed more, I'd negotiate the price down.

Alex got up and, handing me the $100 bill he had twisted into a cylinder, pointed to the mirror and a huge line sitting there. "See if that line suits you. It's from a batch of Bolivian. I looked at the line; tiny crystals and flakes ran through it, no real powder that I could see—the coke was pure, baby. Alex walked to the front door, looked through the peephole for a few seconds, opened it, walked onto the porch, and gave a huge whistle. He waited, then gave a head-cock like he was beckoning someone. Sure enough, up and in walked Kurt, back from wherever. The gang's all here. "Hi guys, doing lines?" It was a joke, a play on a scene in the film *Animal House*, where the character named Flounder walks up to a group of guys playing cards and says, "You guys playing cards?" Stupid but gets me laughing every time.

Patrice was still on my mind. As I've said, that was a date I had no plans of missing. There was something about that chick that I couldn't put my finger on, besides the things I could put my whole hands on. I mean, she was just dynamite to look at and I was sure that getting to know the Patrice underneath that exterior she wore would be endlessly exciting. She seemed to be the kind of chick who gave as good as she got, too. I didn't know except I wanted to spend the night with her and if all went well spend the next fifty years with her. I know, obsessed much? So what, it's my daydream, stay out of it.

I looked at my watch. It was 8:45. I had over two hours to conclude business and get back into Boulder. A few minutes to find a place to park and I'd be at the bar right on time. If Sean didn't want to go, he could stay up here and get a ride from Kurt or Alex in the morning. What I didn't want was to be stuck up here with these three drug-addled dipshits, clearly on their way to an all-nighter, and miss the date. Also, it was time to quit doing coke or I wouldn't have the mental acuity to carry on even the simplest conversation about anything: dinosaurs, volcanos, kamikaze pilot ideology, you get the point. Also, getting hard might be difficult, but I project. The thing was to get out of there on time. Once bitten, twice shy.

Here's what I mean. I once went up to a house in the mountains above Nederland. Nice house, mountain vacation-style with four bedrooms fitted with double bunk beds for lots of guests. An old roommate of mine, his girlfriend, and I had gone up there to do a little partying, as in drink, do cocaine, smoke pot, and potentially fuck one of the other guests. I barely remember my roommate's name at the time (Stuart something Chinese) but I remember her. Her name was Pauli Haverford, who was the second cousin of the ex-governor of California. She had great legs and an amazing ass, world class. She was pretty in a California beach chick sort of way, with long, straight bleached blonde hair. And she was a party queen, loved to dance, laugh, do cocaine. On the way up to the house, she said at least twice from the back seat that she was so in the mood to get high she'd blow someone if it got her a line. I glanced through the rearview mirror. My roommate was looking pretty glum. Holy shit. I thought to myself, I think I can help you, Little Red Riding Pauli. I didn't say anything but just fingered my tall vial with the eight-ball of Bolivian Babble

Dust and felt a twinge and tingle as my cock responded to the verbal trigger. No guilt though, so I had that going for me.

Yeah, she was Stuart's girlfriend, but my ears heard what they heard. What's your point?

So, we got to the place and made ourselves comfortable in the sunken living room. The house was big, more like a country home for the rich and shameless than the cabin I was expecting. The main room at least a thousand square feet, bigger than my whole apartment in Boulder. There was a metal fireplace shaped like a cone with a vent coming out the top and working its way into the wall. The fireplace was open to a 360-degree exposure so that you could sit anywhere and still get warm. The fire crackled nicely, and the flames licked the screen. There were a couple of leather couches and a nice deep leather chair with a cotton throw over the seat and back. Conversation alcoves were set up near the windows. In the center of the room, there was a large rectangular oak coffee table with a beveled glass top. It must have been four feet wide, twice as long, one huge glass surface. I thought to myself that there didn't seem to be a lack of space to lay out lines. I looked around and saw a few others, including my roommate and Pauli. I don't remember the names but, in the end, there were eight of us, maybe nine. Wait, I do remember that a guy named Steve was there. Steve was an old roommate of mine. He didn't talk to me anymore.

Steve liked to "combo buzz," a euphemism for combining pot, liquor, cocaine, quaaludes, and acid, even heroin into one huge buzz. In military terms, he went FUBAR: it fucked him up beyond all recognition. One night he took two hits of blotter LSD and followed it up with a half-bottle of Wild Turkey bourbon and who knew how many lines of blow. It didn't take long before he started running around the apartment threatening to stab me with a Henckels five-star chef's knife. He then sped up the stairs and locked himself into his third-floor bedroom, screaming and crying like a two-year-old. When I got to the bedroom door, he hollered that he was naked and was going to jump off of the balcony to the parking lot thirty-five feet below. I had to break the door down, grab him from behind, twist the knife from his clutching fingers, and punch him in the face twice before he went down. My knuckles hurt a little after that one. I didn't call the cops. Instead, I put some jeans on him and put him to bed, tucked him in nice and tight. I then went back down the stairs where his girlfriend Jane was waiting. I told her that everything was going to be okay. I then laid out a line of blow for her. She did that line, and the next one too. Then she got up and took off her yellow tube top and jeans. She got down in front of me, undid the waist tie on my Riggers, and thanked me in an oral manner. We then retired to my room and got busy. That girl was nasty. Steve didn't know what he had. Or maybe he did. Maybe he knew his girlfriend was a dirty little coke whore. Maybe that's why he wanted to kill himself. And no, I didn't feel bad. I had just saved his life, you know?

Even though we were only at the Nederland party house for three or so days, I only have two other snapshot pictures in my mind from the adventure. I say three or so because that night it snowed about two and a half feet, and we couldn't get out. What I remember was the coffee table covered with cocaine. Remnants of lines, bindles, and cocaine residue were everywhere. There were at least four or five large piles dumped on the table. Each pile of coke was the size of a small snowball. There must have been an ounce on the table; they looked like heaps of crystal sand on a clear glass beach. People were reaching all over the table, pulling the shaved and chopped blow toward them with all manner of instrument from razor blades to credit cards and driver's licenses. Everyone was mixing and matching the coke into personalized lines like they were mixing paint to get just the right color. There was enough coke on that table to feed all of us for a week. It was gone in less than three days. Real food, like Frosted Flakes? I don't remember.

The other thing I remember was Pauli saying yes and smiling when I asked her if she wanted to have dinner with me when we got back to town. Her eyes glittered and shone in the light, like she was possessed by some silver-colored nymph or something. Then she kissed me, sucking lightly on my tongue and biting my lower lip as she pulled away. There was one bedroom I remember with a double bed covered with a tropical floral bedspread. The room had a window overlooking the back of the house and the steep drop into the ravine below. You couldn't see any of it because of the snow. The snow was so thick that whether something was a tree, bush, rock, or railing, you couldn't tell the difference. It was all so beautiful. I know I fucked her in that bedroom a couple of times in that three-day period. I just don't remember that part. Or how I explained it to Stuart. Or Pauli's phone number.

Chapter 21

As I looked at the two of them, Sean and Alex, I should have been ashamed of myself, the kind of person who would callously manipulate people and fake friendship for personal benefit. Of course, I was coming down off the cocaine binge we did in the car on the way up to that house in the middle of perdition. I figured I could be excused for a little sentimentality. I was a little impatient to get the show on the road, take a look at the weasel dust Alex had. Now I knew we were going to make a deal; it was just a matter of time before Alex got around to busting out stash. I considered just coming out and asking. And then I did. "Alex, that is really excellent blow. Can I buy some from you and we do it before I go back down to town?"

Alex said, "Whoa there. Hold your horses; don't get all in a rush. I want to hear some music first, smoke a joint. You're welcome to join me, unless you have something better to do. You could always go wait in the car."

There was the Alex I expected. Now that we were on his turf, he had the upper hand, and planned on milking us, or at least me. I should have known that was going to happen. The guy knew I wanted to get back to town, he even saw the chick I was getting back to town for. Fucker.

Maybe the tables would turn. I swear, as Rodney Dangerfield says, "I don't get no respect." For all I know, he was secretly planning on bamboozling her for himself. All the more reason to conclude our business. Sean, as usual, didn't seem to care one way or another. He just sat there with that easy smile of his, like he was some Buddhist Rinpoche or something. Like he knew a secret about the meaning of life, and I wasn't in on it. At that moment, I really wanted to seriously choke him. Hell, he had something at stake here too. It was those Kelly-green high-tops. They looked really stupid, with the socks sticking out of the top and the glowing black laces, too long for the shoe. They dragged on the floor like a couple of strands of blacker than black pasta. All Sean needed was a big red nose to look like a clown. Not like someone behaving like a fool, the circus kind, or maybe a TV host for infants who told really childish jokes and had a human dressed like a dog for a sidekick. The sidekick would be named Doofus and the TV clown Sean reminded me of would be named Asshole.

We sat there for another ten minutes, listening to *Led Zeppelin III*, the three of them taking pulls of their Heinekens and then all of us passing around the spliff. Yeah, I took some hits. I still had an immediate agenda, and that was to keep building on the friendship and comfort range of our host. I took the time to check out the house from my seat facing the big picture window and the back space and view on the far side of the glass.

From where I sat, I could see two big pines, branches thick with needles. I couldn't tell how tall they were. I decided to play a little game with myself, try to figure out the full height of the trees based on what I could see and what I knew. The trees started about twenty feet below us. This I knew because I knew the house was suspended about that much room from the ground in back. The ground dropped away very quickly, and while the front door was at ground level, the big redwood patio suspended out fifteen feet from the back of the house. The trees grew up from an area even farther down the slope. Okay, so the trees started twenty-five feet below the patio and the trunks appeared to be about four feet in diameter. Where was it I had seen proportional drawings of coniferous tree trunk height to width? I couldn't remember. See? That's what you get for being high, Bruce. You idiot. There's still a chance this deal isn't going through, and then where would you be? Fucking stupid idiot, you're going to blow it because you're not paying attention. PAY ATTENTION! All right. Trunk width equaled about four feet. That means that the tree height was...wait. You need to know the length of the shadow. That's right, and you gotta compare yourself first to get a reference point. Yeah, so if I know the length of my shadow and I know how tall I am, and the angle of me to the ground—ninety degrees—the tree would mirror that proportion. And if I know what the two lengths are, I can figure out the third because in a right triangle, $a^2+b^2=c^2$. Ha, gotcha. I was paying attention in high school geometry class, even if I was high four days out of five, head resting in the crook of my arm, seemingly asleep. They shouldn't have made me take math after lunch. Everyone knows that food makes you sleepy.

I waited for a couple of seconds to realize that I had a basic problem, one I couldn't solve through geometry, calculus, or Middle English literature. I didn't know how long my shadow was because it was dark outside. Obviously, fool.

I came back to earth from my travels to the math moon in time to catch the end of a conversation between Sean, Kurt, and Alex that I thought was titled, "What's. wrong with the Denver Broncos?"

I piped in, "It's fucking John 'Elzeek' Elway. He's the problem. They pay the guy a gazillion dollars, and he throws three interceptions every time he goes out there. Give me Craig Morton. He's a plug, but at least he knows how to eat the ball when there's nobody open to throw to. Trade fucking Elway. Fucking Stanford dirtbag." God damn, I'm getting edgy. Living up to my nickname, the Edge Master. Alex stared at me.

He said, "Wow. I guess you have an opinion on Elway. You can calm down now. What's eating you anyway?"

Sean chimed in, "Yeah, idiot. Quit being an idiot, idiot."

Kurt went, "Humph."

I took a deep breath and said, "To tell you the truth, I'd kind of like to get back to the main reason we came up here. I want to do business with you. The sooner we get to it, the sooner we can all get back to town, find a place, and drink another great bottle of wine. Man, you've been really generous, and I appreciate it, even if Sean snorts up more of your coke than an elephant can eat peanuts. But you guys know I have a date at midnight. It's after nine and I gotta leave here by eleven fifteen to make it to the hotel, park, and get to the bar. I want to see this chick, gaze into her eyes, whisper the moon. Then I want to be eating her out at my soonest opportunity, and I want that to be like, yesterday."

The three of them looked at each other. Alex said, "Poetic. Except for the part about grinding her, which I guess is poetic too, but only if you let us watch. That bartender is seriously smokin'. You're really getting a shot at greatness."

Kurt said, "Bruce and Patrice? Oh, you've got to be kidding."

I know, what a dick, but he was just jealous. I said, "What I think, bud, is that you had an in with her, the opportunity was yours, and you blew it. Now it's my turn." Then I flashed a small smile. "What I know is that I'm going to climb her peaks and valleys tonight."

Sean: "Oh my god, that is so not poetic. Pathetic is more like it. What a cliché. Is that the best you can do?"

Me: "I know you're into her but you can't have her, bud. I saw her first. Don't make me come over there…"

Kurt: "I saw her first." He scowled. We all grinned.

There was silence in the room for a long beat and then Alex said, "You've got a point. Okay, I want to get to town as well. There's a new band, The Red Hot Chili Peppers, playing at the Blue Note, the second set starts at eleven thirty." That's a weird name for a band. Must be from California. Another long silent beat. Alex looked at me directly, his eyes burning a gap between my ears.

241

"So, Bruce, Sean told me you can provide me with the kind of distribution I want and the time constraints I want. I mentioned earlier that I have someone I work with already. Are you sure you can deliver on your word with deeds?"

"Before I answer that, what kind of quantity are we talking about?"

Alex replied, "Now that's a good ask. Don't ever make a commitment without all the information. How about we start with a key and see how that goes." We looked at each other for a second. I watched his eyes carefully. His gaze was steady, and I realized that he was clear and focused. There didn't seem to be any remnant of his behavior in the car on the way up to the house.

"How much do you want for your blow? Wait, before you answer that, let me thank you again for your generosity, the coke is amazing."

"You're welcome." He said, "You don't have to kiss my ass. I have a good feeling about this too, so we're going to get this done. The price to you is going to be twenty-four five a key. How much ya got?"

"Enough. Can I see the key before we finalize?" I quickly supported the claim on financing. Because trust was everything. "I brought cash, full funds. We'll always do it in cash."

"Okay," Alex said, "I like cash. Cash has always been king. If I don't have to front you any product, the price will be twenty-three. How's that?"

I looked at Sean, whose eyes reflected the anticipation of success. He was leaning slightly forward on the couch, arms hugging each other. I saw him grind his jaw. He started to say something until he looked at me and I shook him off with a very subtle shake of my head. Sean, Mr. Cool-Head. I had to concentrate and didn't want him piping in, saying something I couldn't deliver on.

"Do you have any broken up into something smaller, like maybe some of the kilo in ounces?" I asked.

Alex looked at me and then looked away, his eyes getting that thousand-yard stare. That's the look you get when you're either remembering the past, something you wish you didn't remember, or you're contemplating something you may live to regret in the future. Sean and I didn't say a word. The room was silent as an old mine shaft. We waited. Alex looked up again. His eyes pierced.

"Yeah, I think I can manage that, maybe half a pound in ounces, to get you started." He slowly turned his attention to Sean. He leaned forward and took the razor blade from the tabletop and started cutting lines the size of pencils, four of them. When he was done, he tapped the blade edge against the surface a couple of times to get the jumping dust off. He put the razor down in front of him and looked at his handiwork. I don't know what he could have found wrong with it; the lines were really huge, maybe a quarter gram each. Alex then reached into his shirt pocket and pulled out a rolled-up one-hundred-dollar bill. Even from eight feet away I could tell that the bill was brand new, uncirculated, and fresh from the bank. He unrolled it, then re-rolled the bill into a cylinder widthwise and tucked the corner into itself to keep the bill from unraveling. He leaned over the glass top, put the straw-like cylinder into his left nostril, and with a strong, sharp inhale, he took half the line. He inhaled sharply again and pinched his nostril to keep the flake from coming back out. He held it for a couple of seconds and exhaled calmly. He then repeated the process with the other nostril. When he was done, he leaned back and closed his eyes. Then, without opening his eyes, he lobbed the rolled bill to me.

"Your turn." I followed suit, though my way of doing coke differed from his; I didn't take it in sharply, I inhaled in a strong, continuous fashion. The result's always the same, though. Sean followed suit, then Kurt, and the four of us sat back, basking in the brightness of the high.

"I want to show you guys something. We have to go outside. Do you guys want to borrow coats?"

Sean looked at the green Converse high-tops. I could read his mind just like it was my own.

"Sean," I chimed. "How do you feel about frozen toes? Maybe you should consider plastic bags over your feet. It is surely cold outside." I snickered.

"Maybe you should consider a plastic bag over your head, and don't call me Shirley." Alex and I both laughed at the old joke. Alex went to the closet under the staircase and pulled out four down parkas, one for each of us. He threw ours. Kurt took first dibs, of course, a blaze orange one to protect himself from getting accidently shot. Or whatever. The green one to Sean to match his stunning shoes and the black one to me. He put on a fourth, this one was red and had a black cross sewed onto the back.

"What, Alex. You are ski patrol or something?"

Alex said, "Yeah, I started when I was still in college, in Nevada. I worked at Heavenly and just sort of continued it out here. I patrol at A-Basin. The good part is I get to ski for free a couple of times a week."

"And it doesn't hurt that it's A-Basin. I dig that cornice." I said.

Sean jumped in. "Like you jump the cornice. I've never seen you jump the cornice. The biggest jump I ever saw you take was the jump from the ski lift to the ground. And then you had to be pushed. Remember the time that you missed the jump and ran over that four-year-old kid with the Donald Duck ski outfit?"

"That's complete bullshit," I said. "I never ran over that kid, I was pushed into him by an assailant, identity unknown. Besides, the kid loved it. The whole time he cried he kept gibbering about how much fun that was. And that was after they sewed up the gash on his cheek."

Alex smiled, snickered, then said, "That's one of the things I like about you guys, when you get at each other like a bunch of girls, you're pretty funny." Smile.

Sean garbled, "Yeah, he is funny." No smile from me though. I just hate it when someone teases me in front of a stranger. I was trying to make a good first impression and there was Sean, totally incoherent, shooting off at the mouth. I didn't understand how he could be so dense when his comments reflected our trustworthiness and professionalism.

"Donald Duck is the wrong character though. For Sean it's more like the purple Teletubby, the one that's supposed to be a faggot." Stares from all three. "Well, I'm exaggerating a little. I'm pretty sure Sean is straight. What I meant is that he likes it that way with chicks, or so he told me just the other day. Yeah, that's it. That's the story I'm going with." By that time, we had all put on our coats and shoes.

Kurt slapped me across the back of the head. "Now, now, no need for rancor." Alex looked down. Fuck. First impressions count for everything. Don't screw the pooch, lighten up, just bring this home.

The three of them moved to the door, and I followed. As we got to the walkway off the front porch, I held back a little, still uncomfortable about the way the last little snippet of conversation had gone. What Sean said was just a joke; I had blown it all out of proportion. Bruce, you are such an idiot. How many times do I have to tell you to just shut the hell up? The rule "silence is golden" is there for a reason. It means, shut UP!

We moved forward through the center garden in the circular driveway and past the car. The driveway was plowed, edges shoveled. I figured that Alex had either done it himself or paid some little sixth grader to do it. Maybe his girlfriend did it. Huh. I wondered where his girlfriend was hiding. I could have sworn that Alex said his girlfriend was going to be up here.

"Alex, where's your girlfriend? Didn't you say her name was Mary?"

"I thought she'd be home. On the other hand, I'm pretty sure she went to Cozumel. There was a note on the refrigerator, but that note could be a couple of days old. I don't know. We don't keep really good tabs on each other. It's a good thing she's in I think Mexico 'cause she wouldn't be a big fan of all the partying we've been doing. Wait till you meet her; she's great."

We kept trudging about seventy-five yards through the feathery snowfall, then made a sharp right detour into the dense trees and down a moderate decline. No trail cut out and our pace slowed. The good news, especially for Sean, who didn't have warm shoes, was that the snow was really light on the ground, and powdery; most of it had been caught by the tree branches overhead. We walked slowly, our feet crunching each time we took a step. It was see-all-the-stars dark; the trees and ground cover were thick with branches and snow. It was also really freezing, a lot colder than when we drove up to the house. My fingertips started to ache, and I watched my breath reflected through the light from the three-quarter moon coming through openings in the branches. My nose started to dribble, and it wasn't from the cocaine I had hoovered but from the frigid temperature as the air hit the inside of my nostrils. At least I didn't think so. I clenched my hands into fists and shoved them deep into the pockets of the parka. It seemed as though we were astronauts marching through a foreign landscape, at once wholly unfamiliar and slightly perilous. I noticed Alex stumble up ahead and made a quick note to watch the spot for the branch or whatever that had caused the slip. I worked hard not to tumble on my ass; I definitely didn't want to spend the rest of the evening with wet jeans and a frozen pair of balls. That would have been disastrous. I don't think Patrice would have been too impressed. More likely, she would laugh, tell me she needed to powder her nose, and disappear down the back stairs. And if I showed up at Michel's to see her, she would decide I was a stalker and probably get one of her climbing friends to throttle me. Sean was right ahead of me, walking with a lot of confidence; head up, hands swinging slightly at his side, feet making good contact and leaving sharp footprints. I could see the footprint pattern of the shoes, and I noticed that Sean put a lot of emphasis in his heel strike. The runner in me was analyzing his footfall pattern. If he was striking so well with his heel and keeping his balance, I figured to try it. It worked; I felt an immediate stabilization in my stride. Thanks, Sean, bastard. I hated not being the one to get the trick first.

Chapter 22

So, there we were, slowly making our way deeper into the trees, now almost a hundred feet below the patio line of the house, barely visible by moonlight and a good two hundred yards away. After another eight to ten minutes of walking, wiping our noses, and discussing the merits of the Gibson versus the Fender guitar, the trail was more visible, and the trees got less numerous. Finally, up ahead, I saw a small cabin; it couldn't have been more than the size of a one-car garage. It was made of logs and had a pitched metal roof. Fancy. It looked like it had come as a kit you put together yourself. There were two steps you had to walk up to get to the front door. A window, just right of the door, was currently dark. There was also a small porch surrounded by a narrow-gauge log railing. On the porch sat a couple of café chairs and a small round table, covered in snow. They looked comfortable, if it were summer. Nice place to sit, enjoy a cognac and a cigar, admire the solitude and peace of the space. I wouldn't have wanted to do any blow out there, on any day; too much quiet, I would have gone nuts.

We got to the doorway and on the left side of the door, about shoulder height, was an electronic keypad about four inches square. It was the kind with a green screen and a ten-key pad below. I had seen them in the doorways of offices at places like Storage Tech on the road to Longmont, the place that stored other companies' files and stuff. I never really found out; actually, it was a wild-ass guess.

Alex said, "Turn around or look away. Don't look." Okay, fine, I won't look. Alex turned his back on the rest of us and started to push the keycode into the pad. I didn't turn around. Instead, Kurt slipped behind Sean and I slipped behind Kurt. He peeked quick enough to see Alex punch in the last four numbers, 1947. I had heard five little beeps, so I knew that I only needed the first number to open the door on my own. I wasn't stupid; I knew that we were at Alex's stash place. The stupid part would have been if Alex had seen me looking. Deal off. Probably blunt-force trauma. That would have been kinda fucked. It might have even earned me a visit from Alex's friend, Mr. SIG Sauer. No, the idea of ripping off Alex was incredibly stupid. The guy hadn't become one of the biggest dealers in Colorado, or so it looked like, by being careless. The chances were that only he and his girlfriend Mary knew the code, so he would only have us to suspect. Hmmm.

I quickly turned away, pretending to watch the wind in the trees. What the hell was I thinking? Earlier I had been reveling in the idea of Dick getting ground into the street and squeezing IV bags. Now I was contemplating a different stunt that would maybe see me permanently sleeping among the pine tree roots, three hours away, down some anonymous culvert on the road to Gunnison. Or broken legs, at the very least. Even in my cocaine fog, I pretty much knew putting a plan together to rip this guy off would have been half-witted.

Still...

Alex opened the door, reached to his right, and flipped on the light switch. The place lit up, revealing a sitting area with Danish-style furniture and a beautiful organic glass-topped coffee table. Under it all was a Kashmiri carpet, the real kind, at least eight by ten. I crossed the threshold and took my shoes off again, this time leaving them at the inside entrance. I knelt down and felt the rug; it was the real deal. The thing probably cost a good twenty grand. The furniture included a low-slung couch with a one-piece back and chrome legs, maybe two to three inches off the floor. The chair looked like those chairs in the old film noir movies, like *The Maltese Falcon*. They have sort of rounded backs and armrests, you kind of slide back into them; I think they're called club chairs. You see them sometimes in fancy bars where everything seems to be served in a crystal snifter or martini glass, like that. It was white with a beige throw. The couch was black leather. It was going to be cold to sit on, I was sure of it. I decided on the chair and put the throw over the seat. Better to warm it with.

On the right, just on the far side of the small living room, was a small sink, cutting table, and refrigerator. There was a bowl of lemons and limes sitting on the counter. I had no idea why Alex would leave a bowl of citrus fruit in this place; the heat wasn't on, and the fruit was no doubt frozen. That gave me food for thought. Get it?

I said, "Holy shit. This place is radical! Ummm...do you have any heat?" Smile.

"Hold on, let me turn it on. This place warms up real fast; we'll be able to take our coats off in just a couple of minutes. You guys take a seat. Beer?"

While I don't think Sean wanted to make house out here in the boonies, he said yes, as did I. Kurt remained quiet. What I didn't want to do was raise suspicions, now that we were in the proverbial lion's den. We were going to get to see the rumor proven true or false; no need to be pushy. Patience will win out, though I was keenly aware of the time.

My gaze went to the far side of the cabin, where a queen-size bed rested over a beautiful platform built right into the floor. Walnut probably three feet high, smooth as the side of a fine sailing yacht. You could see grain all the way across and around the side of the bed, one giant piece of wood. The tree must have been huge to have allowed for this big a cut. Amazing. I would have guessed the coke would have been under the bed, but I wasn't so sure. Now I thought it was under the rug, if it was even there at all. I started to second-guess the situation and think maybe there was no stash, and the rumor was false. Maybe it was somewhere else, and this was Alex's getaway from his mountain getaway. Maybe I was still high and needed to come down in order to think straight. Now that was a clever idea. Patrice. Eye on the ball. Patrice. The rest of this delusional thinking was just going to get me into killer trouble, and killer was the operative word.

And no Patrice.

In the time I had been sitting there contemplating the circumstances of my night, Alex had gotten four bottles of Guinness out of the fridge and opened them. He brought them back to the sitting area and gave three out, keeping one for himself. He then dropped into the couch, leaned back, and took a deep, somewhat shaky breath. The cocaine, I thought. He's so high he can't take a regular breath. Maybe this relaxing in the woods with a beer was a good idea. I felt calmer, but still wanted to wrap up the deal. It was now going on nine thirty. That gave us at most an hour and a half to conclude our transaction and discuss the logistics—distribution, ground rules for fronting to potential consumers, and other stuff like that. The kind of stuff we should have been discussing when we were straight, though at that point the concerns were moot. It was going to take a team of six pachyderms to get me to go backward when we were so close. So, we sat like that, all taking sips off of our beers, and I was just about at the end of my rope when Alex said,

"Do you like the place?"

"Yeah," Sean said. "When you said there was something you wanted us to see, I wasn't expecting a hobbit house. Who lives in here, munchkins from *The Wizard of Oz*? Sean ground his teeth. That was the second time he had done so; he was coke-blown to the gills. Join the crowd. Alex turned to me, right eyebrow arched inquiringly.

"I like the place, very cozy. Nice place for a chick hideaway. You can do nasty things in here and nobody would know. I have to ask. That headboard doesn't have any bedposts. How do you tie up your girlfriends?"

Kurt looked at me quizzically and asked, "What the fuck, Bruce. Have you ever even had a girlfriend? Have you even been laid? You sound like some preteen zit kid whose total knowledge of sex came from the *Penthouse Forum* he keeps stashed under his bed."

Sean cackled. I smiled. "You're a funny guy, Kurt. Funny. I'm crying. It is to laugh. I'm so glad we met." I got my breath and went for it. "I know, you fucked her first, so I know you could have fucked things up for me, and for that I am grateful. Remind me to throw you a twenty, you know, for the effort. Which reminds me, I don't want to rush things but...actually, I do want to move things along." My brain turned left. "Wait, I didn't respond to your accusations of preadolescent foolishness. So, okay, let me answer your questions. I have a girlfriend named Jill. She gives great head and shakes the bed when she's on top. We've been dating for about eight months. If things go as planned with Patrice, I won't have a girlfriend named Jill. Yes, I have been laid, many times, even on the telephone. No, I'm not a zit kid, and yes, I do get my ideas for sex from the *Penthouse Forum*. But the story I told you about the two sisters at my house in Hawaii? That really happened, I swear."

Kurt finally responded, "What are you, twelve?"

Alex gave me a fleeting look and let out an audible breath tinged with a little sigh. "Okay," he mumbled. "Check this out. There are only a couple of people who've seen this. If you ever repeat a word of what you see or hear, you will die. I mean for real die. Literally. Chopped up." Alex pointed to a fireman's axe he had hanging over the front door. He went to the back of the cabin and knelt down in front of the bed platform. He put his right hand down on the ground next to the left-hand corner and pushed. I saw the floor sink slightly, and a small piece of the floorboard popped up on the other side. This piece he pulled on, and as it separated, I could see a metal rod secured to the bottom and going into the floor. Alex then twisted the small rod and a door in the front of the bed frame popped open. I would have never believed it if I hadn't seen it. There was no way to see the door, the wood matched beyond perfectly. Still, there was the door, open. Sean and I both leaned forward from our perches at the same time and peered into the hole under the bed. Inside, stacked one on top of another, like sandbags protecting from a flood, were what looked like bricks. Black bricks that were covered in plastic. A shitload of them. Holy shit, the rumors were real. I did a mental calculation from the first quick glance I got. Eight bricks up, twelve bricks across. That was ninety-six kilos of cocaine at twenty-plus thousand each. $1.92 million. Plus. Alex watched us with a smile.

"What do you think?"

My eyes popped. Boiyoiyoing. Aooogaahhh. "I've never seen that much coke in any one place, ever," I said, a little breathlessly. Sean just stared at it. And sniffed. The idea that we were going to purchase just one of those bricks was a little daunting in that it would barely make a dent.

Then Alex said, "There's more. The stacks go back four layers deep. I have about four hundred keys. That's why nobody comes in here. You guys are the third, behind Mary and Rocky, of course." It occurred to me that Alex was probably the biggest distributor of coke in the Rocky Mountain Region. When he said he had one other distributor in Boulder, it never occurred to me that he had distributors in about a hundred other cities up and down I-25, east and west on I-70. I kept staring at the coke. Holy shit. Fuckety fuck.

Alex pulled out a baby cocaine scale and grinder, a little green one that isn't very accurate but worked in a pinch. He pulled one of the kilo bricks out of the cubbyhole and shifted it to his left hand. With the other he pulled a switchblade from his parka pocket and made a little slit in the plastic. The eggshell-white powder and chunks tinged with crystals had the consistency of loam. It didn't pour out of the package like sand but sort of flowered out of the package like potting soil. Alex put his knife into the coke and scooped out a batch. He held it up to the light, and I saw the distinct clear windowpane consistency that identified the Bolivian variety. I also smelled a slight tinge of the acetone wash, one of the most important steps in cocaine production. I figured the coke was very well manufactured, for something that was probably produced in a cleared-out meadow, under a tent with mosquito netting, by women in their underwear, in the middle of a jungle somewhere.

Alex put the pile of coke into the scale and checked its weight, about a gram and a half. He then dumped it into the grinder, a stacked cylinder that has three sections. The lid with a small crank attached to it, the middle where the screen is, and the bottom section, a catch container for the well-ground blow. Using a razor or credit card to chop cocaine of this quality was useless; you really needed a grinder to mill it to a consumable consistency. This is what Alex did. The mound left when he uncovered the bottom piece of the grinder was the size of a half a lemon. He then sectioned four smaller heaps and placed them next to each other on the tabletop, lengthening them with an American Express Gold card.

This isn't a good idea, I said to myself. You gotta go down the hill and get to the bar. If you want any chance at Patrice, if you want to have sex, you gotta stop. You know coke and a hard-on mix like stripes and plaid. I thought about my quandary and decided it would be better to protect my business than to worry about Patrice. She probably knew we were doing weasel dust in the restaurant and would know what to expect. Hell, she was a bartender; she knew the score. In fact, she probably wanted to do some, that's why she said yes to the drink. A couple of lines and good tequila and we could go for it. She was the sexiest thing. I doubted it would be that difficult to take care of my side of the sexual requirement, and all she had to do was get naked. My eyes would do the rest. If I stopped doing blow…right after this line.

"Bruce, you go first," Alex said.

"Don't mind if I do." I took the first hoover and jolted with the shock. Purity, there was no substitute. I realized that I didn't have to worry about getting too high before my date. This kind of purity would only have an energizing effect, no shakes or cotton brain. The bill we had been using at the house then passed to Sean, who made short work of his rail. Kurt did his, leaned back, did a little snort to capture any still in his nostrils, and smiled, eyes shining like

261

diamonds. Finally, Alex did his, inhaling violently, leaning back into the couch and holding his nostrils shut. After a few seconds, he opened his eyes and looked at me. They were psychedelic.

"Bruce, I'm going to make you a deal. I'll take your money for one of these unopened packages. Twenty-three thousand, five hundred. You'll have to take my word for it that they weigh exactly one kilo because I'm not going to open it and dump the blow onto the electronic dial-a-gram. I'll also front you the rest of this kilo at, say, twenty-two thousand. This way, you'll make a little more money and can have a few grams for yourself and as product for your clients to sample. My suggestion is that you leave the cutting to someone else. If you want to do more business with me, that's the rule."

"Deal," I said. I looked at Sean and he nodded his agreement. That was good, since Sean was going to be responsible for lining up the buyers once we divvied up the blow into salable quantities. If he hadn't been okay with this, we could have had a problem. Alex took a big chance bringing us all the way out here and bringing us into his trust sphere. To have the deal go south because of last-minute distribution problems could have been disastrous. I said, "Alex, um, I really have to head back to town. Can we wrap it up? After getting all of our shit together, stashing the snow in my car, and getting down to the road, I still have to drive back to town."

Sean said, "And picking up my shoe. We aren't going back to town without my shoe." I looked back at Alex, ignoring Sean's plea. Alex smiled again and stood up, stretching his hands overhead. He knelt down by the door of the bed pedestal, pulled out another kilo, and closed the door. It latched with a sharp click. Once again, you couldn't see the opening at all. Amazing. Alex then stood up.

"Actually, it's only about three minutes to the driveway. I took you guys the long way around. When we go outside, we'll go straight up the side of the hill and be at the house lickety-split. Then we can finish our business."

We all stood and reached for our coats hanging on the pegs where we had left them.

Kurt said, "I need a ride back to town. I call shotgun." I looked at him, he shrugged and smiled. I nodded.

Sean said, "I'm with Bruce. Let's giddy-up. If he's going into town for some wine and women, I'm for it too. Except that I won't have to use blow and wine to get a woman." Oh, that hurt. I had to give as good as I got.

"Maybe not, but I know I'm meeting a beautiful babe who wants me—tonight. For all you know, your partner for overnight festivities could be female, or not. The chances are you won't know until the morning, like last time. I'd be frightened of my situation in the morning if I were you. You might have to chew your arm off to get out of bed." Sean gave me a look that could have melted steel. Ha, motherfucker, touché. I win again in the game of one-up insults. Of course, Sean never really spent the night with another man. At least not that I knew. Not that there's anything wrong with that. Kurt repeated himself.

"What, are you guys twelve? Just stop, you're hurting my ears."

"Alex," I said, "you never answered the question. Are you coming?" I wanted to buy the guy a bottle of wine at the bar, the least I could do. I considered it my way of showing respect and gratitude, my way of cementing the partnership. There was this other bar in the hotel, on the main floor. The bartender there had access to the same wine cellar as the Alcove 201, the fine dining restaurant located next to the Mezzanine. This meant French first growths like Château Mouton and Château Latour. Yummy. Strangely enough, the bar was called the Hemingway Bar. I guessed Hemingway spent some time in the hotel writing a book, or magazine piece, article, whatever, maybe a short story. That would be poetic, to name a bar after someone whose creativity only produced a short story in all the time he spent there. I didn't know it for sure, but I'd heard that his great-granddaughter still drank there. I also heard she needed to be poured into a cab about three every morning. If Alex wanted to have some wine, that bar was our destination. Then I could regroup and head up the back staircase to the Mezzanine bar for my rendezvous.

"Yes, I'm coming," Alex finally responded. "Since Mary is apparently in Cozumel for two weeks; what else am I going to do? Thanks for the invite."

"My pleasure," I said. Sean cast a quick glance at me, and his brow darkened momentarily. What the hell? Did Sean know something I didn't? What's going on? Is this going to turn to shit?

We put on our parkas and while Sean opened the door, Alex took one last look around. He shut off the heater and turned off the lights, and we stepped outside into the snow and stillness. It had gotten colder. The snow sparkled in the moonlight, like diamonds. The moon cast a spotlight on snow-covered trees, turning them into giant rotund topiary creatures. To my drug-addled eyes, they looked like marshmallow Peeps, the kind of gooey candy you eat during Easter. The moonlight also exposed dark, spooky cracks and crevices filled with the black of infinity. The depth of our primal fear, the deepest place of our souls, revealed to no one's eyes but our own.

We set off back up the hill, at first following a meandering path for a short while and then climbing steeply through snow up to our knees. It was hard to believe that I had woken up just eight hours earlier to a clear but windy day. Down in Boulder there wasn't any snow on the ground, just a winter chill. Well, the weather was different up here. Finger-numbing cold, snow puffing up with every step, hitting our faces like stinging sand on a windy beach. Snow got into my shoes and up my jeans leg. My feet and knees felt the cold, the joints aching and popping every time I raised my knee above my hip to avoid dragging my foot through the powder again. My toes were tingling like when you get hit in the funny bone. Sean followed behind me; he kept his head down and hands in his parka.

It wasn't long before we came to the final steep section and navigated the last hundred or so meters to the driveway by the house. When we got to the top, we were no more than fifty meters from the front door. As we came to a stop at the door, I turned away and said, "I'll just be a minute, let me get your cash. Be right in."

Again, Sean gave me a look. What the fuck did he want, or more to the situation, what the fuck did he mean by that glance? I couldn't tell if it meant anything or not, and my imagination was in overdrive. I was fueled by a shnozz of coke, addling my brain; so much snow in my sinuses it felt like brains leaking out my eyes. I was cold too, my whole body shivering. At that point, my toes were frozen like little pigs in icicle blankets.

I reached for the trunk latch, pushed in the metal button, and slowly pulled up. There was a creak and then a pop as the hinges released and then locked in at the open position. I heard the front door open. I heard some stamping, shoe kicking and shuffling. Getting the snow off their boots, in Sean's case, his now-soaking shoes. Jeez, Sean's feet must be frozen solid. I wouldn't want to be him. Maybe that was the reason for the glance. Maybe it wasn't anything except a look of pain, like let's go already. I'm freezing, I can't feel my toes, and I'll beat you silly if you continue to fuck around. Hey, my feet hurt too. He was just being a baby.

In the trunk compartment I found and grabbed a handle sticking out from underneath an Indian-style blanket. Or maybe it was a Mexican-style blanket, but I preferred to think of it as Indian. Thing is, you can't trust

Mexican workmanship. It was beige and green and had what looked like a Pueblo or Toltec pattern, so it could have gone either way.

I pulled a black leather briefcase from under the blanket and checked the locks. Setting the tumblers, I snapped the case open. There, in neat stacks of hundred-dollar notes, was the twenty-five grand. Three stacks, one half as fat as the others, they took up about a quarter of the case. The other part of the case was taken up by a velvet sack with a drawstring closure. I reached for it, opened the drawstring, and pulled out the Webley Mk IV .38; it was the gun you saw in World War I movies. British officer says to the Kraut, "Pip-pip, there you are, old boy, nice queen's sendoff, hello to the kaiser and all that," and pulls the trigger, blowing the guy's brains out. Only in those movies, you don't get to see the blood splatter. In this case, I had inherited the gun from my grandfather, who got it from a guy who got it from a guy. I kept it oiled at all times, cleaning it after every trip into the mountains for target practice. It was loaded. I was a good shot. Not to brag, but I could blow away five Heineken bottles in about nine seconds from thirty feet away. The Webley was a six shot; sometimes I missed one. I looked at it for a second and then held it close, next to my belt, one hand on the grip, the other cradling the barrel. If anyone was looking out the window, they wouldn't be able to see what I was doing. All the better, since I didn't know what I was doing. Actually, that was a lie. I knew exactly what I was doing. I was protecting my investment against any last-minute changes in the plan. Maybe someone, maybe this Rocky guy, could be lying in wait in one of the bedrooms with larceny on his mind and a loaded weapon in his hands. Couldn't have that. And twenty-five grand was a lot of money. Plus, I had to guard against Alex having a gun himself. For all I knew, Alex had been planning on ripping me off this whole time, even when we were having dinner. You know, the craziest guys are the ones who have all the wealth. Plus, how was I going to protect Sean and Kurt, and get us out of there in one piece in case it all blew to hell? And finally, I had to admit, what if I wanted to get away with the coke and not pay the fucker? What then? Hmmm?

I moved the Webley to my side as I closed and turned around with the case, quickly stuffing the gun down the back of my jeans. Holy shit, the barrel was cold! The local temperature at Crack Of My Ass immediately dropped a good thirty degrees, and I pulled in my butt cheeks like I was trying to stave off a bout of diarrhea. I then closed and locked the case, then reached up with my left hand and pulled the latch down, closing the trunk of the car with a slight creaking sound, then a solid thunk. I gotta get that fixed. A little WD-40 should do it.

I stepped from behind the car, took a deep breath, and walked to the front door. I swung the case in front of me for a moment, using the motion to cover an adjustment to the position of the gun behind my back. A song came to me; who is that band?

"Landlords are mad and getting madder, ain't we got fun...times are bad and getting badder, ain't we got fun..."

Fucking earworms. My body started to buzz, and my brain became foggy. When I reached for the door, I heard voices coming from inside, then a couple of people laughing and a voice I recognized but didn't expect. I put down the briefcase and reached for the door with my left hand, keeping my right free to draw the gun. What the fuck was I doing? The song kept playing.

"The rich get rich and the poor get..."

I looked at my watch.

Chapter 23

It was 10:25 p.m.

I pulled on the latch and opened the door. The scene was pretty much as we had left it except for two glaring changes. Dick Dickmann was there with that stupid grin on his face, yukking it up like a Bozo the Clown wannabe. Motherfucker. I couldn't believe my eyes. Standing next to him was a skinny little poof named Octavian, who went by the name Ocho. I know, what were his parents thinking?

I took my attention away from Dick Puffer and took in the whole scene. Sean was sitting with his back to me, Kurt was at the stereo looking at albums, Alex in the lounge chair with his back to the kitchen, and Dickhead and Ocho standing in front of the coffee table, the centers of attention. There was a giant mound of coke on the table with five lines laid out; I guessed one in front of each of them. And none for me. Alex had a cut-off Pixie straw in his hand and I watched as he bent over to snarffle up his designated line. Dick's expression did an about-face, going from grin to frown in less than a second. I liked that. Now we matched expressions, fair fight. The gun suddenly felt comfortable behind my back, like an old friend standing with you in a fight, so I had that going for me. Sun Tzu once said that all battles are fought before they even begin. I would add that the winner would be the one most prepared. And the one who started it. I knew Dick the Prick. He was an asshole, a bully. He was also smart. And arrogant. I hated this guy enough to kill him. Wait, did I? I'd contemplated burning his house down earlier; now I considered shooting him in the head. I had the gun and the drop...what the hell was I saying? Could I really burn down his house? How many steps was that to just drilling him into the great unknown? That was foolish talk; I wasn't going the shoot the guy. Preposterous. The other voice in my head started calculating the ways I could get away with ghosting him.

I shook it off and concentrated on the current situation. But what the fuck was he doing here? How did he get in? What was going on? Confusion blew around my brain like a cave full of bats. Well, there was only one way to find out. I took a breath to get my head together. I tried to find clear sky within the growing dark cumulus clouds of the coming storm and succeeded. Alex looked up from his task, leaving the straw dangling from his left nostril. I guess he was trying to be funny. Funny as in levity. For me, the joke fell on its ass. Alex. Sean, Kurt. Ocho, Fuckhead. A pile of coke and five, now four, lines as big and long as a Bic pen.

Stay calm, I said to myself. Gauge the situation. I looked directly at Dick, who stared back. No emotion in his eyes, just the return of that fucking grin.

"What the fuck are you doing here?"

Dick said nothing and the room stayed silent for a couple of seconds, long enough to get uncomfortable. Alex finally spoke up.

"Brian, last-minute change of plan." Brian? My name is Bruce, asshole.

"I thought we'd stay up here for the night and discuss the overall strategy for the Boulder distribution network." Alex said. What the fuck was he talking about?

Alex said, "I guess you know Richard. I kind of had that impression from our conversation earlier at dinner." You mean the dinner I bought?

Alex went on. "Richard also informs me that the two of you have issues. He seems to think that you're not a trustworthy guy. You know, I mentioned a little of your story while you were outside, and my friend denies the whole thing. Says you have it in for him or something. He doesn't seem to have anything against you, so I have to wonder about your story at dinner." Sean said nothing. Kurt said nothing. Dick, still grinning like a Cheshire cat. Back on. Backfire, my little plan to put him in the shit was going astray. Oh man, Bruce, think! Okay, Sean and Kurt aren't backing you on this, maintaining neutrality. That was good, because as ugly as this got, they would stay out of it. That just left me, Alex, Ocho, and Dick the Prick. Something took my eyes away from Alex and to the table. Who put out the coke? Dick was the one standing. A temporary authority position. Was it too much of a stretch to assume that the blow was his?

Chapter 24

My mind flashed back to a party I was once at in Pasadena. I don't remember what it was for; some California surfer swimmer model dude friend of a friend probably got a national commercial deal or something. Anyway, I didn't know anyone except this Asian chick I had met on Will Rogers State Beach earlier that afternoon. The beach was covered with sand volleyball courts; there were about a half dozen games going on, at least four of them were women twosomes smacking at each other with some skill. I figured that they were probably college players, USC or Pepperdine. The chicks on court were very hot, bikinis and tans and the occasional nipple shot. I picked the game where the players looked to be the best and sat down. I took off my shirt and leaned back, hoping to get a glance from some of the other spectators of the female persuasion. Only one taker, the Asian chick. So, I got up, slithered over, and struck up a conversation with her. She was sweet to look at and seemed to have a brain bigger than a pea. She said she worked in the movie business as the "second-second-third director's assistant," or some nonsense. I figured it was a flunky job, kind of like the fluffer job in the porn industry, but I gave her my undivided attention. Once again, I reiterate that she was very hot. Maybe she was a fluffer; one could always dream. Surprise, slithering was worth it, we talked for a while, watched a game, then agreed to meet later.

Now it was later, and the party at the Cali model dude's house was cranking. I was there about a half an hour, and the chick was nowhere to be seen. Fuckety fuck, I thought. Stood up. Fucking LA. Shallowest people on the planet; they had no problem blowing you off and even fucking you over for their own enjoyment. The perfect place for a guy like Dick Dickmann. I looked around and sniffed. Self-involved, entitled fucks.

I left the backyard and walked around the side of the house, past some bougainvillea running up the wall. There was a three-step rise to an Italian tile patio and a set of french doors that led to the dining room. Time to exit, stage left, before I decked one of the pretty-boy poseurs hovering near the door, shifting their feet and passing a doobie that smelled like old shoes. I crossed the patio and went into the dining room...and wouldn't you believe it, there stood Dick. He was standing around the dining room table with at least eight other guys, one with a bill shoved up his nose, another with one in his ear. Two were laughing at something Dick said. When they turned toward me the laughter doubled. Huh. Very funny, like entertaining three-year-olds. On the table was a framed picture of a smiling family, formally posed, like for Christmas, boys in green, girls in red. There was also a gap on the wall, nail hole in the gap, nail on the floor. Family picture on the table, cocaine on the picture, face in the cocaine. Way to respect the host. Fucking Dick, that's why I hated that guy.

And I said so. "Dick. I can't go anywhere in the country without you around. What the fuck is it, you need to constantly smell my asshole, you can't brown-nose one of your butt-boy pals?"

"Bruce, buddy! I'm surprised you came; this party is for men and hot chicks. What are you doing here, and more important, when are you leaving? Nobody wants you here."

What a clever comeback. For a smart guy, he wasn't. Foolishly, I engaged. What could I do? "If this is a party for men and chicks, which one are you?" I noticed all of the guys with him were now staring at me, only one of them was smiling. No groans, cackles, giggles, laughs, or snorts. I thought my comeback was pretty good. Tough crowd. The blow was Dick's; only conclusion that could be made. Okay, how to extricate myself from a battle I was winning but a war I was going to lose.

"Actually, you guys all look so enthralled, I'm sure there are lots of men, I mean hot chicks, out there who would fuck incoherent, mumbling gadoots such as yourselves," I said. "Great party, but I have to go, it's been a pleasure. Oh, and by the way, if you don't know what a gadoot is, you are one. Just ask Dick, your hostess with the mostest."

I walked past them, making sure to push back hard as Dick moved to give me a good bump. It was a standoff, like almost all of our exchanges. What was it about that guy? Just as curiously, what did he have against me? I'd known the guy since elementary school, and he'd been a prick to me the whole time. We're talking like ten or twelve years. Maybe it was my aura. Yeah, that was it. Aura. I figured I'd talk to one of the space cadet palm readers about it when I got back to Boulder. Or not.

So. That's the story of the Pasadena surf party. And now here I am in Alex's house at 10:30 at night, trying to get out so I can meet Patrice. That's what I thought, but I said something else.

I said, "If we're going to stay up here, then I wouldn't mind a line to catch up." I know if the coke was Dick's the chances were pretty slim he'd lay one out for me, even at Alex's house.

Nobody moved for a couple of seconds and then Alex said, "Step on up, my man." I bent down and untied my shoes, careful to take them off left first, then right. I placed them on a towel, moving the green Converse All Stars Sean was wearing. Did I detect a change in vocal tone? Did he look at me slightly askew? Did Dick's stupid-ass grin get smaller? Dick laid out another line, this one about a third of the size of the others. I was right, his coke. He looked up and his grin had returned. Ah, that was the Dick I knew and wanted to put into the hospital. The revolver tickled my lumbar. Deep breath, I couldn't do anything stupid. Just finish the deal, I thought to myself.

"Alex," I said. "We're both here now, so you can judge for yourself. One of us is serious, the other is grinning like the cat that got the cheese. This is serious business, no room for clowns. Who do you think is telling the truth?" Man, if I could just swing this around, I could still save the original plan. "You did me the honor of revealing what was only a myth. I take that very seriously. You, Sean, and I are about to conclude a business arrangement." There, I got them involved. That should sway things a little in my favor. While Kurt was unpredictable, Sean, he was agreeable. But when Alex searched Sean's face, his eyes stayed on the table, perhaps contemplating a deal gone sour. Oh fuck.

That was bad. Alex was only going to take that one way—Sean wasn't behind me on this. When I needed him to back me, he bailed. Story of my life. The thing is, he knew more than anyone what type of person Dick was. He also knew of our rivalry and how personal it was. He and I were doing this deal and now he was bailing. Best friend. Fucker. Once again, I misjudged the situation. What was it about me that moved people to such disloyalty?

I took a couple of deep breaths and scoped the room again. Alex sitting back in the comfy chair on the left, looking at me, Sean on the right, eyes out the window, Kurt stepping into the kitchen. Dick standing, facing me, grinning. Ocho had moved away and was now in the kitchen, searching the refrigerator for who knows what. A sausage maybe. All were about fifteen feet away. I could close to eight. By this time, the buzz had blown past third into fourth gear, and winding. I felt my knees shake, my heart flutter. I could hear the ocean in my ears, the loud booming of giant surf as it breaks over shallow reef. Enough to feel the crash from miles away. My hand shook slightly. Another deep breath, willing it to stop. I tried to keep my voice level and my eyes from bugging out. Oh fuck, man. Oh fuck. Okay. Here we go. I turned slightly toward my right and approached the living room from the couch side, covering my movement with a swing of the briefcase. I reached for the Webley and drew it real easy, dropping it to my side. I watched. As I had hoped, Alex and Dick watched the case; elementary use of distraction. Sean didn't look, he stared down at pure blackness. I thought I heard the wind blow through the evergreen giants, muted by the window. It was like a dream I had planned: I saw it all in slow motion. There was not going to be any going back. Dick first, he was standing and the most logical threat. Alex was leaning back in the chair so he would have to lean forward to pull any weapon he carried. Alex second. Ocho would duck and so be a difficult target. Sean didn't have a gun. He might live. Simple. Kurt? I already said that you don't bet against him, ever. Two steps forward to about two feet away from the couch and no more than four feet away from Sean's head, I quickly raised the Webley and calmly and methodically aimed it at Dickhead's right eye. And squeezed the trigger. I felt a familiar shudder run through my right arm. The gun smoked. Dick's eye was missing. No sound. I quickly leveled the barrel at Alex, aiming carefully, and pulled the trigger. A red hole popped from his chest. It quickly became a splotch, then a rose. Alex leaned forward, protecting the hole. His forehead exposed, I fired again. The familiar shudder, his forebrain splashed on the mirror, the back of his skull splashed on the leather, again silence. Mist of red, like looking at rain from a couple of miles away. I noticed that I wasn't breathing and took a breath. Time stood still. The gun smoked, I felt a mild heat coming off the barrel and tickling the top of my hand. I felt the pinch on my index finger made by the trigger. I walked up the steps to the kitchen, aimed at the now-standing Ocho's head.

"Please, Bruce, don't."

"You'll talk, Ocho."

"I won't, I swear."

"I know." I squeezed. He went down in a blast of noise and spray. I turned the sound off in my brain. I looked at Kurt. He stared back, stone-faced. Then he looked at the three dead guys, back to me, and shrugged. He turned, kicked Ocho's body out of the way, opened the refrigerator, and grabbed another Guinness. I finally looked back at Sean. He lay down on the floor, next to the couch, hiding, or so he thought. His jaws flapped but no noise came out of his mouth. I saw the fear in his eyes, though. I dropped the gun back to my side, and his bugged eyes pushed back into his head.

Fucking Dick. I couldn't see him, but I did see a hole in the window. Around the hole, blood splattered, and organic matter spread and leaked. The space where his body had stood just seconds before, now empty but for his ghost. Some pieces of his skull dripped down the window too, leaving a trail like slugs across pavement. There, no more Dick Dickmann. The end. Fuck yeah. The bullet had blown out the back of his head and disappeared into the forest. In a millisecond I calculated the likelihood of this coming back on me. Negligible. In fact, it was a good thing the bullet hadn't stayed in his head. And even if the cops found it, the bullet was a Smith & Wesson .38, very common. My gun, very uncommon. No record of it, never registered, never been used in a crime. I had to junk it though. Sorry Gramps.

Alex. He was slouched in the deep cushions, blood and cottage cheese brains covered the back of the chair. Somewhere I remembered someone saying that if you kill someone, double tap. First shot to bring the guy down, second one in the brainpan. Blood trickled from his eye into his mouth, both forever open. His front tooth was stained red. The front of his jeans was wet, and I figured that he had taken a piss on himself. I read somewhere that when someone died, their colon and urethra let go. C'est dommage. Too bad, so sad.

Now Ocho. He was on the floor, dead. Wait, what? Not. I moved closer. Kurt got out of the way, taking a seat on the stairs. Ocho was on his side, head buried under his left arm, all curled up. Rocking ever so slightly. I aimed at him again, this time for the temple. I waited. He stopped rocking and we all heard a long wheezy breath leave his body. That ended it for Ocho. And I felt bad, until I didn't.

I stepped back into the sunken living room and looked down. Sean. What to do about Sean. I decided to find out how much he wanted to get out of our situation with his life. Stupid question; he'd do anything I told him. To coin a phrase, I had the gun. I stepped away from him to a distance of about eight feet. Once I let him get up, what if he tried to make a play? Sound on.

"Sean. What. You have a choice, and I think you know what I'm talking about. Shut up and think about it."

Sean screamed and cried at the same time. "What the fuck? What did you do? What are we going to do? Oh Fuck." Fucking hell.

"These questions are already answered," I said. "It's kind of obvious what I did. What are we gonna do? I know what I'm gonna do. What are *you* gonna do? You have two choices. A. Live. B. I shoot you in the head. I'm serious. It'll happen, count on it. This might be the last minute of your life."

Kurt: "Bruce, take it easy."

Me: "This isn't about you, Kurt. I know what you think. This is a Sean thing. He has to choose. It's either the two of us or the three of us."

I aimed the Webley at Sean's teeth and his eyes popped. I saw him. Short intake of breath. His face turned the light greenish yellow that you see when someone gets ready to puke. Strange, he didn't turn blue-and-purple polka dot, like the opera singer in that one Bugs Bunny cartoon. And he's such a fan.

I smiled, showing no teeth. I narrowed my eyes, laser into his skull. No fucking around.

Kurt: "Bruce..."

Bruce: "Stay out of this, Kurt. I still have two bullets, enough so I can walk out of here alone."

Kurt: "Let's settle down, this doesn't have to get any gnarlier that it already is."

Bruce: "That's right. So, Sean, what do you say?" I aimed again. Serious business, right here and now. Sean, throat gulp. Fear. Got him. Nice. "Think about it. And fuck you very much for not backing me against Dick. This wouldn't have happened if you had stuck to the deal we worked out in the cabin. This is your fault." I waited. He didn't move his mouth, so I helped him. "You've got about ten seconds to decide. That'll do 'er." Tick-tock.

He opened his mouth. I cut him short. "If the answer is no, don't even bother. You don't want the last word out of your garbage hole to be no. You've got eight."

Sean said, "Okay, Bruce, of course I'm with you on this. What do you think? I wanna get shot to death?" He took a deep breath, shoulder shudder. Blink, blink. He looked at Kurt. Kurt looked back, impassive. Sean turned toward the window, glanced at what was left of Dick's half skull, and vomited. I saw him.

I backed up to fifteen feet and said in a dead voice, "Get up. I'm so fucking sick about this. I should just shoot you. You fucking pussy fuck."

Kurt: "Bruce, stop. Now."

Bruce: "No."

Kurt, sigh: "You know how this goes, you fucking haole. I should beat you, then kill you for doing this."

Bruce: "I have the gun and as you can see, clearly a pretty good shot. This isn't the Kurt show this time. Back off, and fuck you, you're as much haole as me." I turned back, looked at Sean with eyes as dead as I could make them.

Sean said, "I'm part Hawaiian so count me out of that argument." He had a point, and his effort to dial down the situation was commendable.

Still. "If you'd just...we are not friends anymore. You sided with that fucking asshole Dick even though you knew he was lying. You both did, you fuckers. If you want to survive until the sun, don't fuck with me, I mean it. That's your future lying over the couch with a hole in his head if you fuck me. I'll fucking leave you in the forest for the wolves. Maybe I'll pop you in the spine, leave you out there alive, no knees to crawl on. I'll even tape your fucking mouths so you can't scream when you get eaten." I stared. I sneered, pursed my lips. I stared at Sean. "Now get up, put on those ridiculous green shoes, walk over to the front door, and stand there. Oh yeah, I want you to put your fingerprints on the table when you get up." Sean put his hands on his thighs and leaned forward.

Chapter 25

Kurt: "Bruce, you fricka. Wait. We get away clean if we don't fuck it up. I have an idea."

"I don't give a shit." I watched Kurt. I re-pointed the gun. He stared. Looked away, shaking his head slightly. Fuck him. I took a deep breath, forcefully calming myself. I then contemplated the circumstances for a couple of seconds and lowered the Webley to my side. Then I gave it another think. "Wait, stay right where you are. Not yet, don't move yet." Pause. "I've changed my mind. Here's what we're gonna do." I looked at Sean and Kurt. "We are going to wipe this place spotless, so find a couple of rags in the kitchen, and be careful what you touch. We'll get out of this. We're then gonna tie some pine branches to the back of the Saab and drag over the tire marks. We're gonna get more branches and wipe our footprints into the house and along the drive and down the long path to the cabin. Okay. Then, we'll get into the car and stop next to the path down to the cabin. Then, we are gonna take the steep path to the cabin and load all the blow we can drag back up to the car, then we'll wipe that path with branches and then we're gonna drive away. We're gonna drag the branches around where we got stuck in the mud too." I glanced back at Sean. "And find your shoe." Sean smirked. "Then we'll go down the hill and decide what to do. Just stay with me on this." I gave Sean another withering look and brought the gun up to his eye level. That wiped the smirk off his face. "If you don't, you're dead." I turned to Kurt as he took a sip of his beer. "What?"

Kurt said, "That was my idea too." I knew it. Kurt was going along to get along, pragmatism in human form.

Sean, still sitting perfectly still, opened his mouth and out popped a pretty good question. "What about the code?"

The code. I forgot the code! What was it? Think. I looked at Kurt. Said, "Kurt looked at Alex's fingers and knows the last four digits. All we gotta get is the first one. We try all ten combinations, we get it. I figure we can carry twenty-five, thirty kilos if we use our jackets."

Kurt smiled. I know, I'll make them both partners. Yeah, good strategy, threaten death and then throw a life raft. Sean would do what I wanted; I was sure of it. I said, "We can make lemonade here if we keep our heads. If you have any other ideas, I'm all ears." I didn't put the gun away; it still hung at my side. Kurt shrugged.

Sean ventured a reserved smile. He spoke at a murmur. "If we get sixty kilos at $25,000 each, that's almost

$1.5 million. $500,000 each. If we got more, maybe $600,000."

Thirds wasn't what I was thinking. "Worry not, we'll split it so's we can disappear." Sucking them along like we were partners. I thought back to earlier in the evening to when Sean called me a liar. When I was telling the story about the twins, Judy Geezer and her sister, thinner Judy. And I considered how this was gonna end for Sean. As far as I was concerned, Kurt would stay the course as long as it was in his interests to do so, money being the operative concept.

I flicked the gun barrel to send Sean into the kitchen. He got up, disappeared for a couple of seconds, and came back out with three red-and-blue-striped dishtowels. He threw one to me, gave one to Kurt, who looked at it like it was a bag of dogshit, and kept the last; we proceeded to wipe down every possible surface; walls, light switch, armrests, even the tile floor where we had stepped. Then we found a vacuum in the other front closet next to the front door and I vacuumed the whole living room rug except for where Dickhead's body lay, blood pooled around his dead head and against the floorboards. Kurt collected our bottles and caps, leaving the ones used by the three dead guys. We saved the coffee table for last. I picked up the rolled-up hundreds, I put them in my pocket. I left the coke and straw.

Kurt said, "Let's wipe this down, then the entry area. Then we can walk outside and wipe down the door handles. From there we should be clear. We'll get some branches to wipe away our footprints to the car and then we can attach them to the bumper and drive away."

I had a thought and said, "Yeah, no harm done." Ha, that was a nasty play on the situation. I was really getting into this criminal mastermind gig. Good fun.

Sean just looked at me. "Very funny," he said, voice dead of emotion. I hoped he would stay that way for a while more. Less to worry about. No baby shit, crying, whining, boo-hoo. I wondered if Kurt felt this way about me when he sent Jimmy to his permanent rest home.

We wiped down the table and tiles, making sure to cover our steps to the front door.

"Get your shoes on, I'm going to check those assholes for whatever green they have." Still in my socks, I went over to Alex's body, head turned to the side, eye still open. Using one of the rags, I reached under his right ass cheek, careful not to mess with the blood, and fished out his wallet. DL, Visa, American Express Gold, and about $3,800 in cash. Good start. I then went around the couch and looked at Dick. It was all I could do not to pull down my pants and take a shit on his face. He also had money, about $600. Mine now, justified treasure for a good night's work. I looked at Ocho. Sorry buddy, wrong place, wrong time. Shouldn't have been friends with Dickless. I didn't bring you here, Ocho, you could have stayed home, but no. So, karma. I dove for his pockets, came up with bupkes but a pipe, a little bit of weed in a pill container, and his house key.

I went back to the front door and put my shoes back on, left foot first, then right. I tied them carefully, making sure that the loops and extra laces were the same length. I even adjusted the laces twice to make it happen. Sean was still on the floor tying up the green Converse All Stars. "Hurry the fuck up, I have a date. You can troll the bar, there's always chicks at the Mezz this time of night looking for a quick taste of salami. You never know. Oh, and the green All Stars should make a splash."

"Shut up."

We looked around one last time. I thought about the shoes again. Wait. I said, "Go upstairs and check the closet.' He did, taking the stairs two at a time. Sean disappeared. A long ten seconds went by. I called up to him, "What does the closet look like? Is there a gap where the shoes you're wearing used to be?" Two questions, one open ended. How do you answer with yes or no? Come on, Bruce, focus.

"Closet's all good and no, these didn't have a box and they were at the end of the row, on the floor. No rug, no box or shoe print."

Perfect, I said to myself. See? We're already halfway through. As Sean came back down, I directed, "Outside, find some good branches and I'll get the twine from the back seat. Don't forget to drag the branches behind you." I spoke to Kurt without looking at him. "Can you open the cabin door?"

"Yup." Just like that, no more anger, no more kook behavior, all serious about finishing this scheme. We each took off on our separate tasks, and I loaded the money back into the trunk of the Saab and closed the hatch with a metallic squeal and crunch. I kept the gun behind my pants next to my spine. Two bullets left.

I watched Sean but he didn't even look up. I guessed he felt pretty safe, and I still hadn't decided what to do. Better not feel that safe, bud, I thought. I went around to the driver's side, opened the door, and reached under the front seat, felt the ball of twine. Once I had it firmly, I pulled, and it came out without unwinding. Another sign of good luck. By the time I had cut the twine into manageable lengths with the Swiss Army knife I stored in the glove compartment, Sean was back, dragging three branches the size of four-foot Christmas trees. We looped the twine around the trunks of each branch and tied them to three sections of the bumper, front, and sides. The three branches made an unbroken pattern about twice the width of the car. Perfect. We got in. Kurt turned over the engine, let it warm up for a couple of seconds.

"Look carefully. Do you see any evidence of our being here?" I asked. Sean looked, head and eyes scanning the road and the driveway roundabout. We had even wiped the little path through the grotto between the car and front door.

Sean said, "I think we got it. Fuck, I think we're good."

"Kinda like the Jimmy thing, yeah?"

He looked out the front window and his eyes saw the past and future. "This was way more intense. I never thought you would do something like this. Fucking psycho. I thought only Kurt would do something like this."

Kurt responded, "Fuck you, Sean, if we weren't in so much trouble, I'd beat you for drills. Those were olden days. I never would have done something like this."

"I guess that's not really true anymore, is it? We're all in it together, so buckle up, buttercups. I always wanted to say that."

A quiet "Fuck," from Kurt.

Sean: "No shit, this is so fucked up. Why did you do that?"

"Why do you think? I mean, Dickhead needed to go. That's a fact. Plus, we're gonna be rich, or will be soon enough, and no witnesses. I could have shot you too...but I didn't. You're welcome."

Kurt put the car into first gear and rode the clutch, creeping forward. "Look out your window," I directed Sean. "Are our tire marks wiped away?"

"Yeah, it looks like it."

"Looks like it or is it. Which one, don't fuck around."

Sean looked again, leaning out until his body hung half out the window. "Is it."

He slipped back into the car, making sure his head didn't strike the window frame, and we made another loop around the parking area. Our tracks were indeed clear. When the cops showed up, they would think that Alex, Ocho, and Dick had come up in Dick's car. No sign of us. A little more luck and some more snow and the footprints would be hidden permanently. No way to tell the size of the footprints so again, no evidence tying us to the scene. Nice. Now for the rest of the heist, as I had begun to think of it. We crept down the drive and parked in front of the path to the cabin. It was gonna be an easy traipse down and a bitch coming back up. We'd have to drag a tree branch behind us as well as carry all that beautiful, pink-tinged, glittering snow. Jackpot. My nose drooled with the thought.

Sean went first back down the trail, more like a ravine, steep and slippery with snow and mud. I followed, moving down the path facing sideways, step/match/stop, step/match/stop, like I was a little infant walking downstairs for the first time. Sean and I were very careful not to touch any branches; triggering snowfall from the treetops would leave evidence of our presence. It didn't take long to get to the bottom, maybe three minutes. I looked back at the path we had descended; it was fucking steep. This was going to be really fucked on the way back. I was inclined to take the long way except we hadn't wiped our footprints. Buck up, you faggot. Winners don't whine. This one you're going to win. Believe in yourself. Just get the blow. One step at a time, eye on the prize.

Sean and I stood there catching our breaths, watching the plumes of condensation clouds explode from our mouths with every exhalation. It was kind of fun to see how thick you could make the cloud before it dissipated. We had a short contest, both smiling like nothing was amiss, like we were two friends just out for a hike in the snow, moon and biting cold at our faces. Except we weren't friends, just two guys dancing to the chorus to "Jungle Boogie." My head spun; my body felt electrified. I still hadn't decided what to do about the end of the song. "What do you think, Sean? Can we do it? The alternative is that I go back up and wipe the path down, we get the blow, and then hike the long way back."

"Am I still in the shit?" Sean countered. "And Kurt? What about him?"

What did that have to do with my question?

Let's digress for a minute. I looked at this situation as an umpire in a baseball game, Sean was the batter. Strike one, Sean. I mean, I could have done this with Kurt alone, and he would have been willing, I think. But here we were.

"A, you're earning your way out. My suggestion is that you figure out how I can trust you. B. Don't worry about Kurt." I looked at Kurt. He gave a slight nod. "And fuck those three guys. Except maybe Ocho. Him I kind of feel bad for."

Sean: "I'm not sure you do. That's the problem."

Bruce: "Really? That's what you think is the problem? I will put a hole into your skull, then you can see how to solve *that* problem." I took a breath, slowed down. "What happened up there is our secret that goes to the grave." And yours could be dug right here...friend, pal, buddy, I thought to myself. Right here and now.

Kurt said, "Lighten up, both of you. Focus. Dumb shits."

Sean said, "Let's just get this over with. We do this, hike back up, and get the fuck out of here. I just want to get out. Sell a couple of kilos, put the rest in my car and drive to Canada."

I said, "Okay, good. Glad to hear that you feel that way. Kurt'll drive, I'll take the back. Besides, as you know, I have a date."

"You're bullshitting me, right? You're gonna go out with that chick, after all this?"

"I look at it as a test in mental toughness," I said. "Do I have the character to take care of business and then handle a date with my dream woman? That's the question I want to answer tonight, and we have to move it if I'm gonna face the challenge." Sean's jaw dropped slightly, and he let out an audible breath, condensation cloud puffing out of his mouth.

"Fucking idiot," he mumbled. He turned and began walking to the cabin. I flipped him the bird. Man, don't fuck with me, I thought. I pulled the gun from the back of my pants. Sean, you fucker, that's strike two. Fuck Kurt.

Kurt: "Just shut the fuck up, will you? And I mean both of you. Sound like a couple of magpies or little old biddies, squabbling. Just shut the fuck up."

He was right. I put the gun back. We got to the cabin in less than three minutes and stopped at the front door, all of us examining the keypad. While Sean stomped his feet to warm up his toes, Kurt started with the code breaking, leaving his gloves on for fingerprint protection. On the fourth try, I heard a distinctive click, and the lock gave way; he got it. I opened the door, and we looked inside, saw the same room we had just sat in a lifetime before. I did a mental swoon. I lost concentration on the task at hand and my attention drifted to what had transpired. I saw the blood, felt the gun at my spine, Alex slouched down into the soft chair, Dick Asshole's skull and brains splattered all over the window. The window. The bullet hole leaking bloodied air into the wind. And Ocho.

I focused on the next step, smiled. I stepped into the room. I heard the creak as my shoes pressed into the wood plank floor. Sean reached for the light and the switch for the heater. He turned them both on, and there was a hum from the furnace outside. I took a deep breath and said, "Might as well turn off the heater, we aren't gonna be here that long." Huh. No words of wisdom or complaints, no whining about his feet. We'll call it a ball. Ball one.

Kurt looked at Sean, said, "Have a seat, warm up your feet if you can. I'll get the cabinet door open." Sean sat down in the seat leaning against the front wall, about eight feet from where Kurt knelt. From the doorway I kept an eye on him through my peripheral vision and watched as Kurt opened the hidden door. There, just as before, were the stacks of kilos, all 394. I stared at them, nice even rows and columns. The structure and efficiency of the stacking relaxed me. I thought for a few seconds and a light bulb clicked on.

"You guys, I have an idea. This coke isn't Alex's, right? The chances are he got it fronted to him by someone, Pablo Escobar, whoever, some fat drug kingpin with a sloppy haircut and bad breath. That guy is going to wonder what happened to his marching dust." I let my mind roll, tongue following. "We take as much as we can take, then rearrange the rest to cover the theft. Then we leave a note, maybe from Alex to his girlfriend, suggesting Alex sold it to some guy in Louisiana, South Carolina, wherever. Just not around here or anywhere west of the Mississippi River. We'll even give him a name—John Smith. The Escobar motherfucker? He's gonna go after the invisible man in wherever we say in the note and try to get the rest of his coke back. And he's gonna try to find the money too. Once the situation is uncovered, we know the Bolivians are gonna be so busy trying to get those answers we can already be in Southern California or Seattle or Vancouver undetected, trading the coke for dollars with one of the triad gangs or Hollywood highfliers. Then we can charter a private yacht for Asia and get lost in Nepal. Stay low profile." I stopped for a couple of seconds. "What do you think?" Before they could respond, I went even further, my mind whizzing at light speed. "We can even tip off the cops in a few days; make sure they get here first. Then the Bolivians have to deal with the cops too. And won't see the note. And then the cops will be chasing John Smith. And once the Bolivians find out about the note, maybe paying off a crooked flatfoot, they'll be chasing too. The wrong way across country." Awesome. Ha. Okay, okay, okay.

Sean and Kurt had been listening patiently this whole time and it felt like the old team was back, everyone quiet, focused, serious. I liked these guys. Especially this Sean, the laid-back, irreverent guy. Not the other Sean, the man-baby whiner back at the house. That Sean, not so much. So, maybe ball two.

Sean looked like he couldn't wait to say something, like a kid who had to go to the bathroom. "Whatever you say, Daffy." He gave a tentative smile. Still scared for his life. If I had been in his position, I would've been too, and he didn't even know how close he was to the bullet. However, his attempt at humor in the face of oblivion: ball three, for bravery. The count was three and two, ladies and gentlemen, Sean moving in on the pitcher. He was in a strong position, needed only one more ball for the walk, and he would get the extra added attraction of one-third of the loot. Of course, If Sean struck out, I'd have to drill a hole in Kurt, too. That weighed on my mind, for sure. Keeping it all for myself was on my mind too.

I wasn't gonna give away their predicament, or my own, so I said, "From my count, there are three down, three standing. How is my math? Are we on the same page or does that make me a functional illiterate?"

"I'd say you are both literate and definitely functional. What got you thinking about doing that?" Sean Said. Kurt nodded slightly.

I thought about it for a couple of seconds. Was he asking me in order to cover his ass later if I let him go? Was he going to use it against me? If I tell him the truth, that I liked it, would he fuck me in court? Should this be another strike against him?

"I guess seeing Dick, and the fact that you turned away when it came to him or me. You left me no choice, I had to do it. Alex might have had a gun. And what about earlier, when he pretended not to know Dick? What was that about? Dickless was obviously invited up here and a confrontation was gonna happen, you knew that as soon as we walked in the door. It was them or me, and I included you with them. You should both be half-blind and brainless with a third hole in your nose, but you're not. Just us here now. The question yet to be answered fully is: since you're not dead, are you with me?"

Kurt bristled but kept his trap shut. Sean took a shallow breath, then another, his eyes never leaving my right arm, though he tried to mask it. I moved my hand to my right jacket pocket to make him feel safer. Maybe this would give him enough safety to answer me truthfully. I watched his eyes. My left hand disappeared. I took a breath, conscious of the moment. It was cold, even in the room. My toes felt like they were being stabbed by tiny needles and my nose ran, this time from the temperature. I didn't care, I just noticed it. Another breath, focus. My eyes went dead.

I was cold. Sean looked me in the eye and uttered in a small, even voice, "Don't shoot me and leave me here for the lions. I don't wanna be a Christian in Rome."

Ha, funny. Ball four, the batter walks. I shifted to Kurt. "What about you, bud?" My hand came out of my pocket and drifted posterior. I reached.

He watched me. He knew how quick I was.

"Let's just get this done. I'm with you guys, getting rich and safely away to Indonesia sounds great to me. I can always go home when this is done, and a few years go by." Kurt let out a breath and some of his bravado, looked at me, my arm, and turned away.

I pulled my hand away from the Webley and took off my jacket. "I'm not going to shoot. Open your jackets and put them on the ground. Here's mine, do the same. I'll hold the door to the bed frame open and pass you the blow. We'll put as much into the jackets as we can, zip 'em up. Then we'll tie them to our backs, like backpacks with the arms as straps."

And we got down to business, me passing the coke out of the hole in the frame, Sean and Kurt stacking them efficiently into the jackets. As we piled the cocaine into the jackets, Sean asked, "How much should we carry? If we load too much, we'll never get back up the ravine and wipe the path clean in time."

He had a good point. That's the Sean I like, the thinking one. I said, "I figure twenty kilos each, forty-four pounds. What do you think?"

"Good." I noticed that Kurt grabbed at least thirty kilos. No biggie, he was stronger than us.

When me and Sean got to twenty kilos in each, we added another three for good measure. What's another 15 percent? We tied the ends of the sleeves together and zipped the jackets closed. This left us with three lumps with holes at the bottoms. I looked around. The lamp cord. Good for one at least. I ripped the lamp cord from the wall, putting us into shadow with only the moon on the snow for reflective light. I then pulled the cord from the lamp and wrapped it around the bottom of the one jacket, closing off the only hole. I looked for something else. I looked everywhere on the floor and walls with my hands as well as my eyes, using my memory as a guide. Nothing. I glanced at the stash hole, bent down, and felt around. Plastic bundles only. Fuck. I felt around, reached over to the corner where there wasn't any stash. And would you believe it, baling twine. "Sean, I got it." I pulled the twine out; there was a good eight feet of it, enough for the leftover jackets.

We split the twine into two equal lengths with the blade on the table; Kurt took his jacket, Sean the other, and we made short work of the problem. We lifted the jackets, and nothing fell out, even when we shook them up and down. Kurt took his and did the same. Success. Okay, okay. We were on a roll. I slid one jacket over my head, one arm through so it fit like a knapsack. Good fit, good enough for the hike. I repositioned the blow to make it look like everything was normal. I then leaned back and closed the bed frame, using my fingertips to gauge the fit. I stood the lamp back on its end and rearranged the coffee table, blowing any residual coke onto the floor and wiping down the razor blade. I turned to Kurt, silhouetted in the moonlight, and whispered, "Is there anything else we need to do?"

No answer from Kurt but Sean whispered back, "No, except we need to get some tree branches. And why are you whispering?"

"I don't know." Pause. "Okay. Kurt's strongest so he can lead, me next, and since you're taller and have better shoes, ha-ha, you can wipe the path after us." Snickers from two of us, Sean not so much.

Sean stopped moving. "You're really not going to kill me?"

"No. How would I get out of the situation? We're too far gone to consider the alternative. Not that I am not thinking of it."

"Okay then, why do I go last?" he said. "That's complete bullshit."

"You have better footing; I watched when we went back up last time. Sorry, you lose. That's what you get for my keen powers of observation." I smiled at him, and he must have seen me 'cause he smiled back, I could see his teeth glint off the snow's reflected light. He turned around and went out the door. Kurt and I stepped after him, turning and giving the room one last look-over with the limited light available. It was all good. I pulled the door shut and heard the lock engage. I said over my shoulder, "Well, that's it. Next stop, the car." I turned and Sean was already pulling a couple of large branches from a pile a few feet away from the corner of the cabin.

"I got a couple." He showed me. "What do you think?" One looked like a fan, the other like a small, skinny Christmas tree.

"Keep the one that's thickest but narrowest. You gotta swing it and push it and stuff, so you have to be able to move it like a broom." Sean dropped the big one and kept the broom. As we made our way up the incline and back to the car at the top, Sean said, "why are we wiping out our footprints again? The cops are still going to see the path and there are three of us. Kurt's prints blend."

Fucking idiot. Maybe I should give him another strike, making three, then just shoot him in the head and watch his body tumble down the ravine. Hey. If he did that, he'd tumble over the path and obscure the prints with his sliding body. Hmmm.

Wait a minute, Bruce, not so fast. You've got to establish some semblance of principle. Are you really that far gone that you won't even live up to commitments you made to yourself?

I said, "We've got to erase the prints anyway. If the cops catch us before we get outa town, or find us in LA, they're going to ask us questions when they find those guys, since we are known associates of Dickless. So far, we've gotten rid of any evidence linking us to this situation. We're clean, up till now. If it snows, even better, but we can't take that chance. The cops are going to find the path, no doubt. But we don't have to give them prints or anything to go with their spectacular discovery. And at this point, let's just keep our eyes on the fucking ball. I've got it all planned. We have the goodies, everything's good, wait and see." I looked up to make sure Kurt wasn't getting any ideas about throwing me down the path. I mean, if I could think of it, they could, too. Actually no, Sean couldn't think of it. He was irritatingly passive. Good for the situation when I needed him to donkey the blow to the car. After that, who knew? I looked Kurt in the eye. Nothing there, nobody home. Frightening. Maybe I should just plunk him, leave him to rot here. Less worry. Oh, come on, stick to the plan, Bruce. You gave them the choice. Kurt was in from the start. Sean, he got the walk, and now you want to change the deal. Eye on the ball? How about keeping *your* eye on the ball. Get moving, you got a lot of stuff to do. Almost home, don't drop the ball now.

We took another two minutes to reach the top. When Sean steadied himself at the edge, we both looked back down the ravine. The moonlight caught the path perfectly, exposing every section of the route so that it looked like a meandering stream, frozen in life. There were no prints that we could see, and I wasn't about to go back down to check closer. I asked Sean, "Are you sure you got it all?"

"Yeah, I checked with each step we took back up here. Fuck you, let's just get outa here. I just want to go."

I didn't blame him. The sooner we got the blow stashed in the trunk and got back down the hill, the sooner

I could put this little mishap behind me. And Kurt had delivered; the Saab was parked, tail facing us, trunk open and waiting. I did have one question, which I asked while we put the three jacket-bags in the trunk. "Are you sure you know where your shoe is?"

Sean said, "No, I'm not sure, but I'm pretty sure I know about where it is."

Kurt scoffed. "Fucking Akana."

I looked at Sean. "When you say 'about,' what do you mean by that?"

"As in, it's within about a six-foot-diameter area, buried in the mud. I'm pretty sure the heel is sticking out; I kind of walked right out of it."

I said, "Well, we have to find it and then clean up the area too. When it freezes tonight, the prints we left will be frozen in the ice and we'd be fucked, and we can't take that chance. Let's hope the ground is still wet and your shoe is sprouting like a weed."

Chapter 26

I got into the back seat; Kurt started the car while Sean went around the door with the broom. He then got into his side and repeated the process. We all looked out our windows and did another last check for prints around us, any kind of print, but we were greeted with nothing but snow that looked freshly cleaned, like groomed ski slopes. If the cops got here tomorrow, they wouldn't find anything except groomed road. By the time they found the bodies, it wouldn't matter if they figured out that others were here, no way to figure out how many, let alone what kind of car. And if they didn't get here for a couple of days, we'd be a long ways away.

Kurt put the car into gear. We moved on down the driveway toward the place we got stuck; we could hear the sound of the pine branches attached to the bumper doing their appointed job. Every couple of seconds, Sean leaned out and checked our getaway; all good. We drove to the end of the driveway and turned right to go down the mountain. I kept track of the mileage, and we soon came upon the scene of our earlier festivities. There were tire marks everywhere, shoe prints and a right-side footprint where Sean had stepped in his pathetic attempt to get us out of the hole. We stopped, leaving the headlights on so we could scour the area for his shoe. Sean got out. I started to get a little tipsy, like I had just had that one extra drink that makes you go over the edge, and then you realize you've gone from feeling great to fucked up in the space of about ten seconds. What to do about this. We still had a long drive down a windy road with seventy-plus kilos of coke, a focused and together navigator, a surly onboard pilot, and a copilot whose hands still shook from the scare I put into him.

I thought about it for a bit and the solution presented itself...more cocaine. What was I thinking and how did it take me so long to figure *that* out? I reached into my pocket and pulled out the vial with the spoon attached to the cap that I still had in my pocket. I handed it to Kurt, who took it and proceeded to take three spoons in each nostril, about three times the amount he would have normally taken. Fucker. I yelled out the car window, "Sean, have you found it yet?"

"No, but I've gotten the tracks erased."

So, there was that. I reached for the open vial, exposing the pink-tinged snow, still flickering in the moonlight through the glass. I reached overhead to turn on the inside light and just as I switched it on, Sean cried out,

"Got it!" I saw Sean start back for the car, holding his shoe aloft like some trophy he'd won in a one-legged ass-kicking contest.

I leaned out the window and said, "Okay, hurry up and get back in the car. And don't forget to wipe off your footprints. And be careful, there's coke exposed in here." Kurt said nothing.

It was 11:00 p.m.; We had an hour to finish this shit, get to town, park, and go to the hotel. And do it all while trying to clear my head as fast as possible. Okay Bruce old buddy, no more blow, put it away. You have to straighten up and fly right. You know the saying. Well, after this one last bump.

I capped the vial and slid it back into my front pocket just as the passenger door opened and Sean climbed in. He settled into the seat and took off the All Stars. These he put under his legs and gave me his muddy shoes, which I placed under the front seat. He then tucked his feet under him Indian-style and took a deep breath. He said, "I think we're good, I got it all."

"Five more minutes. Let's drive to Left Hand Canyon Road and then we'll take the branches off the car. Then we'll be free of this whole night." Though none of us would ever forget it. The car was quiet for about half a minute. I said, "I want to say a couple of things. I was shitting you back there when I said we weren't friends. To me, we are, always have been, since freshman year." Me, trying to cement the loyalty so I didn't have to use the Webley again. Truthfully, I didn't know if I had it in me to fire another shot.

"In my mind we're all tight friends in this car, right here and now. We're also guilty of a triple murder, and don't think they won't come after us; they're fucking cops, that's what they do."

Kurt started, "What do you mean we, ass—"

I stopped him. "We've been through something like this before, like I said, Jimmy Fuckwad, I know we can get away with it again. So, there's some stuff we have to have clear." Silence.

"Here's my take on this. One. Cops aren't like Columbo, they're more like Kojak; they're not that smart, but they can be persistent, and they don't give up. They mostly hope people like us fuck up, so they get a clean bust. Two. I'll split the blow with you both; we'll split it even." Sean's eyebrows rose and his eyes took on a curious look. I said, "What?" Nothing.

"Kurt?"

Kurt shrugged again, again said nothing.

"Three. I figure we have twenty-four to forty-eight hours to sell enough to get us to the coast, say a kilo, twenty-three K. After that, we head for Los Angeles, dump all or most of the rest through Sean's connection, rent a boat, with crew, sail for Australia and Southeast Asia in style. I figure we can get lost in Indonesia or wherever for the rest of our lives. Do you know of anyone who has connections in Sydney?"

Both of them looked at me like I was from Mars.

We reached the road, drove about a half a mile down, then, it was time to dump the branches. I leaned over the seat, spoke to Sean. "It's easiest for you. Would you get out and take the branches away, leave them in the street for the other cars to run over. And when you cut off the twine, bring it back to the car with you. No evidence. Okay?"

Sean sneezed, tied up the All Stars, swift intake of breath and grimace as the cold canvas met warm feet. He stepped out and I felt some tugging from under the car, a creaking sound, then I felt the car shake as Sean released the branches. The car rocked back and forth a couple of times and then Sean stood up from behind the bumper and held up the cut twine. I looked out the back and saw the branches scattered across the road. Perfect.

I yelled out the window, "Get in, let's go!" Sean ran around the car and got back in, unzipping his borrowed coat before settling himself. He quickly removed the green All Stars and wrapped his feet underneath him once more.

I asked to the ether, "Have you given any thought to an Indo connection?"

Kurt tipped his head slightly, indicating some brain cells were engaged, how many I didn't know. He thought for a couple of seconds, and I thought he was going to have someone in mind, but no. "See?" he said. "Look at yourself. No plan. What would you have done if you'd shot us too?"

"But I didn't." I looked at him through the rearview mirror, I made my eyes go dead again, then I flashed anger, blood pressure going up a good ten points as I let the rage wash over me, sending me into a maelstrom of heat and shaking tension. I could feel the blood pumping through my ears.

"Do either of you know anyone who can help us offload this stuff?" I asked again, voice quiet, forceful.

Sean, rapid-fire speech, I could barely follow him. "Amazingly enough, I know this guy from old canoe-paddling days. He lives in Kuta. Good surfer. If anyone has contacts for large quantities, he'd be that guy. I once saw him lay out a one-gram line at a party and do it on a dare.

Get this. The bet was for a gram, so he did the line for nothing. The guy couldn't walk or talk for an hour."

Who the fuck cares if the guy can snort a gram of marching dust? Fucking Sean, oblivious. You need him, Bruce, so let it go. Let him strike out later.

"Can you get in touch with him tonight? That would be tomorrow afternoon sometime because of the International Date Line. Get some idea of his exposure, but don't tell him anything, including that we want to visit him." I leaned forward and whispered into Sean's ear. "And when I say nothing, I mean it." The coke was starting to weaken, and my brain felt like a flaccid penis in a condom. I shook my head and saw stars.

"I don't know about that. I don't have his number; I'd have to call information and see if he's even listed."

What? Backing out? Strategizing his plan B? Or just being a puss. Did he want to gain a third eye?

"Fuck, Sean. *Who. Do. You. Know. I don't care about anything else right now, this instant.* You said something about a guy in LA? Do you even know Los Angeles? Right now, you're the man on this. Find a way to get with that guy, or someone else at the other end, or we won't be able to finalize this. We won't get this coke over the border unless we take it on a private charter. No baggage search means

317

we get away. No connection at the other end means we eat it. This is it for you. Savvy?"

"Settle down, Bruce," Kurt said from the driver's seat.

Sean, contrite. "Yeah, I can get him. His name is—"

"I don't want to know. Just call him when we get to the bar. Use information, from a pay phone. Yeah, perfect, the pay phone. Okay? And when we get to LA, call your friend in Kuta. We got to set that up too."

Sean said, "Okay, okay. Got it. Don't worry. Dude, what's gotten into you?"

My eyebrows went up like a steroid bodybuilder's shoulders when they are doing a shrug. I had no response. How can I tell the truth, that I was seriously considering a pirate ending, all the treasure for myself, like Blackbeard; that I was probably gonna shoot 'em both once I had a plan to get to Australia? (That's right, not Indonesia. Yeah, I am a liar and a sneak, so what?)

Kurt looked at me through the rearview mirror again. "What?" I said. He shrugged. What's with the shrugging and no talking? If the fucker wasn't driving, I'd plug him. Well, maybe not, no place to hide the body.

Chapter 27

It was 11:25 p.m. and we were about five or six miles from downtown, maybe fifteen minutes. Another couple of minutes to park and I'd be in the bar by midnight with minutes to spare. Good.

Yeah, I had done a very bad thing, and I didn't have to be reminded of it. I'd see it through my mind's eye for the rest of my life. That was bad. And I felt bad, in the pit of my stomach. My ears still rang from the gunshots.

We drove for a couple of minutes more and then I said abruptly, "Man, I feel bad. We need to pull over." Kurt looked at me through the mirror. We were down the road, on Broadway, out by the strip bar and the hot tub place. And we all wanted to get as far away from Alex's house as quickly as possible. The road out there wasn't very well lit, streetlights about a hundred yards apart. Kurt slowed the car, looking at the storefronts for the perfect place to stop. After a couple of hundred yards, he found it, the parking lot of a small used clothing store, closed for the night. Avoiding the window light, he drove around to the back of the building, into shadow. Engine off. Car door opens. I get out, stretched my legs one at a time, and stayed in the shadow of the building wall. Sean, out of the passenger seat and watched me over the roof of the car, resting his chin on his crossed hands. I'm sure his palms were cold against the metal of the car, but he didn't move, watching. A quick thought, maybe I should take the gun out of my jeans, just to remind them who's in charge of this escapade. Ummm. No. Let's not tip our hand. Plenty of time for the lights-out.

I took a couple of deep breaths and tried to calm down. I turned toward the wall and leaned on my hands. The cement wall was cold to the touch. The Webley in my back was colder. Wait a minute. What was I going to do about the Webley? I couldn't trash it; I might need it. On the other hand, I had already used it in a triple murder so...it had to go. But when? I looked at the boys. Sean still watching me over the car roof. Kurt looked like he was sleeping. Quick thought. What if Sean got back in the car and they left me out here? Wait, what?

Flashback. Quick pulling the gun, careful aim, firing away, skull, brains and blood spattered all over the walls and furniture. Four shots, four hits. Nice shooting, Tex. The gaping black hole in Dickhead Dickmann's eye socket, the gunpowder-tinged brains oozing from the wound onto the floor and down the glass window. Fuck, I'm gonna be sick. I got sick. I landed on my knees, hunched over and aiming for a porcelain bowl that didn't exist. Projectile sick, every heave leading to another, beefier one. The splattering on the lot surface sounded like when you threw a steaming pile of cow shit against a barn door. I thought I was gonna throw up part of my spleen and my eyes watered so much I couldn't see. The acid taste in my esophagus burned my throat with a pain I hoped wouldn't be reflective of my journey to hell. For what I had done. For what I had to do.

I gagged, heaves and coughs. Spit, spit again. I finally took a breath and opened my left eye. The right was still sealed by my drying tears. Not that there was anything to see except the remains of a great steak, sautéed veggies, and expensive red wine. What a waste. Fuckety, fuck.

The immediate problem was brain fog. What had happened had happened so fast, like I didn't think about it, just did it. But I know I thought about it. I was sure of it. And it was for the best. Besides, the two of them had been in cahoots. Why else would Alex have kept his friendship and business relationship with Dick Dickmann a secret? Why? I'll tell you why. Because they intended to fuck me over, that's why. Dick had probably been the instigator. He deserved what he got, for sure. I might even burn his house down for good measure. In fact, that wasn't a bad idea, maybe burn other evidence. Yeah, that's it. We'll do it together, that way we're handcuffed to the getaway plan.

None of us was going anywhere but far away. Or so they would think. Hee-hee-hee.

What? Oh, Ocho, you say? Fuck him, wrong place, wrong time. Anyone stupid enough to be friends with Dickless...

I took stock of myself. On my knees, hands grabbing parking lot pavement. Deep breath; I glanced up at Sean, who looked back with a blank face. I couldn't tell what he was thinking; suddenly inscrutable, the slightly panic-driven guy coming down the hill was gone. While I had been on my knees barfing out my spleen, Sean had come around the car and was now leaning against the driver's side door, standing on his left leg with the right crossed in front. Cool cucumber. Sean had *his* shit together and he was watching *me*. Seeing what I was going to do. Kurt, now out of the car, sitting on the hood, feet on the tire. Watching. I suddenly felt intimidated, like when I was a kid. Maybe these two were making decisions. Maybe these decisions wouldn't be in my best interest. After all, neither of them was a spatial thinker, only linear, one step at a time, A leads to B and so on. Obviously. Maybe Sean was thinking of going to the cops. Or maybe the two of them were going to jump me, take the gun, blow *my* head off, and skip town *right now*. Oh man, man, fuck. I guess he just didn't get the picture. A lesson was in order; we could switch places, me standing and him on his knees, like at the house. I wouldn't call it Alex's house because Alex didn't live there anymore.

Chapter 28

May 1970

When I was a kid, I was small for my age, but I had a couple of things going for me, or so I thought. One was that I was from a wealthy family, from Balboa Island, in Newport Beach, and started learning karate when I was five. That kept a lot of kids from picking on me. I made up shit about my grandfather being a direct descendant of Comstock, and that we struck it rich from silver in 1859, in Nevada. After a while, I started to believe it too. So, I lied, big deal. Everybody lies, they just deny it. Which were lies too. People have no sense of values, of principles. I never trusted people, they stab you in the back, trust me on this.

Another thing was that I was a pretty good athlete and ran pretty fast, faster than the fuckwads that chased me. You know the rule of survival, fight or flight? I was a flyer. I figured better a thinker than a fighter; use the tools God gave you, that was my motto. The truth was, I had a black belt in karate, but I sucked at it. And one other thing. I had cousins on Oahu who grew great weed in the back of Manoa Valley, where they lived. Whenever we went to visit, I grabbed a double baggie of it, taped it up good, and strapped it to my lower back. Then had an anxiety attack the whole plane ride home.

I hated being bullied, and for the most part I avoided the stigma using the aforementioned tools. However, there was this one guy who just...when I was really small, my parents used to tell me that I was special, that people would see that and that I'd be popular for it. I had my grandfather's gift for gab, and a really quick mind so I could change mental directions on a dime. Anyway, this guy, his name was Keoki Schmidt, who lived next door to my cousins, and he...I don't know, he intimidated me. I always chalked it up to his privileged upbringing and that he was a racist bastard. I think his great-great-grandfather or something was involved in the Hawaiian monarchy overthrow. It wouldn't have surprised me, his family was generationally rich, and he was an entitled fucker, like he was descended from King Kamehameha. On his sixteenth birthday, his parents bought him a Porsche. A Porsche. Fucking spoiled. Whatever, he was a fucking asshole. I always thought it was because I was from California. And it's true, I didn't even speak any Hawaiian, so I stood out when we were visiting. In hindsight, I probably came across as just another mainland kid in need of a beating. Ironic, since I had just as much right to be in Hawaii as most of the people thinking the same about me, especially Keoki

Schmidt. Do I sound sour? Sure, because the guy made me feel inferior.

But I'm getting off the point of the story. Keoki was the only guy I fought. We fought in summer school, three times; I won them all. But there was nobody around to see. Strange, I know, since fights are usually a spectacle in middle or high school. The fights I'd seen had two guys and about two hundred watching. Most couldn't see, they just caught glimpses and followed the cheers. You know, "Fight, fight! Fight!" Pathetic. The fighters just sort of batted at each other with closed fists, at least one of them holding his thumb under his fingers. Good way to break a thumb or dislocate it. I guess Dear Old Dad never taught that kid; hardy, har.

So anyway, this one time, Keoki and I were in Kahala High School library, standing in the stacks away from the prying eyes of the librarian, Mrs. Kahana. We stood in the history section, filled with pop-up picture books about the English establishing Jamestown. I remember one book named "How the War Was Won." I took it down one time and opened it and saw a picture of a Black guy hanging from a tree in Mississippi, a bunch of guys in ghost costumes with pointy hoods standing around watching and mugging for the camera. A couple of them had exposed faces, cherubic features and blimpy bodies. I thought it curious that the book would have the name it had. Maybe the authors had pictures of fat white guys getting hanged in the back chapters. You know, Blacks win? I figured it was a book on the civil rights fight. At least I hoped it was. What kind of high school not located in some mosquito-infested backwater southern cracker state would have such a book on its shelves?

Whoops, off point again.

One thing about Keoki, he was predictable. Big mouth, arrogant, liked to make fun of others in public, used humiliation as a weapon. He also fought like a girl. Always threw his first punch right-handed, loading up from the side, straight at you—or me, as it were. All I did was step aside and grab his arm as it came by, easy. I twisted his arm overhead and stepped under, like when you see a judo flip in an old James Bond movie. Only I didn't flip him. Instead, I got his arm pinned behind him and wrapped my left arm around his throat; half-nelson. Keoki tried to get my arm out from around his neck with his left hand, weak. He tried to step on my foot and kick my shin, pussy. I whispered, "Let's see how you explain this one to your friends," and I pulled up on his right arm as hard as I could. I heard a "pop" and felt a shift of his arm in my grip. There, you fuck, feel it and weep.

Keoki let out a sharp howl, more like "eahh!" than "ooww!" and I let go. Exit, stage right. I immediately tucked around the stacks, scurried down the main aisle, and grabbed a seat in the audio-visual room, jamming the headphones over my ears and flicking the tabletop switch that turned on the foreign language lesson. About a minute later, I felt more than heard a commotion from behind me and felt the strong grip of Mr. McMillen pinch around my neck, pulling me out of the chair, which fell backward and hit the wood floor with a thud and clatter. He turned me around and gave me a quick shake, wobbling my head on its axis.

"Keoki seems to have hurt himself. He says you did it. What do you have to say?"

"Why would I do anything to Keoki? I don't even know him. I'm just here for summer school, I live in California. Mr. McMillen, every time I see him, he's bragging about something. I just stay away from him."

Mr. McMillen just stared at me and squeezed a little harder. I winced, and he pulled his hand away. I knew he knew I was lying, but so what? Keoki couldn't prove anything, as I said, there were no witnesses. As far as I was concerned, Keoki got what he deserved. Now he was the humiliated one. Fucker.

The next summer, Keoki attacked me in science class with a metal crank, the kind that you use to move modular walls around in conference rooms. The thing looked like an oversized ratchet and weighed about ten pounds, and all I remember is Keoki chasing me around the room, swinging it around overhead like a demented camel jockey with a saber. That time, there were a lot of people around, but the teacher was gone. I think his name was Mr. Yim. He taught trigonometry too, I'm pretty sure. Anyway, I ran between chairs to make it harder for him to get near me, ducking under tables to avoid getting hit. Nobody stopped Keoki, even when I called for help. They just watched; my surfing friend Chris watched too. Some friend. See what I mean? You can't trust anybody, not even friends. That one ended with Keoki, on the floor, whining and holding his head after I threw a chair at him. There was bleeding.

I read in the paper some years later that Keoki Schmidt had been out surfing at Malibu, had pissed off some locals, and gotten beaten up so badly that he had to be ambulanced to the hospital. Where he died. Well, he always had a mouth on him...

Chapter 29

I got off my hands and knees, stood facing the wall, collecting my thoughts. Fucking Sean. I still had the Webley pressing into my coccyx and I needed to move it, maybe behind the back seat in the slot that goes to the trunk. Hell, if we were pulled over and the cop opened the trunk, the gun wouldn't be my only problem. After I'd puked up the sheer brutality of what I had done, my head cleared, and I realized the utter stupidity of the Webley situation. With seventy kilos of blow in the back seat, the gun was just icing, and the search would be clean, whether I wore the gun or hid it. Busted, murder and drug possession. I would need Perry Mason to get me out of my predicament.

I decided to let things lie. I looked at Kurt, in the driver's seat. "I'll drive, I'm good now," I said. He just looked at me, all blank-faced. I repeated myself. "Seriously, I wanna drive into town."

"Your car." Then Kurt cocked his head a little sideways and clambered into the back seat. Sean walked around and got into his side of the car as I got behind the wheel. I sat down, took a deep breath and turned the key, but didn't turn over the engine. I could see my breath as it fogged up the window. Sean asked, "What are you waiting for?"

"I've been thinking." Chuckles all around. "Seriously. Get out, man, pop the trunk, get the blanket, the one that has Indian shapes in it. Let's put as much of the stash inside the tire storage area as we can, put the cover back down, latch it. Then put the rest in the blanket folded up next to Kurt, like we came from a picnic or something. That way if we get pulled over for gum-chewing, there won't be any evidence in plain sight, trunk or interior, and anything the cops find will be inadmissible in court. It's getting to be witching hour and Boulder's Finest will be on the lookout. That is, after they put their vial and spoons away."

Kurt, sniffs and a little chuckle: "That'll work." What? Words from Kurt? Perhaps the window of survival cracked open, and I wouldn't have to shoot them after all. Even though I felt like Blackbeard and still kinda wanted to.

Sean gave a short snicker and we both smiled. What I said wasn't far from the truth; it was common knowledge that one of the Boulder assistant DAs was a degenerate Peruvian partier and all-around hose beast. Never met her but had seen her on TV—very nice looking, great legs. Sean pulled his sweater around himself tighter and got out of the car. When he pulled up the trunk and reached for the blanket, I quickly reached behind my back for the Webley. Grabbing it by the grip, I pulled it out and stuck it into the pocket in the driver's side door, grip up. Kurt noticed. We looked at each other. Big trust moment. Sean raised the trunk lid and held up the blanket with a small smile of success. I looked in the back seat and I noticed something I hadn't earlier. My borrowed jacket had a small tear on the right sleeve. Did it come from the trees near the cabin? My brain did a somersault. I had to dump them, all the coats, burn them. They had all kinds of stuff in the fabric: coke, liquor, sweat, snot on the sleeves, whatever. And some of it was going to be from us. Burn them for sure. Sean came around the car and leaned in the window.

Me: "In case you guys haven't noticed, we have a clothing problem. We gotta burn the coats."

Sean: "Good point. People who get questioned later about Alex and Dick and Ocho might remember that Alex owned these coats and then remember us wearing them. They could say to the cops that they saw us wearing them. Then we'd be good and properly fucked. I think we should leave them under the back seats. In the back." Sean made exactly no sense. Okay, stop with the suspicions. He's your partner now. Kurt too.

Kurt said, "Let's leave them in the trunk for now. Maybe we can get rid of them on the drive to LA tomorrow. Some stream or river we can throw them into. Let 'em float away, never to be seen again. Easy." Sean handed the blanket through the window. Kurt handed him the coats to put into the trunk as well. My thoughts were, if we didn't take them with us tomorrow, we could always toss them into a dumpster up on the Hill for the transients to find. Or set them on fire and throw them through a window into Dickhead's house. Burn it down. Hey, two birds, and all that. It would put some suspicion on Dickhead so that when they found him, they would think that this was a cartel sicario thing. Maybe. I was pleased with myself for the quick thinking given the circumstances.

"I've got another idea about what we can do with them, but it needs to wait for later, later," I said. "Trust me, it'll work out."

Sean said, "Trust, me...two words that should never come out of your mouth. Ever."

You know, when I was a really little kid, like three or four, I had a friend named Bret, whose parents owned a VW Bug. We used to sit in the little space in the back-back and watch the sky out the back window as his folks motored their way to McDonald's, back when McDonald's still had those two yellow arches on either side of the drive-in. One time, Bret broke my nose with a head butt in a scuffle between friends, the kind that happen sometimes when you're really little. I ran home, bawling like the little crybaby I was at the time. A couple of hours later, when my dad woke up sober, he was pissed at me for my broken nose. He just cleaned up my face with a washcloth, making sure to get around my nose real good. I screamed from the pain, cried. "What are you crying about? You should have beaten that kid up." Then he sent me back to Bret's house to make things right. "Don't come back until his nose looks like yours." So, as scared of the violence as I was, I did. And lost the first friend I even had. Nice guy, my dad. A real positive influence. I still have the broken nose to tell the tale. For all I know, so does Bret. I know, what does that have to do with our predicament? Well, it's like this. Fucking Dickless deserved more than just getting shot in the head. He deserved to be blamed for everything too. My dad would have been okay with me getting him blamed for the dirty-dog deed that I (we) pulled, since he spent so much time fucking me over. There. Got it? What?

After burying the coke in the trunk, in the tire area and making sure it properly latched, Sean got back into the car. I let the moment stretch out for a couple more seconds, then started the car. I took a couple of deep breaths, put the car into first, and we pulled out of the parking lot and onto Broadway, heading south toward downtown.

Chapter 30

11:45 p.m.

When we got to Boulder proper, we obeyed traffic laws like good citizens, stopping at a couple of traffic lights, including the one on Maxwell and Broadway. I pointed out Maxwell with my chin and nudged Sean. "Speaking of Jimmy..." I said.

His response: "Shut up, don't remind me. I don't want to think about Jimmy, Alex, Dick, Ocho, or any part of then or tonight again. Ever." He paused. "Did I say ever? I meant never, ever. I want a beer. Hotel, and step on it. Please."

I looked at Kurt through the mirror. He smirked. "I remember," he said. "How's your ear?" Funny.

I guessed that getting Sean to burn Dick's house down later was questionable. Oh well, maybe Kurt will buy in, and it'll be two-against-one and democracy will rule. One can only hope. We finally got to the corner of Broadway and Pine, and I turned left a couple of blocks until I got to 13th Street, then turned right and drove past the hotel's front lobby. There was a parking lot directly across the street behind some trees, where I pulled in. Each parking spot had a designated number and there was a box at the entrance for the parking fee. If you didn't want to get towed, you had to fold up the cash and put it into the designated slot. Parking police, at that hour? For a couple of seconds, I toyed with the idea of slipping a folded bindle of coke in the slot instead, but rationality got the better of me and I did like a good little boy and forked over the dough.

We got out of the car. I looked at the Saab and I figured, we were going to drive to LA tomorrow and from there, disappear forever. No more Saab, no more problems. I had already decided to leave the car somewhere in South Central LA to be stripped by some beaner gang. Done, simple.

By my watch it was ten minutes to midnight. Not bad, considering the way the night had gone. Timing was perfect. My balance shifted a bit, the world tilted. I sniffled and tasted the remnants of Alex's marching dust still in my sinuses. Top of the world, Ma.

We strolled into the hotel and into a sea of people walking, pacing, marching in all different directions. Some were going to the front desk, a middle-aged couple walked into the bar next door, the one with the sign overhead that said the Hemingway Bar. There were people coming down the grand staircase to our right, and I could see that the Mezzanine bar overhead on the second floor was just packed with people. We slowly climbed the stairs overlooking the lobby and I made my way to the bar on the far side of the balcony, Kurt next to me, Sean following about five steps behind. The Mezzanine bar was a U-shaped room that encircled the stairs; most of the tables had a view of the marble lobby and front desk below. People populated all the little café tables next to the railing and along the wall, even the small conversation nooks in and around the main bar. I noticed to my left a bunch of musical instruments, guitar, electric piano, a small drum kit. Live music and we were just in time for the next set. I stopped someone going back down to the lobby. "What's the entertainment deal?" I asked.

The woman I had stopped, a short chick with butch black hair and a waddle walk, hollered, "A great band named The Saucers."

I paused, waiting for more, and when none was forthcoming, I asked a second question. "What kind of music?"

The chick stared at me with a mix of condescension and sadness, like I was a child asking for extra time to finish a test I was sure to fail. "You don't know The Saucers?" she yelled over the din. "They play techno country. Kind of like Devo meets Asleep at the Wheel meets Willy Nelson.

They're great!" She smiled and slid past me and down the staircase. I forgot about her less than immediately as my mind wrapped itself around the concept of the Saucers. Oh my God, you have got to be kidding. It occurred to me that I was going to have to go through some ear-splitting torture if I had to wait for Patrice until after the band went on. Fuckety fuck. Hi Mr. Sajak, can I buy a break? I turned to Kurt standing against the wall and raised my voice. "Let's go to the bar. Keep your eyes peeled."

"For what?" he responded. Funny.

"You know what, or whom," I said.

He said, "I'll stay here. Your future blowjob might think you need a babysitter." Another funny.

The Flatirons is on the National Register of Historic Buildings, and the decor was Old West, perfectly restored. The seats and coffee tables placed around the balcony were oak; the bar had to be original, at least a hundred years old. Like the bar at Michel's, there were four rows of bottles stretching a good ten feet off the floor. There was a library sliding ladder parked to the side for reaching the really good stuff at the top.

Sean and I stepped up and took a position behind and to the left of a fraternity dork in a pink oxford cloth shirt with a polo player on the chest, and lime green sweater tied around his neck, geekball casual-like. Like he was going to the polo matches, hardy har. I slid sideways and moved in, pinching between him and the blonde he was trying to make time with. The guy was annoying; he had Ken doll looks and a kind of whinny/snort for a laugh. Still, from the googly eyes and tongue-to-lip tell, the Barbie was into him. She wore a slight smile, like the cat that ate the canary. Her eyes widened and I flashed the dilation. This guy was getting laid later. And the pathetic part was that he didn't even know it. Unbelievable. Well, I guess even losers have to get laid, how else were you gonna get another generation of losers? He caught me scoping. He gave me the nose-to-nose stare like he was going to do something about it. A moment passed and I saw him. Scared eyes, light sweat to his lip. I saw him roll his lower jaw, but he didn't set it. He wasn't going to do anything. In a moment of lucidity, it occurred to me that the last thing I needed was a conflict in the bar. Patrice would bail. Cops would show up. Nothing but trouble.

"Excuse me. Thanks for giving me some space," I said in a nice tone meant to calm him and alleviate the tension. I turned to the bartender and ordered three Guinness, and when I got them and paid, I thanked the guy again and apologized for the inconvenience. I even turned to the chick and gave her a nice-guy plastic smile. See? I could be nice if I wanted to. It's just that in the last couple years, I've wanted to less and less often. I turned away from the two loser lovebirds, gave Sean his beer, and sliced through strangers, coming to rest at the corner nearest the main staircase. I gave Kurt his beer, which he took and then made himself scarce, setting off through the crowd, passing two guys and a girl with matching, black-banded cowboy hats and Buddy Holly–style glasses. Shit-kicking nerds? The thought made me smile for real. Sean beelined for the pay phones. Good boy. I let out my breath and leaned against the wall with a perfect view of the staircase and the bar. I crossed my left leg over my right, stretched my head left and right to get rid of the neck tension. I rebalanced my feet and with that was struck so hard by the prospect of a new life and my knew buckled. Patrice. If we were to have any sort of future together, I'd have to mend my wicked ways. I had been living for so long with my paranoia and jealousy, I didn't know if I could change. But change I would have to. In a moment of clarity backed up by the raucous music and stench of sweat, everything opened up for me through my mind's eye – the restaurant, the cabin, killing three men, attempting to get away with eighty kilos of cocaine with two coconspirators. And now Patrice, who I just knew was my soulmate, even through the fog of drugs and alcohol. I couldn't fuck up again. Ever. Ok, I know that the circumstances for my awakening were somewhat constricted, but who knew when or where lightning would strike, you?

I stepped away.

Chapter 31

12:12. Chick didn't show. Disappointed was being kind in describing my feelings at that moment. I'd just gone through hell to get to the bar and meet the bitch and here she was standing me up. Look at what I had done. The night wouldn't have turned to such shit if I'd known she was going to blow me off. Fucking Patrice, she could have told me upfront; break my heart.

There's nothing worse than having someone give you the shine on, the high hat. How would you feel if the chick of your dreams gave you a taste of the goodies and then forgot that you were even alive? I felt just like that, only worse. It wasn't like getting stood up hadn't happened before; I just chalked it up to my inability to stay in reality. I got stood up by lots of chicks, but that was my fault for not seeing them for the spoiled, stuck-up bitches that they were. This time it was different. Patrice was a good person, and we had stuff in common, and she liked great tequila, and we even knew the same people. And Patrice had given me plenty to look at, and she knew what she was doing all along. And best, or in this case worst of all, she'd accepted the invitation. What kind of chick accepts an invitation for a drink, an offer to learn more about her? I thought that's what women wanted. She talks; I listen. What could be simpler? What the fuck?

I was getting very edgy, my mouth was dry; my jaw was on overdrive from the coke, and my eyes couldn't seem to focus on anything for more than a few seconds. It was like I had vertigo or something, and the room started to flip on me. What to do? A couple of little spoons of the killer Peruvian, that's what I needed. I reached into my right front pants pocket, casually pulled out my vial and spoon set, and let my hand drop to my side naturally. A quick glance showed plenty of coke; the vial was almost full. I set out to find Sean. I found him standing at the other end of the bar, inconspicuous, beer about finished. I leaned over to him, mouth to his ear, keeping my eyes on three mustached cowboy hats sitting at the table a couple of feet away. It turned out that one of them wore an earring in his right ear. I stopped for a second just short of opening my mouth and stared at his earlobe. What was that rule again? Left is right and right is wrong. Right earlobe, faggot. Wouldn't you just know it, those guys were everywhere. He looked away from my blossoming smirk. Once again, I half-yelled over the din and background music.

"Hey man, I'm going outside for a little while. You wanna come or are you staying?"

344

Sean looked at me and smiled; he knew the score and wanted in. His head did a quick swivel around the room, probably for my benefit, and he placed his beer bottle on the table in front of the Alice. Sweetie looked up. Sean turned away.

Sean spoke. "So what, no Patrice?" He saw my scowl, short intake of breath. "Sorry. Okay, we go. Basement. Quick stop, right back. She could just be late." He wormed himself into the Aran wool sweater he'd been wearing since morning. He nodded to the yahoos and the gay one tipped his hat, Clint-style. Oh sister, please. We ignored him and set off for the back stairs.

When we got to the lobby, we made a quick U-turn for the basement stairs door. I quick-checked my watch, timing our scheme, hoping we'd be back upstairs and occupying the observation posts within five minutes. On the way down, I tracked the sound of our footfalls against the wood steps. They seemed almost as loud as the music upstairs, at least to me. Paranoia, raising its ugly head; fuck. I had a mini-crisis of sanity as I thought of all the little things that could trip us up, in one second. Had I covered all the bases until we could get out of town?

I asked, "Sean, have we covered all the bases until we get out of town?"

Sean kept on descending the stairs, and I wasn't sure he'd heard me. He got to the bottom and grabbed the door handle, opened the door, and we looked into an indigo, carpeted hallway. It extended about forty feet to a foyer and was cluttered on both sides with extra restaurant chairs, wine bottle chillers, and boxes of supplies. The foyer, I knew, was the entrance to another restaurant, one that had closed a couple of years before. It was called Corleone's or Pinocchio's or something woppish. The food hadn't been very good unless you liked watery spaghetti with meatballs that tasted like cow flop. I didn't even think anyone came down to this part of the hotel anymore, not even the cleaning crews. Except us.

I took the lead and we moved quietly to the area that was the darkest. Just in case. I figured we could duck down behind a couple of chairs if someone came looking for some of the supplies. When we got to the spot, I pulled the vial out of my front pocket and once again felt for the top, twisting it off for what seemed like the fortieth time that day. The spoon dangled from the plastic screw-on cap, and using my wrist and a deft swing, I flipped it and caught the spoon between thumb and index finger. As my eyes adjusted to the dim tinted light, a noise caught my attention, a furtive sounding scrape, like a shoe over carpeting.

"Did you hear that?"

"What are you talking about?" Sean whispered. "Hurry up, I'm still thirsty and the view is more interesting upstairs." Change of subject. "Did you see the fag?"

"Yes," I said, "and he had eyes for you, you thweet devil." With that, neither of us spoke again as I spooned the blow out of the vial, careful not to spill any in the darkness. Two for him and two for...a sharp pain, like a wasp sting, below my left nipple. It startled me so much that I dropped the vial cap, spoon still attached. I could feel the cocaine induced sinus drain and reached up to pinch my nostrils. I coughed. I tilted my head back a bit, I saw Sean. For some reason he seemed far away, and he stared at me. I think. It was dark. He looked dead.

I couldn't seem to level my head, every time I tried to move it, I got dizzy. Eyes closed, leaning against the wall. Better. Deep breath and an intake, sharp. My shoulder hurt like someone had smashed me with a hammer. I looked for Sean again in the dark but this time I couldn't see him. "Sean, where are you?" I whispered. "Did you see something?"

A flash, just out of view. What the fuck is that? Then a thwop. Yeah, a thwopping sound. Like the sound you hear when you punch a pillow, only about fifty times louder. And a pain deeper than the ninth gate of hell.

I blinked twice but couldn't get the black out of my eyes, I couldn't focus. I tried to breathe but my nose was still draining. A lot. I reached up and wiped my nose. I coughed, stumbled, and put my hand down on the back of one of the chairs lining the hall. It slipped on the wood and I fell over. My knee banged the floor and I rolled onto my back. I dropped my head back and looked up into the dark. My thoughts felt squishy. I reached up for the chair. Come on, get up. GET UP! The cushion was made of some kind of velvet, the chair oval-shaped. Probably nice to sit in. Like at a French restaurant. I wondered what the chair was doing in the hallway of an Italian place. There was no noise. Squishy Head, that's funny, like Play-Doh. That stuff was fun.

I couldn't hear Sean. I think I said something like, "Sean, do you have the vial?" Silence. I coughed and the pain coming from deep in my chest smacked me like a locomotive. I mumbled, more to myself that anyone, "I think someone's here." I didn't hear myself. Had I even said that? I think my hand was still on the cushion back. Soft. I bet it was maroon. Those chairs were always maroon. I coughed, winced. How did I get on the rug? My nose wouldn't stop running; too much cocaine, I guess. My chest rattled like a car engine that's just blown the pistons. I looked at the ceiling, but if I could have seen anything, I would have only seen black. "Where's my vial?"

I didn't see me.

A noise.

Chapter 32

November 19, 1983

12:19am. Kurt stepped out from behind the darkened corner and used his foot to carefully push on the thing lying on the floor. He turned on a small flashlight and with his right foot he gave it another quick nudge, then a good kick, small of the back. No movement. He knelt down, put ear to chest, and listened.

Sean asked in a quiet voice, "Is he dead?"

"Shut up for a second, I can't hear." Sean waited while Kurt listened for a few breaths. He felt the chest; stab wound right into the left lung. No movement. He turned the body slightly, felt for the second stab wound, mid-back, next to the spine. Blood leaked. Kurt turned the body back to its resting place and stood up. He stayed where he was for a couple of seconds and then he turned in the dark toward Sean's voice.

Kurt whispered with finality, "I think he's kicked it, fucking scumbag piece of shit."

Sean: "Where's his gun?"

Kurt felt around the lump, found he Webley in the crack of its ass. He stashed the gun behind his own.

Sean turned to the lump on the ground, barely visible against the dark carpet and walls. Sean spoke low. "Ho, Bruce, you idiot. Tried to be Mr. Clever, and now look at you. Not so clever now, are you?"

Kurt said, "Bruce was a fucking douchebag, a fucking jabronie. I never trusted him; he was always looking for the angle. Thought he was smarter than everyone. Fuck him." They occupied themselves for a couple of seconds by listening to the other's live breathing, the dull thump, then silence, of the music two floors up, and their own thoughts. The body, wilted, folded on the floor like a deflated mannequin posed for a high-concept magazine cover. Kurt twirled the butterfly knife and put it back into the left back pocket of his Levi's.

Sean said, "There's seventy kilos, maybe more, in the Saab. It's ours."

There was silence in the hallway for a couple of seconds. They could hear the sound of water running through the pipes upstairs. A dish broke in the lobby. The music started again.

Sean said, "I don't hear anybody coming. Think we're okay?"

Kurt listened. "Yup, if we don't fuck around."

Sean said, "Okay, I get that."

Kurt was silent for a second. "Bruce could have shot us all. He turned psycho." Webley, six shots, five targets. Bruce with the element of surprise. "We're the last ones standing. The blow is ours. The car too, until sometime tomorrow when they figure out who this lump is. And nothing to tie us to anything."

Kurt reached back into his pocket, carefully wiped the knife with a napkin from one of the storage boxes, then threw it down the hall. It bounced off the carpet and clanged against one of the metal waiter trays leaning against the wall.

"Fuck, that was loud." Time to scoot. I'll miss that knife, Kurt thought to himself, but fuck it. Kurt said, "I have a story for us." Brain on overdrive, thinking off the top of his head.

"We went for dinner with Bruce and some friend of his at Michel's and then we came home. Bruce went to meet a chick at the Flatirons. Nobody will remember you upstairs, you're probably in the clear." Kurt thought about it, plotting. Sean, breathing, listening for any noise from the exit. Voice getting louder as Kurt's brain picked up steam.

"The car registration is in Bruce's name, so he's busted, only he's also dead, so, dead end, so to speak. Ha, see what I did?"

"Quiet, fuck, someone will hear us. Yes, I get it." Sean said. "You stay cool, I stay cool, we get rich." Silence. They moved slowly down the corridor, opposite from the original staircase, in the dark. "We have a problem," Sean said. He pointed to his shoes, unseen in the gloom of the floor. "I got a jacket in the Saab that matches. There's a black one in there that Bruce was wearing earlier too. What do..."

"We take the jacket you borrowed and burn it. Shoes too. We leave a couple of the bricks in the Saab with the jacket Bruce had, fuck with the door to make it look like someone broke in. When they find it, the cops won't know any different." He let his brain burn some more. "Find the blow and they'll think that they're closer to closing the case, dumbshit assholes. Like leading a cow to slaughter, so easy. Just another deal gone bad. When they find those guys in the mountains, they'll make the connection. Bruce stole from Alex and Dick, killed them. He got killed for revenge by who knows? Someone robs the car. Classic. So Boulder. You clean, me clean. We follow the plan, go to LA, catch a slow boat to China. Perfect."

"Okay, but what about the cartel guys?"

Kurt thought for few heartbeats. He could actually hear his heart, which was in fact beating, unlike Bruce's.

"Fuck them, it won't matter. There's nothing on us, it's like we weren't anywhere near this. We know Bruce, that's it. We'll be good. How many keys are still in the little cabin?"

"Most of it. We took what, seventy? Minus the two or three we leave in the Saab to finger Bruce. That leaves a shitload." This time Sean thought for a couple of seconds. "And that won't matter either. In fact, it'll work *for* us. The cops will find it before the cartel or whoever is onto the problem. Cops get there first, confiscate the stash, the Peruvians are shit out of luck, end of story. We're in the clear!"

By this time the two were at the fire door exit, and Kurt pushed the handle with his forearm, opening the door to a column stairwell. No alarm. Holy shit, Sean thought, we're almost home-free. They ascended the stairs by feel, each listening for the other's breath and the sounds coming from the hotel lobby just above. Sean stumbled and almost grabbed the wall but righted himself. Careful, he thought, no touching. They got to the top. Two doors, one leading to the lobby, the other to the sidewalk. Kurt opened the outside door and took a quick glance. He could see his breath. The air was cold and crisp against his face; his nose started to run. He stepped out; Sean followed. Kurt held the door then wiped the handle and door edge with his shirtsleeve. Smart, Sean thought. They walked toward the crosswalk signal and waited for the light to change—nothing to bring attention. Sean obsessed. I have to get rid of these shoes and this ridiculous jacket. Then I'll be clear. Sean watched his breath, tried to make rings with the condensation. I might as well dump the other pair as well; the one is ruined. And a bad memory too.

Kurt thought, Sean's got to get rid of those shoes. And the jacket. Kurt spoke up as they crossed and started walking for the parking lot and the Saab still parked in the shadows. "Give me your shoes."

Sean turned and spoke with some concern touched with panic. "What, are you nuts? It's freezing!"

"Don't be a pussy. Just give them to me when we get to your house. I'll trash them after I drop you off. You'll just have to go inside in your bare feet. Big deal. Don't be a baby. The shoes and jacket tie you to the deed. That means burn the shit. I can take them to Flagstaff and torch them in one of the giant barbecues in the overlook before I drop off the car."

Sean smiled. "Fuck, you got it covered."

"We're going to do this, get fucking rich. Fuck yeah!"

They got to the lot. Sean fished Bruce's keys from his pocket, careful to check for blood in case the cops check the lock later. Sure enough, a smudge. Sean stuck the key in the snow behind the tree, wiggled it around to get it wet, and then wiped it down on his pant leg. Bright lights coming up the street made Sean duck. He stayed low. Crunch of tires. The Saab sat next to an old black suicide-door Lincoln. The Lincoln had a shallow dent in the hood and cracked windshield. Baseball. For sure. Bad luck.

Sean stood up. He moved his eyes off of Kurt and back to the Saab, crab-walked to the passenger-side door, away from prying eyes, and turned the lock. Nice, smooth pop. He noticed the frost on the bottom of the window. He opened the door, then wiped down the handle with his shirtsleeve. His hand disappeared and thumping sounds, the front seat folding down. His head disappeared, then his body. It was dark inside the car.

"Give me the keys before you lose them," Kurt requested.

Sean responded, "Fuck that." Kurt looked him in the eye. Sean relented.

Another car moved up 13th, past where the two were finalizing their escape. Kurt clocked the driver. Wait. NO way! Patrice? The car slowed, then accelerated. Car, and driver, went past the hotel, turned right toward Broadway.

Kurt sniffed, smiled to himself, watched. The air was crisp. His breath was a cloud. From inside the car, Sean watched as Kurt, keys in hand, dropped into the driver's seat. Ignition. Sweet purr, nothing like the purr of a turbo Saab. Thanks, Bruce. They eased out of the parking lot, turned away from their destination, and headed up into the foothills, where the roads were dark. A final left on 6th Street, then up the hill. Neither spoke.

Chapter 33

November 19, 1:38 p.m.

"Paging Dr. Phwaaa, Please reeachhllih to waeea waathwiawaology." What? My eyes opened. The room was white and antiseptic looking. It even smelled antiseptic looking, like someone had dumped a bottle of grain alcohol in a bucket getting ready for a college blowout. Now that's a party.

I needed a bump and a dump. I rolled my eyes and took in my surroundings. There was a curtain hanging on a semicircular steel rod surrounding my bed and the stainless rails were raised up on either side of me, like prison bars. There were at least three lines going into my right arm, with little twist things to turn on the juice. Fancy, like Frankenstein. I smiled, and immediately felt noxious. And I mean with a capital Heave My Guts right here and now.

I moved my head. Straps held a mask to my face. I breathed in, cold. I dropped a couple of tears and tasted sour bile. Okay. I thought for a few seconds, letting my dysfunctional brain start to whirr. Smiling equals puking, moving equals puking uncontrollably. I guessed if I coughed, I'd throw up a piece of pancreas and a testicle. If a=y and 2a= 5y then b = 1/4c + z. That's what a college education will get you, remedial algebra and reasoning skills. And an impossible answer.

I gotta get out of here. I looked up at the fluid bags, dangling like a bunch of squid with tentacles, slowly poisoning me. What were they giving me? It was sort of clear with a brown tinge. Maybe it was morphine. I heard that morphine made you want to throw up. I thought about *that* for a couple of seconds. I changed my mind.

I took a conscious breath. My chest ached like broken bones only deeper down inside. The more I gasped for air, the worse it got. I held my breath and the pain subsided. Just stay calm. I lifted my head a couple of inches and was rewarded with more searing pain in my chest. My head swam. I clenched my teeth and took it, just like eating candy. I looked toward the noise coming from behind the curtain. What does the Wizard tell Dorothy about curtains in *The Wizard of Oz*? Oh yeah, "Don't look." I should have paid attention.

I pulled the mask down. I whispered, "Is there anyone there?" I was hoping for a nurse, or better yet a candy striper, one with great tits I could stare at while she made me comfortable. 'Owwww, Miss Candy Striper, please stop. No, don't stop that, that you can keep doing.' Ha, ha, snort. Another sharp stab of pain where I was supposed to have a heart. My eyes watered again. The curtain whispered a man-made breeze and revealed my first visitor. No candy striper, not by a long shot. What I got was Johnny Law in the guise of police officer Sergeant—SomeFuckingThing. He had three stripes on his sleeve, but his name was obscured by the gaseous rotundity of the belly he led with as he stormed over and manned up to me, big fat cop to horizontal invalid. He stared me down with bulging brown eyes popping from a huge melon, like two gigantic ticks. He was bald with a bad, hair-coloring-tinged comb-over, slicked down. A jowly face like Churchill's bulldog. He looked like some cheap wrestler on the Podunk circuit. Tough guy, oh my.

The lights off his dome, blinding. I closed my eyes. Click.

"Sir," he intoned robotically. I opened my ears. "We found almost three kilos of cocaine in a car registered to you last night. And a dead body. What do you make of that?"

I closed my ears. I was going to be sick, but it wasn't from any morphine. I thought for a few seconds. I felt the presence of Sergeant Bloatbelly, his flab straining his belt, compelling an answer. I opened my eyes. I made a choice.

I said, "Have you seen my clothes?" I gave him my best deer-in-the-headlights look.

Bloat did a double blink and opened his mouth. "Yes I have, but you're not going anywhere." He reached over and pulled one of those cheap, ergonomic plastic chairs from behind the curtain. He turned it backward and straddled it. His crotch was inches from my face. We made eye contact, and I was overcome with thoughts of the old Beatles song "Piggies."

"We'll just have a nice little talk, you and me. It's much better if you and I get to know each other here in the hospital. The station isn't nearly as comfortable."

The police station. Yeah, right. I glanced at my arm and the tubes going into the belly of the octopus. So not likely. And right, like he's going to be my friend, we're going to go out for beers later, maybe swap spit. I unthinkingly looked over and right at his crotch, almost heaved. Friends? Like in jail? I think not. I looked up at him, made a groaning sound to get the attention of the nurse.

"Nurse?" I groaned. "Nurse! I'm feeling dizzy. My chest hurts." I mewled.

And she appeared. Officious, White uniform, cap. She had nice hands and sandalwood prayer beads wrapped on her wrist. Her eyes, blue and penetrating. And kind. I closed mine, feeling safe.

Nurse to Bloat: "Enough for now, Officer, what, Nelson? The patient needs to get some sleep. You'll have to come back later." I heard her give him a good-natured lift off the chair, his pants sticking to the now-wet plastic. "Now, if you come back, let me know first so I can check with the doctor regarding visitors." As he stood, I cracked an eye. She patted him on the back like a teacher with a child. I smiled like the Cheshire cat in *Alice in Wonderland*. On the inside only, can't be egging on the little policeman. After all, he's only here to serve and protect. Eye closed. Click.

"This man is under arrest. *Nurse*. He will remain here, handcuffed and under guard. I expect a telephone call as soon as he wakes up again." He pulled some cuffs from behind his back; I could hear the metal jingle. Me, eyes closed, ears wide open, calm breathing, trying hard to keep a dead face. I knew what was coming. The nurse responded with music.

"Handcuffing this patient infringes on our ability to treat him effectively. *Officer*." She accentuated the word "officer." She probably knew it would bother Bloatbelly that she didn't use the word "Sergeant," and it did.

"My rank is Detective Sergeant, ma'am. I'm not going to get into the legal aspects of this prisoner's rights with you. This man is someone of interest in an ongoing investigation and I need to speak with him as soon as possible. Am I clear?"

This time I couldn't keep a straight face and a little smile curled my right lip, one moment there and the next, gone.

"Detective," she started soothingly, "we are not in the police lockup, we are in a hospital. This man is our patient, and he is still in critical condition. If he's a 'person of interest,' then he's not under arrest, so no handcuffs. What you are suggesting represents a danger to his well-being, and I will have the hospital file a grievance with the Boulder Police Department if you continue this attempt at leverage and intimidation." She stopped, then proceeded in a quieter tone. "Now please leave, we'll let you know when the patient can speak with you. Oh, and no guard. This man is far from a flight risk. His organs are badly damaged and need time to heal properly. If he tried to walk, he would keel over before he got off the bed." Bloat scowled. I cracked my eye. It made his nose disappear into his face. I closed my eye, smiled inwardly.

The cop said, "There's no need for conflict here. I'll return this evening. Maybe Mr. Keown will be feeling better." I kept my eyes closed, face still, calm. I opened my eyes and watched the drapes slowly come to a stop. I could smell the sick people, the nurse's perfume, my own sweat. I closed my eyes. Bloat had said one last thing.

"Bruce Keown, you are under arrest for the possession and intent to distribute cocaine. You have the right to remain silent. You have the right to an attorney. If you do not have one, an attorney will be appointed for you. Do you understand these rights?"

"Yeshth." And fuck you too, you bilious meat popsicle.

He continued. "Nurse, now he is under arrest. Mr. Keown, if you try to run, a warrant will be issued for your arrest and you will be held in lockup until the day of your arraignment, at which time you will appear in front of a judge to plea and set a court date for your trial. And good luck with that." He let out a bark that could have been a laugh. I closed my ears. I was going to be sick, but it wasn't from the morphine. I opened my eyes and saw my future.

Sergeant Bloat turned and left the room, the smell of hot dogs and sauerkraut following him out. I snuck a look at my Rolex, still on my wrist. That's interesting, I thought.

It was almost two in the afternoon. Considering his size, his breakfast hot dog count probably went into the double digits, lunch right on top. I glanced up to find the nurse standing over me, looking at me with veiled curiosity, scrutinizing. I took another look at the watch, this time scrutinizing the date window. Had it really been only twenty-four hours since this situation had begun? Jesus, it felt like a month.

"I knew you were awake." She paused. "I think the police can wait a little longer before they try to string you up. You've already been stabbed twice, you need a break."

Stabbed. Huh. "What's your name?" I whispered.

"Nurse Mori. You can call me Kalyani."

"That's a beautiful name," I croaked. "What does Kalyani mean?"

"It means 'auspicious and beautiful' in Sanskrit. I was actually born Christina, but I started studying Buddhism about five years ago and changed my name."

Oh my God, an open-minded progressive chick protector. And a babe. *Perfect.* I felt my penis twitch, then the worst pain I have ever felt in my lower back. I'd rather be kicked in the balls with a steel-toed boot than feel that again. Unless it was Kalyani doing the kicking. I mean, she would know how to make it better, right? My penis twitched again and this time I cried out.

"What's wrong? Are you hurting anywhere?"

"I'm hurting everywhere."

"Do you need some more morphine?"

I wanted to say yes but thought the better of it. What if Officer Bloat came back early and I was incapacitated? "No, it's okay," I said. Fuck, I might regret that.

She said, "I'll be back in about a half an hour to check up on you again. Do you need anything else before I go?"

I almost gave her some story about needing a massage, you know the kind. Stop, Bruce. Think this through. I gave it a think. It occurred to me that whatever goodwill I had established would be washed out in less time than it took her to say, "I don't think so." No clever retort from my side.

"No, I'm good." I gave her a small smile touched with what I hoped was humility. I tried for the innocent look I used when I would sponge free Tuesday-night dinners at the Naropa Institute up on the Hill. Kalyani gave me another friendly look and an easy nod. Then she left. Maybe there's something I can salvage from this fiasco.

Things looked kind of bleak. Coke in my car. Kilos of coke. In my car. Holy shit. Oh man, this was bad, cartel bad with a capital Fuck. Oh yeah. And stabbed. Twice, I think. By someone I knew. *A friend* whose life I could have taken *but didn't.*

You know, my week didn't start out this way, obviously. According to my watch, it's November 19 and I'm in the hospital with a hole in my chest and another one right next to my left nut. Yesterday my life was completely different, though I guess you could say I still needed some kind of doctor. For my brain.

Wait, what? three kilos. Where's the rest of my fucking coke? I thought about pulling out my octopus and jetting but knew such a move would be the death of me. Slow, quiet breath. I considered the situation. Do I survive a murder attempt just to die from blood loss and injuries? Hell no. I'll probably die in a prison in Alabama, surrounded by huge jabronies with head tattoos and pierced penises. I fell back into the pillow, resigned. I thought it through. Nope, I am so fucked.

Wait. Body? *Who's body?*

Chapter 34

The Saab pulled up to the Gumby House, turned into the back lot, pulled next to a clean '72 VW Bus, and shut down. Sean got out of the passenger side door, took a few steps, did a quick walk-around the lot and surrounding houses for any lights, and returned. He went to the driver's side and knocked on the window. His breath floated. Kurt rolled down the window.

"What's up?" he whispered.

Sean responded in the same whispered volume, "Looks good. No lights on anywhere, everybody's asleep in their safe little beds." They both smiled.

Kurt: "Let's unload the blow and get out of here. Stick to the plan, leave the Saab, just another thing to confuse the fucking cops."

Sean, thinking. Then, "Nah, we gotta take it somewhere and dump it, maybe burn it. There's our fingerprints and stuff all over the car."

They thought a little more, Sean's fingers getting colder by the second. It seemed that they made the decision together because Kurt got out of the car, pulled some keys out of his right front pocket, and opened the passenger door of the van, then unlocked the slider. He reached under the seat and pulled out two large Zero Halliburton suitcases, the kind that are supposedly uncrackable without the combination. Sean went around to the trunk of the Saab and opened it. He reached down, flipped the tire cover. Out came the blow, a couple of keys at a time. He turned, and into the Zeros they went. Kurt kept his eyes roving, aware that any of the neighbors could see their activity if they were awake, perhaps doing blow and jabbering away about nothing intelligible. It was crucial that they not be seen. Crucial.

"Hurry up," Kurt said.

Sean: "Well, you could help, but no, you wanted to play lookout. So, give me a few and we can get outa here."

Kurt: "Where's Bruce's vial? I need a pick-me-up if we are going to start the road trip tonight. Or this morning."

Sean: "Are you kidding? As if we didn't do enough coke to kill a wild pig?" He purposefully lowered his voice a notch, hoping to be a good example for Kurt.

"What? Boddah you?" Kurt slowed down his movements. He gave Sean a dark stare. The moonlight offered an angled shadow over his face. His muscles bunched and relaxed. A breath of air, frosty, escaped. Menacing.

Sean: "Woah, take it easy, brah. I'm only saying." Sean finished stashing the kilos into the cases. He shut them, locked them. Slid each under the first-row bench seat. Safe.

Kurt said, "Well, don't 'only say'. Give me the vial that I now know you have stashed."

Sean: "I don't have it. I think we left it in the basement, next to the lump that used to be Bruce."

They both considered the situation. Fuck. Fingerprints. What about DNA, on the spoon? Could the cops get their DNA off the spoon handle, or even off the spoon itself? What about the vial? Did they touch it?

Sean said, "I think we might be fucked. We might have to go back. I know I touched the vial and the spoon. What about you?"

Kurt responded, "I know I touched them when we were driving to the hotel. After that, no. But maybe with all three of us fucking with the coke, the cops won't be able to isolate our DNA, and the fingerprints will be useless, too much smudging. And let's not forget the BPD habit of making vials like that just disappear from the evidence listings. Yeah, let's go with that. At least we'll be able to sleep later instead of worrying." See that? Disaster averted. "Besides, we have a plan, LA by the 22nd, sell this coke, charter a boat, sail the fuck out of Dodge. You did find someone to buy the blow in LA, right?"

Sean: "Yup. Would you believe, Bruce's cousin. Ironic, yeah? And the best part is that Jumping Jeff Keown doesn't even talk to Bruce, they had a falling-out. Bruce told me about it."

"Why is he called 'Jumping Jeff'?"

"Apparently he's the next king of BMX trick world." Kurt snickered. Sean snickered after Kurt.

Kurt reached behind his back, pulled the revolver, and put it into the glove compartment of the Saab, locked it. They glanced at each other. Kurt locked the van, up the back stairs, and a quick snag of clothes, toothbrushes, food, and water for the road. Shove everything into the internal-framed North Face backpack. Sean went to Bruce's room to take the only valuable thing he owned: a Rolex Submariner. Bruce always said that Jacques Cousteau gave it to his dad in 1968. He figured he could trade it in for a lot of grands, maybe upscale the charter for one with private cabins. It was gone. Shit, he thought. He went back into the main room and sat on the wood pew, contemplating the circumstances. "Okay, let's see. Do we have everything?"

Kurt, coming out of the bathroom, grabbed his nose, sneezed, "Shitfuck." He said, "I don't know, do we have everything? Beers, food, coats, water, money, toothbrushes and toothpaste, sunglasses...what else?"

"Well, I bet you could use some clothes. We could go by your house, or you can borrow some of mine, maybe take some of Bruce's. He's got nice threads and he doesn't need them anymore."

Kurt went into Bruce's bedroom, looked at the poster on the ceiling, and for the nth time thought, What the fuck? He went to the dresser and grabbed a few T-shirts, some jeans, a couple of shorts, and some underwear. Socks, can never have too many socks. Closet? Bruce's rubber slippers and his Nike running shoes, a half size too big but would work in a pinch. Kurt grabbed what he wanted, kicked the rest back into the closet and pushed the door closed with his elbow. He went to the desk, opened the first drawer on the right, never know, right? Well, would you look at that, Kurt said to himself. He reached in, drew out a six-inch switchblade. Nice ivory handle. Thumbed it open, checked the sharpness on a piece of lined paper sitting on the desktop, growing dust. It cut smooth. Yeah. Kurt heard the TV go on and the music lead into a Bugs Bunny cartoon.

Kurt stepped into the hallway and whispered, in a mildly incredulous voice, "Are you kidding me? We gotta go and you're watching the rabbit? Let's go!"

"Okay, fuck!" TV off. "Let's go then!" came the voice from the pew. Sean grabbed the blanket covering the pew, the backpack, and stood ready. Kurt found a small suitcase in the front closet, unzipped it. He tossed the clothes and other stuffs inside, shut it. Done. Knife in pocket, a great replacement for the K-Bar. Kurt thought about their exit strategy for a few seconds as both men proceeded down the darkened stairs, out the door, and around the side of the house to where the van was parked. Opened the side door, go-bags in, shut the door.

Kurt: "You drive the Saab; I've got the bus."

Sean: "And what? I'm stuck with the gun?"

Kurt: "When we dump the Saab, it'll be in the glove compartment, all neat, for the cops to find. Just another loose end closed. Hell yeah, perfect ending if I do say so myself. With the gun in the Saab, the evidence is on Bruce, and he's dead."

Sean: "You said that already. Where should we go to jettison the Saab? We can't leave it around the corner, duh."

Kurt: "Michel's. There won't be anyone in the parking lot at this hour and nobody will be there until tomorrow after 2:00; remember, dinner only. We'll leave it next to Alex's car. We can torch 'em both there, and it's a quick escape through Estes Park. We can catch the freeway at Idaho Springs. Home-free. You can take first shift."

"Uh, no, I don't think so. You're the driver now, you get to drive until daylight. I'll take over in Grand Junction. How's that?"

"Done. I'll go first; you follow about five minutes behind. Low profile. Okay?"

Sean was silent for a few seconds, seeing if there was anything he had missed.

Sean: "Okay."

They got into their respective vehicles and the VW engine turned over. Kurt backed the bus out of the driveway, into the alley with access to College Avenue. Left on College, right on 11th, right on University, and another left. Out of sight, Broadway, going north. Soon, streetlights faded away and a more rural highway greeted him.

Six minutes later, Sean started the Saab and followed the same pattern, turning left down Broadway, towards downtown. The headlights of the Saab led the way, down the hill, past Marine Street, then Arapahoe, going north. Sean smiled to himself, it was the end of a ridiculous day, but they were free. Drop off the Saab at Michel's, torch the cars, done and done. Utah by morning. Nearing the green light at Canyon Blvd., Sean glanced up through the front windshield and saw the clouds release the moon, offering a bright view of the path forward and the lonely highway up ahead. The Rolling Stones last cut on Let It Bleed was playing, "You Can't Always Get What You Want." Now what should he listen to next? Sean looked at the selection of cassettes scattered in the passenger seat. Picked up Pink Floyd, "Wish You Were Here."

And the earth stood still, just for a second or two. Sean looked left and saw headlights coming his way. He had just enough time to mumble, "That guy is running the light. Fucke_."

It was one-thirty in the morning, downtown Boulder, people going home from the bars. A permissive society, lots of drug and drink-addled students and ex-students behind the wheels of cars, swerving, drifting, paying no attention. Driving recklessly. Until one driver, nineteen-year-old Jordan Goldberg from Staten Island, New York, runs the stop light at Broadway and Canyon. His Toyota Corolla, a High School graduation present from his uncle Bennie, never stood a chance. Neither did the Saab he T-boned. Neither did Sean.

Chapter 35

Kurt pulled into the Michel's parking lot, next to Alex's 528e. He eyed the car, shivered from a whisp of regret about the evening, then leaned back into the driver's seat of the bus and waited. Time went by. Kurt continued to wait and think. This was by far the most awful day, and night, of his life. Compared to tossing Tracy, his one true love, out of the house, this was a hundred times worse. So much karma build up.

Wait. How much of this evening did he really plan and execute purposefully anyway? What happened at Alex's house, not on him. Now, stabbing Bruce, that was karma, but Sean carried half the load.

Kurt reached across to the glove compartment, pulled out a bag of Kailua homegrown with the blue tinge and frosty bud, some rolling papers, and rolled himself a joint. You know, while he waited. He struck a light, lit the doobie, tossed the match, and took a couple of shallow hits so as not to cough. He leaned his head out the window and watched the stars. And took another hit. The stars spun. They drifted in and out of his vision, like bringing a book really close and then holding it far away, really fast. You know how some words disappear when you hold a book close? That's what Kurt experienced. And as he let his mind wander, his memories of the night, and his role in it, took on new life. Kurt no longer saw the dinner as a plan cooked up by Alex, with him as the facilitator. It was all about Bruce's greed. He kind of forced the issue, didn't he? Yes he did, to be honest.

Kurt watched a tape of the events at the house in his mind's eye. Again. And again. So, Alex was dead. Maké Loa. That would hurt for a while. Ocho? He had tried to stop it. I mean, right? And Dick...well, he was a dick. Kurt deliberated. Inhale. Alex was his friend and partner but nothing could have stopped Bruce. Nobody even knew he had a gun. And who would have thought in a million years that Bruce would have the stones to shoot up the place? Or be such a good shot?

Kurt took another hit. He watched the smoke leave, drift up to merge with the clouds. He saw his breath but didn't notice the cold. He blinked. So, Alex was gone, but not all his (their) stash. Some of it was under the back seat, that very moment. Kurt smiled again. Then he frowned. Fucking Bruce, it was all his fault. He deserved what he got. Kurt took a deep breath, and another. Shoulders bunched. The night was quiet except for the sound of the wind. The stars spun. His forehead smoothed, breath calmed, and the stress of the whole Alex affair slowly drifted with the chilly breeze and THC. Kurt would miss Alex. And to be fair, he'd miss Bruce too. Fucking Bruce.

After a while Kurt, who didn't know how long because he was high and didn't have a watch, slowly came to terms with the night, justifying every nuance of the events as they transpired. And his Karma now lay intact before his judgment. Just like that. Easy.

He waited.

THE END

ACKNOWLEDEMENTS

I started this book as a way to hang with my wife, who suggested we do the annual NaNoWriMo writing contest together. We both successfully navigated the requirements and I ended up with a very rough first draft. Little did I know that a decade later, when I revisited this manuscript to maybe turn this into a "real" book that this here would be the result. This is my first novel, and I couldn't have done it without the help of several people.

Deepest thanks to my wonderful professional editor, Stephanie Chou. She and I just hit it off and she was the greatest support through the most difficult part of the writing process, from draft to publish-ready manuscript. Her editing skills are second to none.

Additionally, a big Aloha and Mahalo to Brian (Boogie) Black, who helped me visualize my cover design ideas. He did an excellent job. Boogie and I have been friends for over fifty years and our mutual love of fine arts and design helped make the cover design a smooth experience. He's an excellent artist.

Finally, and most importantly, my deepest gratitude to my wife Catherine, who's sincere involvement, objective feedback and unswerving support for this adventure was instrumental in me starting the process and persevering during the tough times. Without her this book wouldn't exist. Thank you my love.

Bradley Alan Stern
March, 2025

BIOGRAPHY

Originally from Honolulu, Hawaii, Bradley Alan Stern was, by turns, a national-level athlete, a wellness consultant, a motivational coach, corporate strategist and college professor. He also lived in Boulder, Colorado in the early 1980's, and interacted with the types of people portrayed in this book. These experiences helped him create the larger-than-life main characters, the other quirky secondaries, as well as the world that these characters inhabit. He now resides in Kalamazoo, MI with his wife and dog Nicky. He holds an MA in psychology and an MBA and is a member of the International Thriller Writers. This is his debut novel.

COMING IN 2026:
MONKEY WRENCH